THE GOLDEN PRINCESS

THE FOUR KINGDOMS AND BEYOND

THE FOUR KINGDOMS

The Princess Companion: A Retelling of The Princess and the Pea
(Book One)

The Princess Fugitive: A Reimagining of Little Red Riding Hood
(Book Two)

The Coronation Ball: A Four Kingdoms Cinderella Novelette

Happily Every Afters: A Reimagining of Snow White and Rose Red
(Novella)

The Princess Pact: A Twist on Rumpelstiltskin (Book Three)

A Midwinter's Wedding: A Retelling of The Frog Prince (Novella)

The Princess Game: A Reimagining of Sleeping Beauty (Book Four)

The Princess Search: A Retelling of The Ugly Duckling (Book Five)

BEYOND THE FOUR KINGDOMS

A Dance of Silver and Shadow: A Retelling of The Twelve Dancing
Princesses (Book One)

A Tale of Beauty and Beast: A Retelling of Beauty and the Beast
(Book Two)

A Crown of Snow and Ice: A Retelling of The Snow Queen (Book Three)

A Dream of Ebony and White: A Retelling of Snow White (Book Four)

A Captive of Wing and Feather: A Retelling of Swan Lake (Book Five)

A Princess of Wind and Wave: A Retelling of The Little Mermaid
(Book Six)

THE GOLDEN PRINCESS

A RETELLING OF ALI BABA AND THE FORTY THIEVES

MELANIE CELLIER

LUMINANT PUBLICATIONS

For the first Mel in the Cellier family,
thanks for welcoming me so warmly all those years ago and for sharing
life's journey in all the years since

RETURN TO THE FOUR KINGDOMS

KINGDOM OF ARDASIRA

Sultan Kalmir—Sultana Nadira

Parents of

Prince Zain (Zaid)—Cassandra of Eldon

KINGDOM OF KURALAN

Sultan Khalil—Sultana Rabia

Parents of

Prince Tarek (Rek)

Princess Adara

Prince Xavier

Prince Xander

Four Kingdoms
NORTHGATE
Northhelm
RANGMEROS
Rangmere
Arcadia
ARCADIE
Kuralan
The Great Desert
KAREMA
LANARE
Lanoreé
SERRALA
Ardasira
INVERNE
BANISHMENT
ISLAND

CROSSING
SSA'S VILLAGE
Kuralan
The Great Desert
KAREMA
MADDOX
QALERIM
SIRRALA
Ardasira
ARGOT

PART I
THE SERVANT AND THE CAVE

CHAPTER 1

"Greetings!" a loud, cheerful voice called from outside.

Nyla glanced toward the window but couldn't see into the courtyard beyond since she was sprawled across the sitting room's daybed.

"Kasim isn't usually back from his day's business so early," she said with the same irritated tone she'd been using all morning.

I rapidly debated whether to reply and decided it was marginally safer to correct her error than say nothing.

"I think it might actually be Ali," I said, careful to keep my voice free of any hint of criticism. I even peered through the closest window as if I needed to confirm it with my eyes, although I could easily hear the difference between my employer's voice and that of his brother.

"Ali?" Nyla sat up, her look of annoyance growing. "I know my husband's brother likes to take advantage of our good nature most every day of the week, but he usually comes in the morning, at least." Her voice dropped to a mutter. "And why Kasim allows it, I'll never understand."

I suppressed a sigh. It was true Ali often came to his brother's house looking for a servant to assist him in his day's woodcutting. But Nyla's complaints were old and tired by now, especially since she was all too aware of the reason both she and her husband permitted a groom or manservant to accompany Ali.

Much as they might decry being related to someone as unsuccessful as Ali, they feared the situation could grow even worse. Neither of them wanted the humiliation of such a close relative descending into abject poverty.

Nyla heaved herself onto her feet, a calculating look entering her eyes as they turned to me. Her impatience with her brother-in-law usually led her to ignore his daily arrival, allowing Ali to pick from among the available servants himself. But apparently her bad mood on this occasion needed a more proactive outlet, and Ali's arrival provided her another opportunity to take her annoyance out on me.

Obediently I trailed her as we left the room and crossed to the mansion's main door. I stayed several steps behind since it wouldn't do to let Nyla see my lift of spirits at the unexpected reprieve from a day spent in her sole company. She had spent the entire morning complaining about not being invited to a party at the palace the previous evening, becoming gradually more and more annoyed in the process. I had grown tired of her ill-temper long before the midday meal, but she had required my continued presence as a receptacle for her complaints.

Nyla liked to direct any annoyance she felt that was even vaguely related to the royals toward me, as if I was somehow responsible for her exclusion from royal circles. And one of her favorite punishments was sending me along with Ali in place of his usual assistant. But while she might consider the task unpleasant and degrading, I found Ali to be a pleasant enough companion, and I enjoyed getting out of the city and into the shaded greenery of the surrounding woods. Naturally I took great care not to let on about my true feelings to Nyla.

We stepped out into the enclosed entry courtyard, and I lifted my face toward the afternoon sun. It danced off the water in the elegant fountain, lighting up the greenery that edged the packed earth of the courtyard center.

"Ali." Nyla's tone stopped just short of open rudeness, her eyes traveling from her brother-in-law to his son. "And Navid. How… delightful."

Ali's lined face remained creased in a friendly grin, but the carefully blank expression on the tall young man at his side tightened slightly.

I sent Navid a quick smile of welcome, and the hardness in his eyes softened. I'd been explaining to him for years that there wasn't any point being offended at the things Nyla said. It just exhausted you while having no effect whatsoever on her. But such restraint required practice, and he didn't have the constant exposure to Nyla that I did.

"I see you're heading out of the city again, brother." Nyla eyed the three donkeys standing behind the two men.

One of the animals brayed loudly, as if sensing Nyla's disgust, and her look of dislike deepened.

"As always, sister." Ali bowed. "Navid had intended to accompany me on this occasion, but his master needs him in the city today. He's negotiating a deal with a new supplier and wants his most promising apprentice to observe the proceedings."

He swelled with pride as he always did when he mentioned Navid's apprenticeship with one of the leading merchants in the city—an apprenticeship that would have been out of Navid's reach without the assistance of his merchant uncle.

"Indeed." Nyla unbent slightly. "Kasim has had excellent reports from his friend about the apprenticeship of my nephew. Navid brings credit to the family."

Since her pleasant expression faded almost immediately, her eyes straying once more to the donkeys, this measure of praise did nothing to soften Navid's stiff posture.

Ali, however, appeared oblivious to her underlying distaste. "We are eternally grateful to Kasim, and to you, Nyla, for your good nature in recommending Navid to such an illustrious position." He bowed again.

Nyla smiled graciously, accepting the compliment while I rolled my eyes behind her back. Navid had started his apprenticeship before I arrived in Kasim's household, but the older servants had described the scene to me.

Nyla had raged and protested to Kasim in private, claiming it wasn't their responsibility to provide for Kasim's poverty-stricken brother and his family. She had sworn her nephew would bring dishonor to Kasim's own good name—a reputation won not through his own merit but from her unexpected inheritance a short time after their marriage. The fact they had once been almost as poor as Ali and his wife did nothing to engender sympathy in Nyla.

Of course, now that Navid had nearly completed the years of his apprenticeship—having excelled throughout—all memory of her earlier opposition was erased from her mind. I had even heard her claim the entire arrangement was her idea.

"In fact," Ali continued, "I am hoping to trespass upon your good nature once again. Without Navid to assist me, I find myself one hand short." He chuckled as he gestured to the three donkeys, making his request as if he didn't make the same one nearly every day.

Nyla swiveled slightly, her gaze latching on to me. This time I let the sigh escape, assuming a depressed air.

Her mouth curved up in response to my manner. "Zaria is available to accompany you." She turned back to show Ali her falsely sweet smile. "I'm sure she would be most happy to assist."

"Zaria?" My name startled Navid from his silence. "Surely you can't mean to send only her? Just this morning they were talking in the market about the return of the thieves."

"That must be recent news." I stepped out from behind Nyla. "I thought there hadn't been trouble for months. Everyone thought the gang had moved on to other parts of Kuralan."

"Perhaps they did. But they're back on the roads near the capital again now." Navid turned to his father. "Perhaps I could get out of today's negotiations, after all. I could accompany you myself, at least until we hear the gang has—"

"Absolutely not!" Nyla glared at him. "You will not bring this family into disrepute by shirking your responsibilities to your master. Especially not when he does you honor by including you in such important proceedings."

"Certainly you must listen to the wise words of your aunt." Ali's brow creased for the first time since his arrival. "I can assure you I will do well enough with Zaria."

"Perhaps you would do better on your own." Navid's skeptical gaze moved back to me.

"Really, Navid!" I kept my tone stern, although my eyes laughed at him. "I promise my presence will not be a detriment to your father."

Ali chuckled. "No, indeed! Zaria has accompanied me often enough. She and I will deal well together, I have no doubt."

"That's not what I meant." Navid stopped, shaking his head in frustration.

"I see," I said gravely. "In that case, let me reassure you. Despite my small stature and general lack of bulk, I will endeavor to bring your father back in one piece, no matter what cutthroat villains we and the donkeys may encounter."

"Zaria!" Navid groaned. "That's not what I meant either, and you know it!"

A chuckle slipped out, earning me a reproachful glare from Nyla. My casual, joking manner was one of the things she most deplored in me—declaring it irreverent and disrespectful. But even after more than three years as a servant, I hadn't managed to fully curb my old nature.

"Thieves will not be interested in our load of firewood," Ali said comfortably. "You may go in peace, son."

"No, indeed they will not." Nyla looked down her nose at

Navid. "If you do not fear to send your father out into the woods alone, you certainly need not fear on behalf of one of my servants."

Navid's lip curled slightly at the disparaging way she said servant, but he remained silent. He had learned long ago that he wouldn't be the one punished if he spoke out in our defense.

I was elated, however. An afternoon in the forest was far better than I had envisaged for the day. Assuring Ali I would only be gone for a moment, I ran back inside to change my ankle-length outer robe for one of a thicker material. It was always cooler beneath the trees, and we were starting late, so we would be lucky to make it back before sunset took much of the day's warmth with it.

Nyla met me at the mansion's door on my return. "Enjoy the donkeys, Zaria." She sniffed disdainfully. "It's all you've turned out to be good for."

With a swish, she turned, the heavy brocade of her much more elaborate robe brushing the ground as she sauntered down the hallway. I shook my head and dashed outside to join Ali by the outer gate.

Nyla would never forget I had been recommended for a place in her household by one of the palace viziers. She had given me a position only because she thought I would provide an ongoing connection to the palace—an assumption that had turned out to be false. I was fairly certain she kept me all this time later because she enjoyed having someone to punish for her disappointment. Other servants had a habit of resigning after too much exposure to her ill tempers.

"Ah, there you are." Ali smiled and handed me two of the leads.

I took them, giving a soft greeting to the donkeys. They brayed at me in what I was convinced was a friendly manner, coming easily when I gave the two ropes a gentle tug.

As we walked through the streets of the city, I watched Ali. He called friendly greetings to many of the people we passed, a picture of amiable contentment.

Sometimes I marveled that such a man could have produced Navid. I wasn't sure if Ali truly lacked his son's intelligence and perception, or if those qualities were simply masked by his good nature and the fact he most definitely lacked his son's drive for success.

No one of any sense could doubt his gentle heart, however. His donkeys were evidence enough of that. I had never in my life seen such amiable members of their kind—and since they had been raised from birth by Ali himself, I could only assume they mimicked their master's nature.

When we passed out through the open gate and stepped off the road into the trees, I let out a soft breath. I loved the hum of the dusty city, but this sort of peace could only be achieved when surrounded by green, growing things.

"You needn't be concerned," Ali said, misreading my sigh. "I'm quite sure no thieves would be interested in my girls, even when we have filled their baskets with firewood." He patted the head of the closest donkey with affection.

Unlike his brother and sister-in-law, he appeared to have no shame in the poverty that drove him to spend his days pursuing such meager riches as firewood. He made no apology for it but began to talk in a rambling manner, making infrequent pauses that required only the briefest of acknowledgments from me.

I smiled to myself as I listened. Ali's amiable animals could easily be secured in a string and led by one person. But after my first excursion into the forest, I had worked out that Ali's need for assistance had more to do with his desire for company than any more practical requirement.

We wandered for some time before Ali stopped and began to unload the donkeys. He had found a new location since my last time accompanying him, distinctive due to the unusually round shape of the clearing and a large rocky section of ground on one side. It provided plenty of room for the donkeys to graze without moving out of sight, and Ali soon settled into his work, chopping large branches to fit inside the baskets.

Officially, I was tasked with collecting smaller branches to fit around the larger ones. But Ali never commented on my gathering speed, so I wandered around the clearing first. When I caught sight of the large bush to one side of the rocky section of ground, however, I decided it was time to head out among the trees.

I had once loved bushes like that—the deceptively thick growth hiding the perfect space in the middle for children to play. But my memories of such adventures had soured with the years, and I had no interest in dwelling on them.

Walking through the forest soon calmed my agitation. The slight hint of autumnal chill in the air, the smell of leaves and flowers, and the sounds of animals hidden in the underbrush filled my senses. Nothing could be further from the human bustle of the city.

I had gathered four promising branches when I caught a sound that didn't fit. Pausing, I listened more carefully. The jingle of a harness cut through the trees, followed by a distant sound I recognized as the cadence of spoken words.

I tilted my head, straining to hear more. We sometimes encountered other woodcutters, but they came on foot with donkeys, like us. These people were on horseback.

Honest travelers venturing off the road for a cool break among the trees? They were deep in the forest for that.

A pleasure party of nobility, then? The nobles sometimes made it this far, seeking a longer ride than could be afforded in the extensive palace gardens.

I had once been part of such excursions myself.

My heart skipped slightly. Was it the younger royals I could hear? I had learned to ride in their company, and all four of them were skilled on horseback.

Something uncomfortable crawled its way from my stomach toward my throat, but I couldn't tell if it was excitement or anxiety. It had been more than three years since I had seen the princess or any of the princes. Not being a glutton for emotional pain, I avoided the processional days when I might have glimpsed them from afar.

I couldn't deny the desire to see them now, though. Adara was my oldest friend. In that difficult first year with Nyla, I had as often cried myself to sleep over the loss of her companionship as over my father's death.

The itch to see the princess again was strong. But a brief glimpse—or even an exchange of words—wasn't worth the pain of opening old wounds.

And as for her brothers...I had done my best to forget the mischievous twins altogether. My childish preference for Prince Xavier and Prince Xander had been foolish then, and I would be wise not to give way to it again, even for a moment. They had been handsome enough when we were just turned fifteen—the talk in the market suggested they had only grown more attractive in the three years since.

Foolishness! I upbraided myself. The riders were unlikely to be my old royal playmates. Adara and her brothers had always ridden in the morning, and the voices that were growing louder sounded both older and harsher than the voices of my childhood.

I was still standing, frozen with indecision, when the first glimpse of movement showed through the trees. The band of riders was bigger than I'd expected—no wonder I'd heard them from so far away.

One glance was enough to tell me they weren't a pleasure party. Dressed alike, they wore the brown leather and short kaftans of the city guards.

The sight of their uniforms returned the feeling to my legs, and I stumbled back several steps with a sinking sensation in my stomach. Navid's earlier words about danger in the forest echoed ominously in my mind. What were the guards doing all the way out here? Who were they pursuing?

"Have we lost the trail?" called a voice, younger and smoother than the ones I had heard from afar.

I froze again, recognizing the speaker instantly despite the passage of years. The one royal sibling I had no desire to see.

Someone replied to him, but I didn't hear their words, my eyes trapped by the white horse which stepped to the front of the group. A tall, straight figure sat astride it, his eyes turned away from me, toward the captain of the guards.

He had grown—both in height and the breadth of his shoulders—but his dark hair curled at his neck just as it used to, and his voice still carried the same whiplash of command, delivered instinctively with every word he spoke.

In the course of three years, I had turned him into a stranger in my mind, but one glance and my memories rebelled. Happy times sprang to mind—a gaggle of children, running free through the palace gardens, Rek at our head.

But that was before he grew away from us—less Rek and more Crown Prince Tarek every day. And that was before I became a servant, and he convinced Adara they could no longer associate with me.

I knew my friend wouldn't have cared about my change in rank on her own, but her brother had always cared deeply about his role as crown prince. And the worst of it was that I couldn't even blame him—not if I was being fair. They were royalty, and I had no place in their lives anymore.

This tall young man was a stranger, whatever my memories said.

Although I didn't move or make any sound, something drew his attention. His seat shifted as he swung his head in my direction, scanning the now silent forest.

I felt it in my belly the moment his eyes found me, his gaze locking with mine despite the distance. I had no idea what my face showed, but his expression changed as suddenly as if he'd been struck.

"Zaria?" The single word contained astonishment and some other emotion I couldn't name.

Several guards twisted to stare in my direction. But before any of them could speak—and before I could decide whether to approach or to turn and run—their attention was seized by their captain.

"There!" he shouted. "I saw one of them! Quickly now!"

The captain had been looking away from me, unaware of the short interchange between me and the prince, and I hadn't seen whatever had attracted his attention. His men responded instantly, wheeling their horses to follow their captain's lead, streaking away from me through the trees.

Only Prince Tarek hesitated, his eyes still on me. But his guards were retreating further from him, pulling his attention in their direction. With a single look back at me, he muttered angry, inaudible words and spurred his horse after the rest of his group.

Within moments, I was alone again, still stationary among the trees, my breathing heavy despite my continued immobility.

It took several long moments for my brain to sputter back into motion, catching up with the meaning of what I had just seen.

If the guard captain was right, he had just spotted their quarry within sight of where I now stood. And surely a group of guards that size—led by the prince no less—wouldn't be pursuing an ordinary criminal.

I turned and ran, the branches I had been clutching falling from my arms. Weaving between trunks and bushes, I sprinted toward Ali. When I promised Navid I would return his father to him, I hadn't seriously thought we would come so close to danger.

I catapulted into the clearing where I had left Ali and the donkeys. The animals brayed, and Ali regarded me with mild concern while I panted, trying to catch my breath enough to speak.

"Is something wrong?" He peered at the quiet trees behind me.

I nodded. "Guards. In the woods." I struggled to slow my breathing. "Chasing that gang, I think. They're near."

Ali frowned. "Were they heading in this direction?"

I shook my head. "They went the opposite way, but even so…" I frowned, trying to put my discomfort into words. I had never felt so alone beneath the trees.

I glanced over my shoulder. The forest had gone quiet, with not even the most distant sound of riders. The guards must be long out of reach by now, the thieves ahead of them. I told myself to relax, but my body didn't respond.

Ali peered into the leaves, seeming unsure of the best course of action. I took several more steadying breaths and shook my head. I was behaving like a fool. We were in no danger here. The forest was quiet.

I paused, finally identifying the cause of my lingering discomfort. It wasn't just quiet—it was too quiet. I might not be able to hear riders, but neither could I hear anything else. The ordinary sounds of the forest hadn't resumed.

I looked toward the donkeys. The oldest of them—usually the leader—brayed quietly. Her expression was unusually alert as she swung her head from side to side, facing toward the trees.

"Quiet!" I whispered, holding up a warning hand to Ali.

His frown deepened, but he obeyed, honoring me with his instant faith in my judgment. I could only imagine how Nyla would have reacted in the same situation.

An old familiar thought flashed through my mind. If only Ali's wife Mariam had been the one with the inheritance instead of Nyla. Ali and Mariam would make far better employers.

I pushed the pointless dream aside. All my attention was needed on the current situation.

At first my straining ears could hear nothing. I was almost at the point of relaxing when a faint noise reached me.

I sucked in a breath. "Did you hear that?" I whispered.

"Riders," Ali breathed. "That was a harness, for sure."

A moment later the sound of hushed voices reached us.

"The guards?" Ali asked hopefully, but I shook my head.

"The squad was heading directly away from us. And they weren't creeping through the forest, either."

Our eyes met and held, horror growing in both our gazes. I didn't need to voice my fear about who this second group of riders might be.

"We must hide ourselves!" Ali said quietly. "They can have no interest in my firewood, but what if they choose to kill anyone they meet rather than let us live to report their presence?"

I nodded fervent agreement, but Ali didn't move. His eyes flew around the unusually round clearing, jumping from tree to bush.

"We could climb a tree," he blurted out. "No, wait, the donkeys can't climb." He wrung his hands, his eyes making the circuit again.

I waited a moment, but he produced nothing further beyond a concerned groan, so I took charge.

"You climb that one." I pointed at a nearby tree with regular branches and a dense enough canopy to keep a person hidden. "I'll take the donkeys into the bush over there by the rocks. Hopefully the space in the middle is big enough for us all."

Ali hesitated only a moment before nodding agreement and scrambling onto the first branch of the indicated tree.

CHAPTER 2

I rushed to untie the donkeys' leads. My hands fumbled, half my mind listening for the sound of the gang. Were the noises getting louder? Were they coming this way?

By the time I had the ropes free, I was sure the thieves were approaching. Whispering reassurances to the animals—the words unconvincing in my own ears—I hurried them across the clearing toward the large clump of bushes.

With ordinary donkeys this would never have worked, but Ali's gentle beasts didn't protest the strange treatment. The branches scratched at me as I pushed through, although the animals didn't seem to notice.

Thankfully the clear space in the center of the clump of bushes was even larger than I'd hoped. As soon as we were screened behind the thick leaves, I stopped, placing a hand on each of the younger animals' muzzles and continuing my soft whisper. When they stilled, their ears pricking as if they under-stood the danger and need for quiet, I went silent.

Surrounded by leaves, it was harder to make out the sounds of the approaching riders. My whole body was on alert, every muscle tight, and my heart racing. But as the long seconds dragged out with no sign of anyone, I couldn't keep my thoughts from wandering to my unexpected confrontation with Rek.

Crown Prince Tarek, I corrected myself in my mind. That tall young man was a stranger.

But it didn't matter what I called him. Seeing him had brought far too many memories flooding back. And at the worst possible time. I couldn't risk becoming agitated—not when my emotions might transfer to the animals I was attempting to protect.

Not all the memories were bad, though. In fact, if I was honest, the positive ones far outweighed the negative. In the dark days after my father's death, I had let my pain color backward and poison the years before. But enough time had passed for me to see everything more clearly. I had loved my years at the palace, running free with the royal children, however much pain it had brought to me later.

What was Adara like now? Did she still get up to mischief with her younger brothers, her merry laugh always a breath away? Or was she more serious these days—following in her older brother's footsteps and taking on the mantle of adulthood as she came of age?

And what of the twins? Being only a couple of months younger than me, they had come of age recently. It had been impossible to miss the occasion since the whole city celebrated for days. Word in the market gave the twins themselves credit for the festivities. Apparently they had insisted the whole populace celebrate the long awaited day with them.

It was a characteristic move, if so. It seemed at least some of the royals hadn't changed. Xavier had always thrown himself into celebrations and festivities with utter abandon, and Xander always had time and attention for everyone, regardless of their status and position. Combined, they were an irresistible force, and the stuffier courtiers had long ago despaired of the two of them.

It was thanks to the twins I had been adopted into the royal circle in the first place. Arriving at the palace as a motherless five-year-old, I had been lost in the enormous building and grounds. Xavier and Xander had found me, wandering in bewilderment, and demanded I join them. Apparently they were in need of another girl for their latest game of exploration—a necessary balance due to there being one princess and three princes.

As the daughter of a junior vizier—the newest to be elevated to the position and one of common birth, on top—I only just qualified as a royal companion. But the twins charmed their parents and the palace staff as easily as they had charmed five-year-old me, so no one ever attempted to separate us. And when my father proved both his loyalty and his worth in the following years, my place became assured.

Until he died and everything changed.

I shook my head before the memories could veer back toward those dark times. Surely if a gang of thieves was approaching our location, they should have arrived by now, no matter how quietly and carefully they were moving?

It was a large forest, and there was nothing particularly interesting about this clearing, beyond the unusual symmetry of its circular shape. Had they already passed us by, moving on to other parts and new targets?

A soft whicker made me flinch, the donkeys moving uncomfortably until I stroked their muzzles again. Leaning forward, I tried to peer through the leaves. Was it thieves, after all, or was I cowering in a bush for nothing?

The same denseness of shrubbery that protected us made it difficult for me to distinguish anything clearly. But the sounds beyond were louder, making it unmistakable that a party of riders had not only entered the clearing but stopped within it.

"Hold!" a gruff voice said, quiet despite the roughness of his tone. "Are we certain we have evaded pursuit?"

"Davis is the wiliest of us, and the most skilled at forest craft," a commanding voice replied, with a hint of irritation. "He will have successfully led them away. Or do you question my judgment in sending a decoy to mislead them? Perhaps you wish we hadn't come here at all?"

There was a loaded silence before the first man spoke again.

"Of course not. We all know why we had to come." He sounded resentful but submissive.

The leader gave a quiet growl. "We might wish the cave was located further from the capital, but we'll be gone soon enough. Which is why haste will serve us best."

No one responded to the challenge in his tone, the clearing falling into silence.

I held my breath, even as my mind raced. Cave? What cave? There were no mountains within this section of forest, and I had never heard talk of any caves.

"Open sesame!"

The captain barked the nonsense words as if they were of great import.

I wished I could see Ali's face. What was he making of this strange conversation? Did it make more sense to him than it did to me?

A loud grinding sound made one of the donkeys bray softly. Thankfully her call was hidden by the scraping of stone against stone and the swearing of several of the men in the clearing. Clearly they were as worried about loud sounds as I was.

Curiosity overcame my good sense, and I crept forward, trusting in the upheaval outside to cover any noise from my movement. Maneuvering myself into a better position where I could peer through a small gap in the leaves, I got my first good view of the clearing.

The soft gasp that dropped unheeded from my lips was thankfully covered by the continued grinding. The men standing outside were even greater in number than I had been expecting.

What looked like two score men were clumped close together, garbed in high quality leather. But despite the value of their clothes, the dirt encrusted in the material told me they hadn't ridden out from any high-class mansion.

Their mounts were in a similar condition—their finely bred coats covered in several days' dirt, each one loaded with worn and heavy-looking saddlebags. But my eyes skittered quickly over the thieves, not even the underlying menace of the captain holding my attention.

Instead I was captivated by the ground in front of him where an opening was appearing in the forest floor, in the section of rocky ground. As I stared with round eyes, the gaping hole grew larger, the rock pulling away to reveal a dark, jagged cave mouth.

Impossible!

As soon as the stone stopped moving, the captain urged his mount forward. The horse must have been familiar with the strange cave because it gave only the slightest protest, dancing sideways briefly before stepping forward and leading the way into the darkness.

A bright spot of light traveled with him—a lit lantern I hadn't even noticed in the daylight of the clearing. It illuminated the way for the line of men who obediently filed after him. I strained forward, risking exposure in my effort to see inside the wondrous cave.

I could make out nothing but dark rock, however. A tunnel disappeared into the distance, swallowing the men without revealing anything of its secrets. As they disappeared into darkness, I counted them. Thirty-nine.

As soon as the last of them had exited the clearing, the grinding noise began again. Working even more quickly this time, the opening of the cave closed back up. No evidence of its presence remained in the now quiet clearing.

I remained in place trying to make sense of the scene I had witnessed. What had just happened? How was it possible?

My eyes flew to the tree where Ali had concealed himself. Would he now appear and suggest we retreat? It was certainly my instinct to get as far away as possible as quickly as possible. But the gang's captain had spoken of haste and being gone soon. Caution warned me the thieves might re-emerge at any moment.

Apparently Ali felt the same because not so much as a leaf stirred in his tree. A minute passed and then another. I occupied the time trying to make sense of what I'd just seen.

From their accents, these men were Kuralani—if not from the capital, Karema, itself, then from some other corner of our kingdom. But watching them open a cave in what had been solid ground made me think of our southern neighbor, Ardasira. By now everyone had heard of the fabled treasure cave discovered there.

I had a personal link to the dramatic events in Ardasira three years ago, although my involvement had been much more fleeting than most of my fellow servants could be brought to believe. They had plied me with questions about the affair, and especially about the foreign princess.

It didn't matter that she'd turned out not to be a princess at all. Since she'd ended up marrying Ardasira's own Prince Zain, everyone seemed ready to overlook that detail.

They were less willing to believe that my interaction with Princess Cassandra had been brief and—more importantly—that it had contained no hint of the fabled Treasure of Qalerim. Neither had we discussed treachery at the highest ranks. Our conversation had been mainly limited to our respective wardrobes.

It was chance alone that had led me to meet the supposed princess. Kasim was in the southern kingdom on a business trip, invited by none other than the Ardasiran Grand Vizier. Naturally, Nyla had accompanied him, eager for the royal connections sure to ensue—even if they were connections in a different kingdom.

Layla, Nyla's personal servant, should have accompanied her on the trip, but Nyla had just hired me. For that brief period I had been her treasured favorite, the one who was going to give her entré to royal society in Karema. So naturally she had decided to take me on the much-anticipated trip to Ardasira in Layla's place.

It was on that trip that things began to go wrong. After inadvertently helping a traitor, they had been forced to flee Ardasira in secrecy, leaving Nyla's hopes in ashes. And I was the lone witness to her disappointment, fear, and shame.

Even worse, I had managed to actually speak to a royal while there—only to squander the opportunity. At least, that was how Nyla saw it, given I hadn't managed any ongoing communication with Prince Zain's new bride.

It didn't matter how many times I explained to her that my encounter with the foreign girl who would later become a princess had been brief. I had never even left my post in the dressing room where ball guests could go to refresh themselves. I had been waiting obediently for any appearance by Nyla when Cassandra had entered the room instead.

Of course I had heard rumors—every servant in the palace was gossiping about the girl claiming to be a princess from an impossible foreign land. But we had exchanged only a few words —and our outfits. She hadn't even explained to me why she wished to swap an exquisite gown of silk for the garb of a servant. And now she was a princess of Ardasira while I remained a servant. It was nonsense to think I might have any influence with her.

When it gradually became clear I no longer had an ongoing link to the Kuralani palace, either, Nyla's fury was complete. I had thought she would dismiss me—and at fifteen, alone and friendless, it had been a terrifying prospect. But she hadn't done so then or in all the years since.

She had, however, treated me to the full extent of her ill

temper and hatred, and I had felt no obligation to inform her when a single communication did arrive from Princess Cassandra some time after our return. It had consisted of a short letter of thanks and a purse of gold coins. Both items lived under my bed along with several rolls of damaged carpets and a number of tattered cushions. Every month, I added to the purse's contents. Eventually, it would be enough to secure me a new life. Day to day, I didn't think of it at all.

My mind dwelt on that gold now, however. According to the letter, the gold was intended to replace the expensive dress gifted to me by the princess—a dress that had transformed from purest silk to dirty rags in my hands later that night. The shock of the transformation still hit me sometimes, especially since I hadn't known the dress was the product of the enchantments encircling the fabled treasure cave. Only as it changed had I realized the truth, especially given the stories already starting to swirl about the girl who had given it to me.

Seeing the enchantments of the first treasure cave—and of the lamp that controlled it—with my own eyes had certainly made it easier to believe the fantastical stories I heard later. Everyone in the market was abuzz with tales about the events leading up to Prince Zain's betrothal. It might have seemed impossible before, but after the dress, I did believe that a magic lamp had allowed a foreign girl and a traitorous vizier to find and unlock the wonders of the fabled lost treasure cave.

My eyes traveled back to the rocky ground that had been a gaping hole only minutes ago. How many times had I heard someone in the market repeat those stories, always adding a comment about the ancient legends that first told of the treasure cave? No one ever failed to mention that those legends told of two caves.

At first, it had ignited a frenzy of searching. Rumor had long held that the second lost treasure cave of legend must be located in Kuralan, and suddenly everyone was convinced they would be the one to find it. No one ever found as much as a trace, however.

At least, not as far as anyone knew...

Surely I was letting my mind race out of control. How could a gang of thieves have found what eluded the best scholars in the land? Kasim had been one of those obsessed with the cave—and since he traded in ancient texts, he had access to information others lacked. And yet, he had never found even a hint of the location of a second magical cave.

Of course, that might have been due to his own poor understanding and not the content of his texts. He had once possessed a hint to the location of the first cave and had managed to miss it.

Not only had he missed it, he had unwittingly provided it to a dangerous traitor, bent on destruction and conquest—the very mistake that had sent Kasim and Nyla fleeing Ardasira, fearful of what questions might be asked. In any other situation, Nyla would have been shouting their involvement in the cave's discovery from the rooftops, but instead they had spent three years keeping it desperately quiet.

The trip to Ardasira had bound Nyla and me together in ways neither of us desired. I was a constant reminder of her worst disappointments, but at the same time, she couldn't risk turning me loose. As long as I chose to stay, she didn't dare throw me to the streets. Instead, she found relief in ill temper. But I had my own reasons for staying—not least of which was the handsome salary she had agreed to pay when she first took me on.

But despite Kasim's incompetence, it still seemed incredible a gang of thieves had succeeded where he failed.

And yet, I had just seen the ground open in response to a couple of spoken words. How could I not wonder if the missing second treasure cave had been found after all?

More minutes passed. If we'd left immediately, we could have escaped by now. Maybe it was foolish to continue waiting. And yet, so much time had now passed that the thieves must be about to reappear. Surely it was wiser to wait just a little longer.

The grinding sound that split the clearing came without warning this time, hitting my tense nerves hard and setting all three donkeys braying. Thankfully there was no one in the clearing to hear their noise other than the concealed Ali.

I stayed in place, peering through the leaves as the cave mouth once more opened up, revealing the same rough stone tunnel, sloping steeply downward toward unseen underground caverns.

The robber captain reappeared, his mount almost prancing as the mare passed back out into the open air and sunlight. Within moments all the gang were above ground again, a quick head count showing that none had been left within the cave. Many of them looked disgruntled—hardly suggestive of thieves who had just accessed vast and magical riches—and their once bulging saddlebags lay flat against their horses' sides. If there were riches in that cave, they didn't appear to be bringing any back out with them.

"Close sesame," the captain said before barking in a louder voice, "Ride!"

The group kicked their mounts into movement, disappearing far more quickly than they had appeared. By the time the last of them had passed from sight, the cave mouth had closed again, leaving an undisturbed clearing behind.

I remained inside the bush, hardly able to believe they had really left.

CHAPTER 3

A loud thud made me jump. I had barely caught my breath from the shock before a solid four-legged shape knocked me aside, sending me staggering into a sharp collection of branches. The other two donkeys followed close behind their leader, pushing their way out of the bushes.

Grumbling about ingratitude, I extracted myself from the greenery and followed the animals toward their master who was still heaving himself back to his feet. Apparently his descent from the tree had been more fall than climb.

Ali took time to comfort the unsettled donkeys, but his hands shook as he did so, his eyes wide as he stared at me.

"Do you think…Is it possible…" He stopped and drew a deep breath. "Surely it cannot be that *we* of all people have stumbled across the cave of legends?"

"If we have," I said slowly, "then we're not the only ones to have done so." I gazed in the direction taken by the thieves.

"Certainly, certainly," Ali agreed. "But they are gone now." He hesitated, peering toward where the cave mouth had been. "Unless you think one or more of them remained inside? There was such a number of them that it is possible—"

"No." I shook my head. "I counted them in and out. Thirty-nine in both directions."

"Excellent!" Ali gave me a pleased look. "Navid is right. You're a sharp one, Zaria."

I brushed aside the compliment. "Can we be sure they won't return?"

"Surely they will not do so—at least not immediately. Why should they? They seemed most anxious to be away from the capital."

I nodded slowly. That much was true.

"So you want to look inside?" I asked carefully, unsure why I felt so much dread at the prospect. Normally I would have been eager to explore such an unexpected marvel.

"Of course we must do so!" Ali's eyes were still on the ground where the cave had been. "Who knows what wealth may lie inside?"

"And what enchantments," I said. "Don't forget the stories about the other cave. They say the treasure there was protected by deadly enchantments."

"Nonsense, nonsense," Ali said. "Who says so? The market loves to spread sensational gossip. I'm sure those stories have been exaggerated out of all recognition."

I frowned. "Even Kasim believes it likely, though. And you know he prides himself on his knowledge of ancient texts. He's always dismissing tales he believes to be mere rumor or story."

"Far be it from me to criticize my esteemed brother," Ali said, with the closest I had ever heard to contempt in his tone. "But he can sometimes place too much reliance on his own understanding."

I snorted in amusement. I had always suspected Ali couldn't be as oblivious to his brother and sister-in-law's failings as he chose to appear.

His face softened as he examined me. "You may remain out here with the animals, Zaria, if you prefer. I give you full permission to run away at the first sign of any returning thieves."

"Nonsense!" I said, energized by the suggestion. "I promised Navid I would see you safely home, and I don't intend to abandon you now."

"My son has an excellent sense of humor," Ali said with a broad smile. "But you must not consider yourself bound by it."

I considered several retorts but abandoned them all.

"If we're going to do this," I said instead, "let's get it over with."

"Excellent! Excellent!" Ali turned glistening eyes on the rock. "Now what were the words that brigand used?"

"Open sesame," I replied, a tinge of excitement coloring my tone despite myself.

Immediately the grinding sound returned, and the ground in front of us split. As the dark hole grew larger, I regarded it doubtfully.

"I don't suppose you have a lantern with you? I know we usually return from these gathering days well before dark, but..."

"As it turns out," Ali cried triumphantly, "I do have one. Since we got such a late start to the day, I thought it prudent."

He rummaged around in one of the baskets secured to the senior donkey, pulling out a small lantern with a glad cry. I waited with rising impatience as he lit it. Now that we had decided to explore, I wanted to get moving.

Even with the small circle of light from the lantern, neither of us suggested attempting to coax the poor donkeys into the earth. Instead we took a minute to secure their leads to a nearby branch and plunged into the cave entrance alone.

The ground beneath our feet was uneven and rocky, but I couldn't keep my attention on it. Instead I kept looking forward, straining to see ahead of us in the poor light. The tunnel couldn't go on forever. And even if we were wrong about the treasure cave, those thieves had left the contents of their saddlebags somewhere.

We reached a solid wall of stone, explaining why we hadn't been able to see further down the tunnel. It didn't end, however, merely turning sharply. Ali reached the bend first, the lantern stretched out before him, but I was close on his heels.

My forward momentum stopped abruptly as I rounded the corner myself, a loud gasp falling from my lips.

Extending before us was an enormous cavern. I had spent the last several minutes imagining bizarre wonders, such as the carved trees and jeweled fruit famously found in the Qalerim cave. There was nothing like that here. Instead, my eyes swept back and forth across an endless expanse of traditional wealth.

Overwhelmed by the sheer scale of the treasure, my mind struggled to take it in. Everywhere I looked, chests sat open, overflowing with gold. Heaped among the coins were other items shaped from gold—jewelry, crowns, goblets, even plates and cutlery. And interspersed with the gold were rolled carpets of the finest weave, bags of jewels, long bolts of luxurious material that showed no sign of age or wear, and even paintings, all displaying the hand of a master.

Ali echoed my gasp. "This is—"

"Way too much," I said, feeling queasy.

He turned to me with a furrowed brow. "Whatever can you mean, Zaria? This is incredible! There's enough gold here to turn around the fortunes of our entire kingdom—especially now the foreign lands have been discovered across the Great Desert. You know the sultan wishes to establish trade with them. With this much gold, any merchant could create the most lucrative connections."

"And yet," I said, "the only people who know about its existence are thieves—thieves who apparently leave it here, unseen and unspent. Thieves who actually bring *more* gold to swell this unimaginable hoard."

"Some people are never satisfied." Ali's attention was back on the shining expanse before us, disappearing off into darkness beyond the reach of the lantern. "Look at my own brother, the worthy Kasim. He started with nothing, as did I, and then had the good fortune to marry a woman who inherited great wealth. And yet has it left either of them satisfied?"

I frowned at him, surprised at his speaking so openly about his brother's failings for a second time. But his attention was still on the treasure, his mind only half on his words.

After a moment of silence, he seemed to realize what he had said.

"Listen to me, letting my tongue run away with nonsense." He tore his eyes from the wealth to give me a smile. "You must discard my foolish words, Zaria. I declare I've been gold-struck!"

I turned back to regard the immense treasure. It was certainly enough to render anyone devoid of sensible thought.

Yet another reason to be wary of it.

"Do you really see nothing you would like for yourself?" Ali asked, crossing toward the closest chest. "That necklace would look fine around your neck, I am sure."

"Don't touch it!" I said sharply as he leaned toward the chest's contents.

He pulled back, giving me an indulgent look. "Don't tell me you still fear enchantments?"

"And so should you," I snapped back. "Seeing this only confirms my fear. Nothing about this cave seems natural."

"Of course it's not natural!" Ali cried. "We have found the second fabled treasure cave—leftovers from the vast empire that once stood where the Great Desert does now. Could a natural cave preserve these fine carpets like this? Why, look at that bolt of silk! Anyone would think it delivered from the weavers yesterday."

"Perhaps it was," I said coolly. "Those thieves are bringing something here."

"Nonsense!" Ali said. "You are too cautious, my dear."

Stooping too quickly for me to prevent, he snatched up the

golden necklace on top of the closest chest and threw it to me. I reacted instinctively, snatching it out of the air as it sailed toward me.

He didn't even hear my cry of protest, having already turned back to the chest. After a breathless moment, I relaxed, forced to acknowledge that no immediate calamity had befallen us. The ground didn't rumble beneath us, and the roof of the cavern showed no sign of collapsing on our heads.

Ali glanced back at me. "You see, Zaria! There is nothing to fear here. We have stumbled upon good fortune beyond imagining, and you mustn't look so glum!"

I dredged up a smile, but the churning in my gut continued. As I stared down at the necklace, I tried to trace the source of my discomfort. Why was I so sure this wealth wasn't the free gift it appeared?

The necklace was elaborate, studded with small gems and wrought by the hand of a master. Even in the meager light of one lantern it glittered and shone. It was easily the most beautiful jewelry I could remember seeing.

But every instinct in me wanted to cast it away, distrustful of its excess. I walked over to Ali, returning the necklace to the chest it had come from. But even as I straightened, my eyes lingered on the necklace's beauty.

Immediately I knew why I felt a mistrust Ali did not. This was the second time I had held an impossibly beautiful product of a magical treasure cave in my hands. And last time, the dress had faded away, too good to be true, just as it had first appeared. And even the princess who had given it to me hadn't understood the enchantment it was under. Wealth generated from enchantments could not be trusted.

"Wait here!" Ali instructed, the smile plastered across his face losing none of its width. "I will fetch the donkeys, and we may then fill their baskets."

"You're going to take it?" I asked, alarmed. "Baskets full of it?"

"And why not?" Ali demanded. "There is so much here that even were I to take ten baskets full, no one would notice any lack."

I considered his words as he hurried outside for the donkeys. It was possible he was right. There certainly were riches beyond counting here. On the other hand, the thieves would surely come again. And if they did notice the cave had been disturbed, how great would their wrath be? It wouldn't be so hard to trace the theft back to Ali—not when he was about to go from poverty to vast wealth in one impossible day.

"Please think this through," I begged Ali when he reappeared. "How will you explain your sudden good fortune? What if the thieves track you down?"

Ali paused but only for a moment. "I am sure we will think of something," he said. "Navid is always singing your praises, so perhaps you can help me come up with a convincing story."

"Me?" I gaped at him. "What possible story could explain such an overnight change in fortunes?"

"Who said anything about overnight?" Ali scooped gold coins into the closest basket, only giving me half his attention. "I will bury these coins and bring them out slowly, increasing my wealth over time."

I sighed at his heedless method of scooping up the gold, unable to resist getting involved. "At least spread out your theft. Don't take so much from one chest. If you take only a little from each one, perhaps the thieves will miss its absence after all."

"An excellent suggestion!" Ali moved immediately to the next chest, and I followed behind, trying to smooth over the depleted chests he was leaving in his wake.

In a surprisingly short amount of time, the baskets were full. I stood back and surveyed the cave while Ali artfully arranged pieces of firewood on top of the baskets to obscure the gold underneath.

To my inexpert eye, the cave looked undisturbed. Catching a

stray coin out of place, I scooped it up and reached for the closest chest.

"No, no!" Ali protested. "You must keep something for yourself. A single coin cannot bring disaster."

I paused. I wanted to ignore him, but if I did, he might try to foist the necklace back on me instead. I had no desire to linger here, caught up in an argument.

"Very well." I slipped the coin in my pocket. "Can we please leave now?"

"Certainly!" Ali gave the treasures of the cave a final glance. "I feel sure these coins will keep me going for a long time indeed. But if I do find myself in need again, there is plenty more here."

"In need?" I stared at him. "You're taking *six baskets* of gold coins home."

He chuckled. "It seems like a dream, does it not? I just wish I could fit that painting into one of the baskets as it is just the sort of beautiful thing I would like to see every day. Do you think if we removed it from the frame and rolled it up, it might be possible to—"

"I think it's time for us to be going," I said firmly. "Who knows when that painting was stolen or from whom? It is not an untraceable coin, and you would do well to leave it be."

"Yes, I suppose so." He sighed before brightening again. "I shall soon be able to buy a painting of my own with these coins. It is just a matter of patience."

I grabbed the leads of the two closest donkeys and began to tug them out of the cave. They came eagerly, unnerved by the flickering light and the vast cavern.

"Sensible creatures," I muttered as I hurried us outside again.

When the five of us were safely in the clearing, I turned back to the cave mouth.

"Close sesame," I proclaimed loudly and clearly.

For a tense moment, I thought nothing was happening. But then the now familiar grinding began, the hole shrinking rapidly.

Was the entire tunnel flattening behind it as well? I shivered as I imagined being caught in the tunnel when it closed. But the final rays of afternoon sun made it harder to hold on to such dark thoughts.

I shook them off and led the way forward, lingering for a moment on the edge of the trees to check for any changes to the clearing. There were none. It looked just as it had when we first arrived.

Ali hurried to keep up with me, shaking his head.

"You cannot really be so unmoved by the wonder we have just witnessed," he exclaimed. "Think how different this discovery could make your life!"

"I am thinking about it," I said. "I'm thinking of being stalked by forty cutthroat thieves—or being branded a thief myself if I turn up in the market and try to spend golden coins. I'm thinking of living every moment waiting for the enchantment to finally reveal itself and for my new life to dissolve into nothing. Given the danger from the thieves, we cannot risk telling others what we've found. So I would have no way to explain my change in fortune. And I have no desire to leave my friends and city behind and start again where I know no one."

A sharp pang shot through me at the idea of leaving. It was a familiar feeling and one I never prodded too closely. I pushed it aside now, trying to concentrate on Ali's response.

"Goodness, no! We cannot breathe a word of what we've found!" For the first time Ali seemed to understand my reluctance. "The revelation would be inviting disaster."

"On that, at least, we agree," I said grimly. "There is plenty of room for disaster even before considering the possibility of an enchantment. And just because it was not readily apparent doesn't mean it doesn't exist."

"Don't worry so, Zaria." Ali's perpetual cheerfulness no longer seemed a pleasant trait, but I shut my mouth on my frustration, knowing it would do no good to argue with him.

"I'll think of something," he assured me. "And I shall find a way to share this change of fortune with you. We must both of us only hold our tongues, and the future will be bright."

I ground my teeth, wanting to tell him to leave me out of his plotting. But whether I liked it or not, the day's adventures had bound us firmly together. Just as Nyla feared to let me go, knowing a truth that could hurt her, so Ali would now be sure to keep me close.

I sighed as the city gates came into view. Today had turned out to be far more complicated than I could have imagined. And that was without considering my unexpected run in with the crown prince.

Ali's smile seemed a little forced as he exchanged pleasantries with the gate guards, but none of them appeared to notice. He was a familiar figure at this gate, and they waved him through with friendly greetings. As soon as we were within the shadow of the city walls, he winked at me.

I was about to let out an indignant protest when a low voice spoke, startling me enough to forget about the stolen gold.

"Zaria! So it really is you!"

I turned slowly, a single word slipping from my lips.

"Rek."

CHAPTER 4

The prince's white horse stepped out of the shadow of the wall, moving toward us. Ali's eyes grew wide, and he bowed deeply.

"Your Highness!"

Jolted into action by his movement, I also bowed. Rek's frown grew deeper, dissatisfaction on his face as he watched me. The brief anger he'd shown in the forest flashed back through my mind, followed by a surge of my own anger. What reason did Rek have to be so scathing? I had not been at fault for my change in status, and I had never tried to push myself on him since.

"This is an unexpected surprise, Your Highness." The words came out more stiffly than I'd intended.

He raised one eyebrow. "Unexpected indeed. I didn't realize you were back in Kuralan."

"Back in Kuralan?" I repeated, too confused to form a more coherent question.

My one trip outside our kingdom's borders had been brief. After the disappointment of our visit to Sirrala, Ardasira's capital, not even Nyla had left our city for three years.

"I hope you were able to apprehend your quarry, Your Highness." Ali looked between us, his brow creased with confusion and concern, despite the smile pasted on his face.

Even Ali's habitual calm hadn't survived the dramatic events of the afternoon. But at least he wasn't glancing guiltily at the donkeys.

Rek didn't appear to notice anything odd, however, his own furrowed brow focused exclusively on me. But after an awkward moment of silence, he dragged his eyes to Ali.

"Unfortunately we were not successful." His brows contracted further. "What do you know of the matter?"

Seeming to realize his mistake, Ali executed another hasty bow.

"Nothing much, Your Highness, certainly. Merely that Zaria here saw the guards pursuing someone through the forest. Naturally it is my hope that Your Royal Highness and your esteemed family are successful in every endeavor."

Rek looked unimpressed by the fulsome gushing.

"And who are you?" he asked.

"Ali, Your Highness. Merely a lowly woodcutter. No one of any consequence."

Rek glanced at the branches lying on top of the donkeys' baskets. Could he see any gold shining through from underneath? I might disagree with Ali's actions in taking the gold, but I didn't want him targeted by the royal family—for Navid's sake more than Ali's own.

Rek must not have noticed anything amiss because he transferred his attention back to me.

"It's been a long time, Zaria," he said in a disarmingly soft voice. "I thought—" He paused, shaking his head and falling silent, apparently unwilling to finish the sentence.

"More than three years." I met his eyes steadily.

For some unknown reason he wanted to talk as if we were still friends. But while my mind might understand the gulf of station between us now, my emotions weren't as compliant. His abandonment had hurt, and I didn't intend to pretend otherwise.

I couldn't resist asking after his sister, however. "How is Adara? I miss her." The last words slipped out before I could stop them.

A reproachful look came over Rek's face. "She misses you, too."

I snorted, my indignation overcoming my good sense. Adara could come find me anytime. As a child, she had been bound to the palace except for the occasional sanctioned parade through the city or excursion to the forest, but she had been of age for well over a year now. And Rek himself had come of age shortly after my father's death. He, at least, could have approached me almost from the beginning.

My expression soured further as I remembered my excitement as the city celebrated the coming of age of their crown prince. Rek had long been preparing for the extra responsibility he would gain on his birthday—distancing himself from our antics as he approached eighteen. But with that responsibility came freedom from the palace walls. Freedom which would allow him to come find me—if he desired to do so.

I had gone to the palace myself on my first rest day after I started work with Nyla. Alone, shocked, and in grief, I hadn't been thinking clearly. But I had never gotten the opportunity to embarrass myself in front of anyone other than the guards at the front gate. They had turned me away, just as they would any servant who turned up demanding entrance.

In the long days after that, my mind had told me their refusal was a relief. It had saved me from inevitable rejection inside the palace walls since there could be no further friendship between me and the royals. But despite my mind's lectures, my heart had still hoped. I had almost convinced myself that after his birthday Rek would come find me, bringing messages from his younger siblings who were still trapped at home.

But the days had turned into weeks, and eventually my heart had accepted what my mind had known all along. Not only was Rek not interested in pursuing a friendship with a servant, he wasn't willing to be the means of opening communication between his sister and me either. And Adara—always so impetuous and warm—could not be blamed for seeing reason by the time her own birthday arrived. It had still hurt, however, and I couldn't hide that now.

The expression on my face seemed to confuse him, and he glanced again at Ali.

"Sorry, *who* are you?"

"A…Ali? Your Highness?" Ali threw me a bewildered look, but I just shrugged, using all my self-control to bite my tongue.

Despite the strangeness of Rek's manner and his bizarre opening comment, he clearly knew where I had been the whole time. Azzam had informed him I was working for the merchant Kasim's household, and Rek was now surprised to find me with Ali the woodcutter instead.

Azzam—one of the viziers who had worked most closely with my father—had believed the royals would contact me immediately. I couldn't blame him for believing better of my old friends than they deserved. And I hadn't been surprised to receive no visits from him, either. As a child, I had rarely seen Azzam and there was no affection between us—it had been a sense of duty that led him to secure a position for the bereft daughter of one of his closest colleagues.

A horrifying possibility overtook me. Did Rek think I'd married Ali to escape the life of a servant? Ali was old enough to be my father!

"Ali is Kasim's brother," I blurted, the words bursting out despite myself. "I sometimes assist him as he gathers wood."

Rek's frown didn't lighten, and another awkward silence descended over us. But as he gazed at me, Rek's expression softened, an emotion in his eyes I couldn't read.

"Zaria," he began, only to be interrupted by the clatter of approaching hooves.

We looked up to find the guard captain from the forest approaching, a squad of guards behind him.

"Prince Tarek!" The captain saluted, but his expression was forbidding. "There you are. I was beginning to fear I would have to report to your father that we had lost you."

Rek didn't even glance at us, straightening on his horse's back and nudging the animal forward, cutting Ali and me out of the circle of conversation.

I sighed softly. Now there was an audience, the prince didn't want anyone to see him conversing with such lowly persons as us.

"My apologies, Captain." Rek guided his horse further forward. "I had some private business to conduct, but I am ready to return home now."

The captain looked curiously toward us, half obscured though we were, but Rek cleared his throat, an imperious inclination of his head indicating that he expected the guards to lead the way.

The captain nodded back and wheeled his horse toward the palace. His squad formed around the prince, and the column of horses moved into the city. They had nearly passed from sight when Rek sent a single glance back toward us, our eyes meeting for the briefest moment.

Something sharp and heated jumped from his gaze to mine, but before I could identify what it might be, he turned a corner and was gone.

"Come on, Zaria!" Ali hissed. "We must get these animals home." He sent a significant look toward the closest basket.

His words jolted me into action. I had been distracted by the past, but Ali's attention was firmly on the gold. Only once we were both moving did he ask the questions that must have been swirling in his head.

"What was that about, Zaria? The prince knew you!"

I shrugged, having regained some of my equanimity now that Rek was no longer within view.

"Surely someone has mentioned that I came to Nyla from the palace? Before his death, my father was a junior vizier there. I once knew all the royals. But that was another lifetime."

"A vizier!" Ali was surprised enough to stop, but when the donkeys kept moving, he hurried back into motion. "But what are you doing as a servant in that case? What of your mother?"

"She died birthing me. I never knew her."

"I'm sorry," he said, true sympathy in his voice.

I managed a small smile. "My father, and the nurse he employed, gave me all the affection a young girl could need. I noticed no lack."

"But they are both deceased as well?" He waited for my nod of confirmation. "How tragic. Now that you mention it, I do remember something about you having come from the palace. It is so long ago, I had forgotten. But I assumed you must have been a servant there. Surely the child of a vizier would not be left destitute!"

My mouth twisted. "I only discovered after my father's death that he had many debts. It took all his savings to defray them, leaving me with nothing. I am grateful to one of his fellow viziers for using his position to find me employment."

I said the words mechanically, knowing I should feel gratitude to Azzam. My undutiful emotions rebelled, however. From the moment my numb shock had subsided, and I had grasped Nyla's character, I had felt nothing toward him but sour resentment.

I wasn't foolish enough to speak in those terms, though. In society's eyes, Kasim's household provided secure and enviable employment, and Azzam had continued to rise up the ranks of viziers in the last three years. It would be ridiculous for someone in my position to set myself up as his enemy, however much I resented his lack of compassion.

"Ah! Here we are!" The sight of his front door pushed my sad history from Ali's mind.

He drove the three donkeys ahead of him, waiting until we were all inside the simple fence that encircled his modest home before he rubbed his hands together in delight. He closed the gate firmly just as his wife, Mariam, came bustling out to welcome him.

Their house was much smaller than Kasim and Nyla's, with little room for servants. And the courtyard between the fence and house was nothing more than packed earth. But even this house would have been out of their reach if it hadn't been purchased for them by Kasim.

The rumor among the servants was that he had done it in an effort to appease Nyla. His wife had been mortified at having relatives living in what she described as a hovel. But unsurprisingly, she hadn't been pleased at his expenditure. And she certainly didn't seem to like her brother and sister-in-law any better now they lived in a nicer home.

I had always been glad for Navid's sake, though.

"Zaria!" Mariam smiled at me in welcome before turning to frown at Ali. "Navid mentioned she had gone with you, but what is she doing here? You should have seen her home first." Her tone suggested disappointment at Ali's failure of courtesy.

"And you're back so quickly," she continued, worry creasing her face. Her expression relaxed when she looked to the donkeys, however. "Ah, but I see your baskets are full. A good afternoon's work, then?"

"You will soon see how good, best of wives!" Ali cried. "When you realize what is inside these baskets, you will understand why I hurried straight here, not even deviating to see our good Zaria home."

Mariam looked more taken aback than cheered by these words, regarding the baskets as if she thought something inside might leap out and attack her.

"Whatever can you mean?" she asked. "Don't play games with me, Ali, I beg of you. It has been a long enough day without such nonsense."

"Has it, my dear?" He smiled at her. "Well I hope it will be the last such. Why you can hire as many servants as you like now!"

"What do you mean?" she asked sharply, the alarm on her face growing. "Tell me at once, Ali!"

Ali swept aside the branches on the closest basket with a low, triumphant cry.

Mariam cried out in horror, staggering back, her hands flying to her mouth. Ali deflated, looking at her with concern.

"There is no cause for alarm. Don't you see that our fortunes have changed forever?"

"No cause for alarm!?" Mariam glared at him. "Never did I think I would live to see my husband become a thief."

"A thief! No indeed!"

I cleared my throat, and he threw me a guilty look. "Well, not so that it counts. Stealing from thieves isn't really stealing at all."

"Stealing…from thieves?" Mariam regarded him with bulging eyes, her horror apparently too great for proper speech.

"I do not even consider it to be stealing from them," Ali argued with another look at me. "I have discovered the second treasure cave of the younger brother from legend. The fact some thieves found it first means nothing. It does not make the gold theirs."

"The lost treasure cave?" Mariam's expression slowly transformed, an eager look coming into her eyes as she regarded the gleaming gold in the basket. "That is a different matter, indeed."

I looked at the gold myself, frowning. Having seen the cave's contents, plus the way the entrance operated, I couldn't doubt we had discovered the legendary treasure cave. But I still couldn't understand the actions of the thieves. If a gang of robbers discovered such a treasure trove, surely they would have long ago cleared it out? It was true it provided a secure location to store their stolen goods, but why go to the danger of continuing to rob travelers at all? It would take many lifetimes to spend the fortune sitting in that cave.

I cleared my throat, and Mariam turned to look at me. From the sudden concern on her face, she had just remembered her husband had a companion in his discovery.

"I suppose some of this is yours, then, Zaria?"

I shook my head. "I want nothing to do with it. Surely you've heard the tales of the other treasure cave? I fear there's an enchantment on this gold. If Ali had listened to me, we wouldn't have touched a single coin."

"Enchantment?" Mariam looked sharply back at Ali. "We don't want any enchantments here!"

"Relax, my dear." He smiled. "Zaria is overly cautious. As you can see, we were able to bring baskets of gold out without any ill effect at all. There was not so much as a rumble, I promise you."

"Baskets?" Mariam stared with round eyes at the other donkeys. "Are all the baskets full then?"

"Every one!" Ali exclaimed proudly.

"But...but..." Mariam staggered over to collapse on a bench that ran along the house by the front door. She took a moment to catch her breath. "We must count it all!"

"Count it?" Ali laughed. "There is too much to count. And plenty more where it came from."

"More?" I gave him a disapproving look. "Surely you don't mean to return to the cave! What if you encounter the thieves again?"

"I'm sure I shan't need to return," he said complacently. "We will not spend all this gold in a hurry."

"No." Mariam heaved herself back to her feet, having recovered from her initial shock. "We must be wise in how we approach this. We cannot have people asking where our sudden wealth has come from. If we spend a little, people will assume it to be the generosity of your brother. But if we spend too much at once, rumors may spread.

Rumors that may reach the ears of this gang. Who knows how they would react to knowing their hideout has been discovered?"

I nodded approvingly, glad at least someone was showing some sense.

"We will bury it," Ali said. "And dig it up a little at a time while I think of an explanation for an increase in our circumstances. And of course, once I happen upon one, we must be sure to pay back my brother for this house."

Mariam stilled, her brow creasing, but after a moment she sighed and nodded.

"Of course, my dear. Our honor demands it, even if the original gift was given selfishly and begrudgingly. If Kasim and Nyla knew anything of honor, they would have us as part of their household, as do other families in their position. But we must not let their lack of honor sully our own."

"Precisely." Ali beamed at her.

Mariam's eyes returned to the baskets. "If we are already calculating how to part with the gold, we really must know how much there is to start with. If we cannot count it all, I must at least weigh it."

Ali sighed. "If you insist, my dear, although I cannot see the point."

He turned away to remove the first of the baskets from the nearest donkey, and Mariam threw me a conspiratorial look of exasperation.

"Of course he does not," she said in an under-voice. "Does he keep the records of our family finances? No, of course not!" She rolled her eyes before hurrying to assist Ali.

I watched them in growing consternation. The events of the afternoon had all happened in such quick succession that my mind was reeling. I felt sure I was missing some important angle to all of this.

Lost in my thoughts, I nearly missed the glances Mariam kept sending me. When I finally met her gaze, she quickly looked away, but a moment later she spoke in a determinedly cheerful voice.

"Of course you must benefit in some way from all of this, Zaria. I know you are great friends with my son, and I have heard from him of the trials you all suffer under Nyla. We all know the trouble she has keeping any servant for longer than a few months."

The disgust in her voice as she mentioned her sister-in-law didn't surprise me. Ali might wear a perpetually cheerful manner, but his wife had never been as successful at hiding her true opinion of Nyla and Kasim.

Not that she spoke openly against them—she knew her obligation as family, even if Nyla did not. But neither could anyone expect her to like relatives who treated her, her husband, and their son with such contempt and who ignored the family obligations that should have had Kasim welcome Ali's family with open arms.

"I get on well enough," I said warily, unsure where she was going with her comments.

"Oh certainly," she said quickly. "I'm sure you have your own reasons for staying with her, and it does you great credit. But if you don't wish to take any of the gold directly, you must at least come and work for us where I can promise you a much more welcoming home than you currently enjoy."

Her words caught me by surprise. Once again I was hit by a pain at the thought of leaving my current life. But I pushed the complicated tangle of emotions away, sensing the day's unexpected events had only further confused my feelings on the matter.

"That...is a kind offer," I said slowly, unsure how to reply. Something inside me had shifted, I was sure of that much. Maybe I really could leave Nyla and work for Mariam instead. I needed space to think, though. I wasn't ready to commit myself to anything.

"Of course we can't take you on immediately," Mariam rushed to add, providing the opening I needed. "We have to ease into spending this gold carefully. But as soon as Ali thinks of an excuse for a change in our fortunes, I'll begin hiring, and of course you'll be the first to receive an offer."

"You need feel no rush on my account," I said quickly and received a gracious smile in response.

I pretended not to notice the hint of concern that still lingered in her eyes, instead giving both her and Ali a bright farewell. Mariam returned it, bustling over to the gate with me. But when she reached it, her hand stilled on the latch.

"It occurs to me that I don't have a set of scales sufficient for weighing all this gold," she said. "Could you ask Nyla's cook if we might borrow one?"

I hesitated for a moment but could think of no obvious danger in the action.

"I'll ask her," I said. "She's used to sending food and other items to you, so it shouldn't cause a problem."

Mariam stiffened, although I had been thinking only of the strength of our cover story and hadn't intended to reference Mariam's poverty or Nyla's begrudging charity.

"I'm much obliged," she said stiffly. "And if you tell Nyla that Ali has requested your help again tomorrow, then you can bring the scales over yourself tomorrow morning."

"Certainly, if you wish it. But if Nyla proves difficult, I'll have to send one of the other girls over in my place. So I would recommend finding somewhere out of sight to stash those baskets."

"Of course," Mariam said. "We may have spent our life in poverty, but we aren't fools."

"I'm sorry," I said quickly. "I didn't mean to imply you were. I'm all turned around after the afternoon's revelations. And I can't stop thinking of the possible consequences of taking this gold. You and Ali have always been kind to me, and Navid is one of my closest friends. I would hate to see any harm befall you."

Mariam softened. "You're a good girl, Zaria. I'm sorry my sister-in-law treats you so harshly. You don't deserve her ill will."

I smiled back. "Perhaps this gold will do some good after all, and I'll soon be free of her."

Mariam's eyes flashed back to the baskets. "I'm sure it will do much good. I assure you, we will treat it with full caution." She opened the gate, and I slipped out with a final farewell.

Despite her reassurances, I walked the streets between Ali and Kasim's house in a state of high distraction. I couldn't shake the feeling this gold was only going to lead to disaster.

CHAPTER 5

The wall around Kasim's enormous home was a far cry from the one around his brother's house. Instead of a simple door, elaborate double gates gave entrance into the large courtyard. Both Kasim and Nyla loved entertaining merchants and officials—putting on elaborate parties with dancers or fire breathers—and at this time of the late afternoon, it wouldn't have been surprising to find guests arriving.

Normally I loved to hide and watch the dancers, my toes itching to join the dance, but on this occasion I was grateful to slip through the gates to an empty courtyard. My nerves were already on edge, and I didn't want an audience.

"Welcome back!" The cheerful call made me start before I recognized the gray hair and calm expression of one of the senior grooms.

I forced a smile and crossed the open space to greet the mare he was leading back from her daily exercise. She was one of my favorites, a gentle creature who deserved a better rider than Nyla.

"Evening, girl," I murmured, patting her velvety nose.

"Greetings to you, too," said Rowan with a chuckle.

"Sorry." I gave him an apologetic look. "It's been a tiring afternoon. Consider my greetings meant for both of you."

He chuckled. "How can I mind being eclipsed by such a noble lady as this?" He gave the mare an affectionate pat before looking back at me. "I heard she sent you out to the forest." His voice held sympathy, and neither of us felt the need to clarify who *she* was. "You were probably better off, though. She's been raging all afternoon, so you would have just been a target here."

I grimaced, sorry for the rest of them who had been left behind. Nyla's gold had bought her a secure place in the social circle of the merchants of Karema, but what she really wanted was access to the royal circle and acceptance among the courtiers. It wasn't a totally impossible dream since the richest merchants were often invited to palace functions. But for some reason, an initial invitation four years ago had never been followed up by another.

I sighed. "I hope she'll have calmed down by tomorrow. Are there any guests expected tonight?"

When he shook his head, I breathed a sigh of relief. The night would end a lot earlier without guests, and I wanted the sanctuary of my tiny bedchamber to sort out my muddled thoughts.

Images kept flashing through my mind—chests overflowing with gold alternated with the grim look of the thieves and with the face of Rek. I had thought myself long ago adjusted to my new life, but seeing my old friend had stirred it all up again.

"Maybe you should head straight for bed." Rowan watched my face with concern. "You look exhausted, and the last thing you need is to run into her."

I dredged up an approximation of my usual grin. "Don't worry about me. You know I can handle it. I've been coping for three years, and I'm not going to collapse in a heap now."

"That's our Zaria." He smiled back at me. "Irrepressible. That's what Yara always says about you."

I laughed, although I hardly felt my normal self. Rowan and

Yara, the cook, formed the heart of the small group of servants whose positions in the household were of long-standing, and when I arrived here, heartbroken and in shock, they had been my first friends. Their acceptance had paved my way. With an endless stream of servants coming and going, driven away by Nyla's manner and ceaseless demands, it hadn't been long before I was no longer the useless new girl from the palace. I would always be grateful to them for their kindness.

"Tempting as it is, I can't go and hide immediately," I said. "I need to speak to Yara. Mariam sent a message for her."

I gave the mare a final pat and Rowan a farewell smile before hurrying the rest of the way across the courtyard. I made directly for the external kitchen door, knowing I was unlikely to find Nyla inside.

Sure enough, only the cook and her various underlings were inside the bustling room. The evening meal was in the final stages of preparation, but Yara still broke off her work to greet me with a cry of delight.

"There you are!" she exclaimed. "I was starting to think you'd vanished."

I rolled my eyes. "It hasn't been that long. I visited yesterday!"

"Yes, but everyone knows *she's* on a rampage today. I thought you'd have sought refuge in here before now."

"She sent me out with Ali." I took a seat on one of the stools by the long workbench and stole a date from a nearby platter.

As I put it in my mouth, I hummed softly with pleasure. I couldn't remember the last time I'd eaten.

Yara's face softened, and she smiled at me affectionately. "Of course she did. Why you put up with her, I don't know. And don't tell me that you stay because the job is physically undemanding and pays well! I've heard that nonsense from you often enough, but the rest of us aren't subjected to the same constant persecution you are. I don't care if they're only words, she'll wear you away until there's nothing left if you let her, child."

I shrugged. We'd had this conversation enough times before that Yara could recite my side as easily as hers. My friends had never been able to understand why I stayed, putting up with Nyla's verbal abuse. Perhaps that was because I had never fully articulated it even to myself. But the day's events had changed everything—and I was only beginning to sense how much that was true. I needed time to sort out my own emotions.

"You must be even more exhausted than you look!" Yara's voice broke my reverie, and I sent her a guilty look.

"Sorry, were you speaking to me?"

She raised an eyebrow. "I was telling you that you don't need to scavenge from the master's plate. I'll have one of the girls make you a plate of your own."

She waved vaguely in the direction of a small knot of kitchen maids, and one launched into action. I smiled gratefully at the girl before turning back to Yara.

"I didn't actually come about food—delicious as everything you make is."

Yara's eyebrow rose higher. "What's all this then? Flattery? What sort of favor are you after?"

"Not one for me. I've come from Ali's, and Mariam asked if she could borrow your scales."

"My scales! Whatever will she want next?" Yara looked put out, so I hurried back into speech.

"She's very grateful for your continued goodwill. She called that stew you sent them last week divine, and said she hopes Nyla appreciates that she has a true artist in her employ."

"Well, as to that..." Yara's glower melted into a smile. "It's very kind of her to send such a message, I'm sure." Her brows lowered again. "Even if it's just to butter me up for another favor."

"No, no, I'm sure it's not," I said quickly. "She said it well before she asked for the scales. Navid was the one who told me, and he agreed most heartily."

"Well, as for that young scamp…" Yara smiled in a matronly way, shooting me what she no doubt thought a furtive look.

But this was another topic I preferred not to engage with on the day. I knew it brought pleasure to my friends in the household to think there was more between Navid and me than mere friendship, so it wasn't an easy notion to talk them out of.

"As it happens," said Yara, unbending even more, "I have just recently purchased a newer, larger set of scales. So Mariam can borrow my old ones without causing any great inconvenience." Her voice darkened again. "Not that she could have known that."

I jumped down from the stool. "She'll be glad to hear she's causing no inconvenience, I'm sure. Can I take them now? I promised to drop them over first thing tomorrow before setting off with Ali."

"The forest again so soon?" Yara asked, any irritation with Mariam forgotten. "That woman will drive you into your grave." I knew she wasn't referring to Mariam, so I just laughed.

"I'm not so weak, I promise you. Do you really think I'm likely to expire just from a few days of walking in the forest?"

Yara put her hands on her hips. "And have you eaten anything today?"

"Well…" I hesitated, not willing to actually lie. "It was a busy morning, and then—"

"Exactly!" Yara cried triumphantly. "Don't try to pull anything over on me. I was serving Nyla before you were a babe in arms, and if anyone knows her true nature it's me."

"My condolences," I muttered, and her volatile mood shifted again, a chuckle shaking her.

Yara's cooking was famous throughout the city, and her food enabled Nyla to take pride in her dinners. She had to hire outside entertainers for the events, since no dinner was complete without some form of entertainment with dessert, but she never needed to hire a special cook as other households did.

Everyone knew Nyla paid Yara a veritable fortune to remain

in her service, just as Kasim paid Rowan similar to retain his superior skill with the horses. They paid their junior servants a great deal less well, and rarely retained them long as a result. No one had been serving Nyla as long as Yara.

"Just make sure you eat everything on that plate before you let her catch sight of you!" Yara ordered, and I meekly agreed.

Minutes later, I tottered out of the kitchen with a heaped plate in one hand and the scales wedged under my other arm. I took the long way around to the back stairs, successfully making it to my own room without being seen by anyone.

The food was welcome and the sanctuary even more so, but before I could enjoy either of them, I had one final task to complete. Placing my plate on a small table and dropping the scales on the small chest that held my clothes, I pulled out the single golden coin weighing down my pocket.

Safe in my room, without the prickly feeling on the back of my neck that I'd had the whole time in the cave, I examined it. The only difference between this coin and the ones already hidden beneath my bed was the bright shine of the gold. The others had passed through many hands, but this one looked untouched and new. But shouldn't an ancient coin be stamped with a different design than the modern ones used in both Ardasira and Kuralan?

With a feeling of discomfort, I concluded this particular coin must be a more recent addition by the thieves. But once added to the hoard, it had become enmeshed in the enchantment and its protective effects. Once that thought had taken root, I had no desire to keep holding the coin. Dropping to my knees, I retrieved the leather pouch from its hiding place beneath the bed.

Opening it, I pulled out a coin and held it up side by side with the new one for one final examination. I could still see no difference beyond the brightness of the new one which made it stand out against my other coins. Sighing, I put both coins into the pouch and pulled it closed again.

I gazed at the scales as I wolfed down my dinner. In themselves, they were an innocuous item, but they seemed to represent all the chaos of the day.

I had just finished the plate when a knock on my door made me flinch. I hurried to answer it, reminding myself Nyla had never come to my room before and was unlikely to start now.

A tall, thin woman stood on the other side, an impatient look on her face. I knew her well enough to know that was her habitual expression, though.

"Long day, Layla?" I asked with sympathy.

Layla was another of the tiny circle who had been in Nyla's employ for years. Unlike Yara and Rowan she had no particular area of expertise other than the valuable ability to endure Nyla's moods. In exchange for that imperturbability, Nyla paid her nearly as much as Yara. She might not care about the ever changing faces among the maids or guards or grooms, but she hadn't liked constantly having to train a new personal servant.

"Yara told me you were back," Layla said in a hurried voice, getting straight to the point. "I'm sorry, but Nyla has a task for you."

"Now?" I stared at her in dismay.

"She wants you to polish all the silverware. She says it needs to be done by morning."

"Polish the silverware?" My eyes widened. Although I often helped out where needed, that job was usually completed by the kitchen staff and on a set schedule.

Layla gave me a sympathetic grimace. "She's insisting it has to be you, but you'd better do the polishing in here, so you stay out of her way."

My eyebrows rose. "It's that bad?"

"Worse," she said gloomily. "It turns out Yasmine was invited to the palace last night and—in case that wasn't bad enough—she turned up for tea this afternoon because she *just knew Nyla would want to hear all about it.*"

I gasped, my sympathy growing. "If there's one woman who would make a worse mistress than Nyla…" I shook my head.

"She's miserly to her servants," Layla said, her voice making it clear she considered such behavior the worst of all crimes. "At least we're well compensated for Nyla's…moods."

I nodded, not bothering to point out that only some of the servants were well paid.

"I know you're determined to remain in your role here," she said, her voice making it clear she shared Yara's opinion that I could do better for myself elsewhere, "so I suggest you stay out of sight. Or Nyla might finally lose her temper enough to actually throw you out."

I grimaced. The last thing I needed was more upheavals tonight. I glanced at the scales, struck by an idea.

"Ali asked me to help him tomorrow as well. I'll leave first thing in the morning, before Nyla's up. If I can stay out of her way the whole day, she might have calmed down again by tomorrow night."

"An excellent plan," Layla said promptly. "If she asks for you, I'll tell her you're in the forest. Here, you better give me your plate. I've left everything you need for the polishing just here." She gestured to the wall beside my door.

As she brushed off my profuse thanks and bustled off down the corridor, I looked at the piled silverware with a sigh. I'd be up half the night completing the unnecessary task. At least my friend had helped by collecting everything I needed so I could stay hidden for now.

I glanced back up to catch a final glimpse of Layla. She was only fifteen years older than me, but she carried herself as if she were a peer of Rowan and Yara who must be two decades older again. A lot of the newer servants in the household found her too abrupt, thinking it came from hauteur, but it was just her natural manner.

Despite Yara and Rowan's championing, Layla hadn't taken to

me at first. She must have considered me a rival for her position given Nyla had chosen me—a brand new servant—for the grand trip to Sirrala in Layla's place. But given how the visit had turned out, her suspicion and resentment transformed to sympathy within weeks. We had long ago become allies. And while officially I was a general maid, providing help wherever it was needed in the house, I most often worked with Layla.

Bringing the armloads inside, I set myself up and began polishing, whisking my cloth across the silver surface of a candlestick as quickly as I could. I needed to be gone promptly in the morning and couldn't afford to oversleep, which meant I needed to get the task finished sooner rather than later.

As I worked on the monotonous task, my eyes were continuously drawn back to the scales as the events of the afternoon replayed in my head. A magical cave full of wonders beyond counting was enough to distract anyone, but it wasn't the cave that intruded most on my thoughts.

The thieves had made a more intimidating picture and, as I pushed the cloth back and forth, I realized I was even more concerned about them than about the possibility of an enchantment.

As I moved from one piece of silverware to the next, I pondered the unanswerable questions: would they realize someone had stolen from the cave? And what would they do if they did?

A gang of forty cutthroat thieves would be frightening enough, but I couldn't shake the certainty there was something strange about their behavior. Did they steal—despite all the risks —just for the joy of it? What possible reason could there be for someone with access to such riches to resort to thievery?

The idea increased the sense of danger that surrounded them, and a new guilty thought crept over me. In the initial shock of discovery, Ali and I had naturally been focused on our discovery of the fabled second treasure cave. But we had found something else as well—the headquarters of the dangerous gang who had been plaguing the roads of Kuralan for decades.

Rek was looking for those thieves, and I could tell him where to find them. It was almost as if he had known that when he chose to lie in wait for us inside the city gates. But he couldn't possibly have done. Something else had driven him to wait there, and for some reason that was an even more intriguing thought than the cave and the thieves put together.

It was foolish and illogical to focus on Rek in the middle of everything else, but I couldn't help the way my thoughts kept circling back to him.

I put down one item and picked up the next without even looking at it.

Rek had looked so different and yet so familiar. What did Adara and the twins look like now? Would the best friend of my childhood look unrecognizably grown up and sophisticated?

But despite the shock of seeing Rek, nothing had actually changed. Dwelling on the royals was as foolish now as it had been three years ago. Nothing Rek had done or said had given the impression he wished to resume old friendships. Instead he had hovered on the edge of anger, clearly consumed by emotions I didn't fully understand.

What could I possibly have done to provoke him? I had obediently left the palace when instructed to do so, and I had meekly worked for Nyla ever since, putting up with all her abuse and turning myself into a valuable member of her household. And never once in all that time had I attempted to push my unwelcome presence on the royals. What could Rek possibly have against me?

And yet, the more I thought about our two brief encounters, the more his behavior and words seemed as incomprehensible as that of the thieves. What had he said to me?

I didn't realize you were back in Kuralan.

The words made no sense. But if I didn't know better and just took them at face value, they seemed straightforward enough. Rek had been under the impression I no longer resided in Kuralan. But what could possibly have given him that idea?

Azzam had told the royals where I was after he found me this position. If Rek had inquired after me in the years that followed, anyone in the market could have told him that I still worked for Nyla and could be found among Kasim's household. Even though all my new friends said I could find a better life elsewhere, here I still was.

In all that time, even after I received Cassandra's gift of gold, I told myself I didn't have enough saved to start a new life. No matter how much I added, I never had enough. And every time my friends brought it up, I felt the same stab of discomfort, the same instinctual desire to change the topic of conversation.

I didn't like to admit it, even to myself, but deep down I knew the truth. I never had enough gold for a new life because I didn't really want a new life. I wanted my old life back. And living in Kuralan, working for Nyla, was my last connection with that old life.

I knew Rek could have found me at any time because I had made sure that was the case. And while I was being honest, it wasn't just about my royal friends. The palace at Karema was the happy home of my childhood, the place I had lived with my father. How could I admit to my friends that I was still clinging to my inner child, whatever it cost me?

But if I had done everything possible to remain contactable, why did Rek think I was living somewhere far away? He'd always known where I was.

Unless...

Unless he hadn't.

The final piece of silverware dropped from my hands as I surged to my feet. Pacing over to the window, I threw open the shutters. Darkness had now fallen, but I desperately needed fresh air.

Azzam had hurried me out of the palace while I was still in shock and consumed by grief. I hadn't even had the chance to say goodbye to my friends. He had assured me he had informed the royals of his actions on my behalf, and that they would contact me in the following days. But what if he hadn't told them at all? What if he'd told them something entirely different?

It was incomprehensible. What possible reason could he have to lie?

But the more I thought about it, the more Rek's response made sense in the light of this possibility. If he thought I had left without so much as a farewell—moving somewhere out of reach and then never sending a single letter…

It would have been a monstrous betrayal of the kindness and friendship they had shown me over ten years.

But why would Azzam do something so cruel? I couldn't accept the idea without any sort of motivation. What did Azzam have to gain by such deception?

I frowned as I returned to my place and retrieved the now dusty jug I had dropped. I would have to start polishing it all over again, but I welcomed the physical outlet.

Rubbing it so hard I might wear the silver away, I considered. Why had Nyla insisted I polish silverware that didn't need the attention? What did she have to gain by directing her frustration and rage toward me?

Only an outlet for her resentment and jealousy.

But Azzam hadn't been my father's enemy. He had been one of the viziers in the same group as my father. My father had been highly praised for all ten of the years he worked as a vizier, and the two men had often worked closely together. Azzam had been my father's friend, or I wouldn't have trusted him after my father's death.

An incongruous image appeared in my mind. Yasmine and Nyla sitting down to tea, the facade of friendship a thin veneer over simmering jealousy and competition. As a child, I had taken friendships at face value, but I had now worked closely with Nyla for years, so I knew things weren't always as they initially appeared. I couldn't think of a single one of Nyla's so-called friends who she actually liked. She either accepted them because they pandered to her sense of importance, or the friendship was merely an opportunity to flaunt her wealth and position—as Yasmine had done today with her invitation. Nyla might be angry with Yasmine, but she would have done the same in reverse and gloried in every minute.

My father hadn't been like that, I was sure of it. He had been true from head to heart and always kind, regardless of the other person's rank. But that just meant he would never have spoken poorly of one of his colleagues to his young daughter. If Azzam was another Nyla, my father would have privately held him in contempt, but he wouldn't have thought to warn me. Caught up with the royal children, I almost never came into contact with Azzam. And my father hadn't expected to suddenly die.

I was trembling, gasping the cool night air in an effort to calm down. All my foundations, all my emotions from the last three years were shaking along with me.

My first instinct was to run straight out of the house and head to the palace. But my good sense soon reasserted itself. My personal revelation would do nothing to get me through the gates. If I turned up at the palace in the middle of the night, the guards would laugh in my face—if they didn't arrest me on suspicion I was there to cause trouble.

My best hope was to wait for a public appearance—the very events I had been carefully avoiding all this time for fear of the pain they would cause me. If I managed to push my way to the front of the crowd, they might recognize me. Rek had already done so in the middle of a forest, so I clearly hadn't changed that greatly. Adara would surely know me as well, as long as she wasn't so angry at my disappearance that she rejected me before I had a chance to explain.

If only I could have my time with Rek by the gate back again. If only I'd thought faster and understood the implications of his words. I might never get an opportunity like that again.

Finally finishing the last piece of polishing, I placed it carefully on the tray with the others. As I rose to my feet and reached for the tray's handles, my eyes fell on the scales and guilt flooded me. I should have used my one opportunity to speak to Rek to report our discovery of the cave.

Now, of course, the same difficulty applied with the cave as with my own concerns. How could I get a message to Rek or Adara about the gang when I had no way to access them? I wasn't foolhardy enough to give my message directly to the guards. I could only imagine how they would respond if I turned up and announced I had information about the thieves. I had no desire to find myself on the wrong end of a guard interrogation.

Sighing, I hurried out into the corridor to return the pieces of silverware to their cupboard. However much I wanted to do so, I couldn't turn my revelations into action. Not right this second anyway.

It was hard to discipline myself to quietly return to bed and seek my overdue sleep. I had always preferred action to patient waiting. But eventually my fatigue overtook me, and I managed a few fitful hours.

CHAPTER 6

After the rough night, I slept later than intended, leaping from bed as soon as I realized it was well past dawn. With the scales tucked under my arm, I opened my door and nearly stepped on the package just outside it.

The date bread inside the wrapping had probably been warm when it was left here, but it was stone cold now. I sighed. Layla must have told Yara I intended to leave early.

Doubly annoyed at my uncharacteristic folly in sleeping late, I hurried for the closest exit into the courtyard. When I stepped out of the house without running into anyone, I let out a soft breath of relief. But I'd hardly taken two steps when a sharp voice called my name.

"Zaria! There you are!" Nyla swept toward me, remnants of a late breakfast still clutched in her hand. If she was chasing me down mid-meal, then the night had done little to cool her bad mood.

I straightened my shoulders and managed a smile. It was never a good idea to let Nyla see any irritation.

"I'm just leaving," I said. "Ali requested that I help him again today." I allowed a downcast expression to cross my face, and Nyla relaxed a little at the sight of it.

"Yes, you deserve another day outcast from the city. When I think what I went through yesterday with that odious woman laughing into her tea—"

I edged toward the gate, wondering if I dared slip out while she was still ranting. Her eyes speared me, however, her words abruptly breaking off as she focused on the bundle under my arm.

"What have you got there? Are you stealing something?"

I stopped, holding out the scales for her inspection.

"No, of course not." I restrained my anger. "I would never steal. Mariam asked to borrow some scales, and Yara has sent these old ones."

Nyla sniffed, clearly torn between the desire to disapprove of her sister-in-law's actions—whatever they might be—and approval of the fact Yara had only sent the old scales.

"Here, let me see those." She snatched the scales away from me, turning them over as if she wanted to check for herself that they weren't the new set.

"What could Mariam possibly have that needs weighing with such large scales?" she demanded, her eyes narrowing. "You must find out, Zaria!"

I blinked, taken aback. "But I—"

"No!" She held up a hand to stop me. "Everyone is always telling me how clever you are—although I take leave to doubt it myself. I'm sure you can think of a way to discover what Mariam is about. You can report back to me tonight."

With a satisfied nod, she thrust the scales back toward me and pointed at the gate. I gulped and accepted them, hurrying out of the courtyard before she could change her mind. At least I had the whole day to think of what answer I could give her. I certainly couldn't tell her the truth.

I groaned as I rushed through the streets of Karema. As if my list of worries wasn't big enough, I now needed to add the fear that Nyla might learn the truth about Ali's discovery. That would certainly be disastrous.

I took my usual shortcut through the market, waving greetings at the various stallholders but not stopping to speak to anyone as I rushed to Ali's. However, when I passed the bakery on the edge of the market, I came to a halt. A hand-drawn cart rested to one side of the door. Its load of sacks was already half-depleted, the work of a burly man who was slinging another two across his shoulders as I passed.

The miller and his cart were a familiar sight around this part of the city. And standing beside the cart, gazing toward the market, was an even more familiar figure.

"Zaria!" The petite young woman flicked her long black braid over her shoulder and dived toward me, her rounded face alight with joy.

I laughed as she wrapped her arms around me and squeezed. "Kali!" I said back, half mockingly.

She grinned in return, unfazed by my teasing.

I had met Kalila, the miller's daughter, the first time I visited the market. She was full of curiosity about the new girl—especially when she heard I had spent most of my life at the palace. It only took the discovery that we were mere months apart in age to turn us into firm friends.

She pulled back, her face full of excitement. "Have you heard the news?"

"News?" Fear shot through me. Had Ali already slipped up? Surely news of the treasure couldn't have spread through the market already.

"The thieves are back!" She said it like it was the most thrilling thing to happen in the last month.

"Oh." Relief shot through me before I looked at her suspiciously. "You seem unnaturally pleased about that."

A wounded expression filled her mobile features. "Of course

I'm not excited they're robbing people, but..." Her face shifted back to bright animation. "Samir actually saw them! He's been out of the city visiting relatives down south, and he was on his way back yesterday afternoon when the gang converged on a caravan traveling just ahead of him."

"What?" I twisted around, trying to peer back toward Samir's stall in the market. It was just out of sight, however. "Is he all right? Did they rob him?"

"He's fine. I guess his one little cart wasn't an appealing target compared to a whole caravan. But he saw the whole thing! And —!" She paused and looked at me expectantly, waiting for me to show the proper shock and interest before she delivered the climax of her news.

"Were the merchants in the caravan harmed?" I asked, a sick feeling developing in my stomach as I thought of the hard look on the faces of the thieves.

"They probably would have killed them all," Kali said with dramatic relish, "except guards came thundering out of the city and drove them into the forest. And guess who was at their head!"

"Oh," I said, finally catching up with the real reason this news was so sensational.

She gave me an odd look. "Did you already hear the story?" Her voice dripped with disappointment.

I shook my head. "No, not at all. Keep going."

Her smile returned. "It was the crown prince! Prince Tarek himself!" She nudged me, wiggling her eyebrows suggestively. "Your old friend."

I managed to dredge up a smile. "That's ancient history, Kali. You know that."

Two days ago I would have added that the prince wouldn't even recognize me if he saw me now, but it turned out that wasn't true.

But as good a friend as Kali was, I wasn't ready to tell her about my encounter with Rek or my revelation of the night before.

Kali sighed. "You're always so practical and focused, Zaria! Surely even you must be a little interested to hear that someone we know saw the prince pursuing the thieves into the forest!"

I laughed. "Sorry to be such a disappointment, best of friends. Shall I ask with bated breath whether he caught them?"

I had nearly forgotten to ask the crucial question that any uninformed person would surely ask.

"Sadly, no." Kali wilted. "Think how much better the story would be if he had!"

"And the lives of everyone who uses our kingdom's roads," I said wryly.

Kali waved aside my words. "Of course, of course. But think of the celebrations if the prince had caught them!" She rolled her eyes. "Not that you would have come."

"Actually," I said, "about that…"

Kali gasped and clapped her hands. "You mean you've changed your mind about living like a hermit?"

I laughed. "I don't live like a hermit! I'm here right now talking to you, aren't I?"

She wrinkled her nose. "You know what I mean! Whenever there's something especially fun going on, you hide away at home."

I grimaced, and she instantly looked contrite. "I'm sorry. I shouldn't tease you. Of course I understand why you don't want to come." She took my hand and squeezed it with a look of warm sympathy.

Kali was the only one who knew the whole story of my history at the palace. Except she didn't know the true story, I realized with a jolt. Although it had been unintentionally done, I had misled her.

Guilt filled me at having given her the wrong idea about my old friends. Kali was too loyal to accept the practicalities of our difference in station as a reason for the royals abandoning our friendship. Despite every protestation on my own part, she always declared that even if she became a princess tomorrow, she would remain friends with me. And now it turned out Adara might have been feeling the same way all along.

I shook my head. It was too late to think about that, and the present had plenty of worries without piling on ones from the past.

"I think it's wonderful if you're ready to join us at the next celebration, though," Kali said earnestly. "I've always hoped you would be able to move past the hurt eventually."

I winced but made myself squeeze her hand back, promising I would tell her the full truth at some point. Just not right now, with me late to Ali, and her father about to finish delivering the flour to the bakery.

"Thank you, Kali," I said. "You're a good friend."

"The best, naturally." She let go of my hand, giving me a cheeky smile just as her father called to her.

I chuckled, shaking my head as I waved goodbye and hurried back on my way. Kali was one of the things that had made it easy to settle into my life here, providing me with a delightful respite from Nyla whenever I had a rest day.

It was only a few minutes further to Ali's house, but all my earlier worries had returned by the time I reached the gate. I paused in front of it, staring at the festive red material tied around the handle.

The mark was a common enough symbol—seen around the city on the doors and gates of homes both large and small. But while I normally smiled to see a family celebrating the presence of house guests, I couldn't believe the bad timing of someone coming to stay with Ali today of all days.

Their arrival must have been unexpected—had Mariam and Ali already concealed the gold? Or had the visitors caught sight of it? It was a terrible coincidence to have someone turn up just at this moment, but no self-respecting household in the kingdom would turn away guests, even if they weren't expected."

Shaking my head, I tried to open the gate, only to find it locked. Frowning, I rapped loudly on the wood.

It took a long minute for someone to answer, and I heard the sound of a lock being drawn before the latch lifted. A cautious face peered through the gap, but a look of relief filled Navid's features when he recognized me.

"Oh, thank goodness it's you. I thought you'd never get here!"

He pulled the gate slightly further open, his arm shooting out through the gap to pull me inside. I looked around the courtyard as he re-latched the gate in a state of high distraction. There was, thankfully, no sign of the gold.

"What's going on?" I asked.

"I thought you already knew all about it!" Navid looked at me suspiciously. "Father said you were with him when he discovered…" He let his words trail off as if the reality was too unbelievable to speak aloud.

"Yes, I know about that. I meant the visitors." I pointed back at the locked gate.

"Visitors?" Navid stared at me for a moment in confusion before his brow cleared. "Oh yes, my mother's brilliant plan."

He didn't sound at all convinced of its brilliance.

"You mean she invited someone here?" I stared at him.

"No." He shook his head. "There's no one here. She wants our neighbors to think there is."

"But…why…" My brain raced, trying to understand the odd behavior. "Something to do with her plan to account for your sudden change in fortune, I suppose."

Navid nodded. "She says that Uncle Kasim became wealthy through his wife's family, so why shouldn't Father?"

I frowned. "I didn't think Mariam's family had any particular wealth."

"They don't. But they're from out west, so no one in Karema

knows much about them. They live near the edge of the Great Desert, so she's hit upon the notion of claiming they've traveled across the desert to make contacts in the new kingdoms. She's planning to claim they've set up lucrative trade deals, and that they want Father to manage the Karema end of the business."

"It's not a bad cover story," I said slowly, considering the various angles. "If they live near the desert, they would need someone here in the capital. But why would they trust something so important to a woodcutter, even if he is family?"

Navid ran a hand through his hair, looking unhappy. "That's where I come in. Everyone knows Uncle Kasim set me up with a prestigious apprenticeship, and I'll be graduating next week. Most people expect me to work for him after that, especially since he has no children of his own. He's never said he intends me to be his successor and heir, but naturally people make assumptions…" His mouth twisted, indicating he knew just how Nyla would feel about Kasim making Navid his heir.

In my private opinion, a lot of Nyla's antagonism toward her nephew stemmed from her awareness that he was a great deal more astute than her husband. I wasn't the only one she blamed for squandering the opportunities I'd been given. I was just an easier target than her husband.

"I see," I said slowly. "If it's natural to think you would take a position under your uncle, how much more natural that you would choose to work with your father when this opportunity arose. Yes, I can see how that makes sense. You were always meant to turn your family's fortunes around, you're just going to have some unexpected extra help."

"It still doesn't seem real." He fixed me with an intense look. "Is it really all true, Zaria? You and my father found the second treasure cave?"

"It's true, but…" I hesitated, unsure if Navid would want to hear words of warning right now. But he had always showed far more sense than his father.

"We didn't just trip and fall into the cave mouth," I said in a rush. "We didn't find the cave by chance—we followed a gang of forty thieves to it. *Forty thieves*, Navid! And an enchanted treasure. I'm not convinced this is the windfall your parents think it."

Navid's look of concern deepened. "You think the thieves might come after us?"

I shrugged. "We tried to make what Ali took look as inconspicuous as possible, so it wasn't obvious someone had been there. And I'll admit there was a lot of treasure. It's possible they won't even notice anything's amiss on their next visit. But..." I gave him an apologetic look. "We're talking about an enchanted treasure cave. Who knows what methods the thieves may have to detect the presence of intruders? And that's not even considering any potential enchantments."

"Enchantments?" Navid took a step toward me, lowering his voice. "You think there's something wrong with the gold?"

I shrugged again. "I don't know. Which is the whole issue. We don't know anything. The stories say there was an enchantment on the gold in the first cave. Why wouldn't there be one on this gold?"

I didn't mention that I had seen the power of those enchantments for myself—power that could reshape physical reality.

"But the stories say that enchantment made the cave collapse," Navid protested. "Nothing like that happened, did it?"

"Not so much as a rumble." I groaned. "But that just makes me more nervous. Centuries have passed, and the tales from Ardasira say the first cave's enchantments had degraded with time. If that had happened here as well, it might explain the cave not collapsing, but I would have expected at least a little shake, some dust coming down from the roof, perhaps. But there was no response at all to Ali taking the gold."

"And that worries you?" Navid asked.

"It makes me think there was never any enchantment to

collapse the cave at all. Which means the second cave may have an entirely different enchantment."

"Or none at all."

"That seems to be your father's point of view."

Navid ran a hand through his increasingly messy hair. "I see your concern. There's no way I'm going to convince Mother and Father to give this up, though."

I sighed and held out the scales. "No, I didn't think so. I've brought the scales, as requested."

Navid took them, looking down at them with an expression of unbelief. "So much gold it needs to be weighed instead of counted," he said softly. "It does seem too good to be true."

"Precisely," I said grimly, gently pushing him toward the door of the house. "But come on, we might as well go inside. I told the other servants Ali wanted my help again today, so I don't have to head back home yet."

"Thank you, Zaria." He led the way through their front door. "I'm grateful to have your good sense in this craziness—even if I was enormously alarmed when Father said he had to push you to take even a single coin. If you didn't want any part of this, I wasn't sure we did either."

"You're right, I don't want any part of it for myself. I wish I hadn't taken even that one coin, but at the time I was obsessed with getting out of there as fast as possible."

Navid tossed a look of apology over his shoulder. "Sorry. Father can be like that. He's so cheerful and always smiling, that you don't even notice how insistent he can be."

"Zaria!" Mariam pounced on us, all smiles. "Thank you so much for coming. Now we can get started."

"Sorry, I meant to be here earlier."

She brushed my words aside, smiling as she bustled toward the back of the house with the scales in hand.

"You worried me with the material on your door," I added, and that got a chuckle out of her.

"I only came up with the idea after you left yesterday." She stopped suddenly, turning to fix me with an intense look as Navid disappeared through the door. "I assume Navid told you the story? What do you think?"

I considered the question. Mariam was obviously wanting to know the reaction of the first person to hear her invented story. Part of me was reluctant to encourage her, but while I didn't approve of the whole situation, I didn't want to see her family in trouble, either.

And I didn't want to be dragged into trouble myself. I had been at the cave as well, after all. At this point, it would be best for all of us if Ali and Mariam pulled this charade off.

"I think it's believable enough," I said, and Mariam's beam returned.

"The best bit is that it means we can start spending at least some of the gold immediately. Naturally my relatives have left us money to enable us to set up this end of the business."

An objection I should have thought of earlier hit me. "Won't people be expecting you to start buying products to ship to the new lands?"

"Navid is taking care of that part." Her face filled with pride. "He's going to set up an actual merchant business. Who knows, maybe we actually will end up with connections in the Four Kingdoms?"

She hesitated, giving me a look that made me nervous. "You couldn't help there, could you? If you've been holding back from Nyla, we'd all understand. But I know you'd want to help Navid..."

"If I could, I would, of course," I said hurriedly. "Navid has been a good friend to me since I arrived with Kasim and Nyla. But I haven't been holding back. All I did was exchange a few passing words with Princess Cassandra—and that was before she was even a princess. I don't have any royal connections."

Even as I said the words, I saw Rek's face from the day before.

Was Mariam's query only based on old history, or had Ali told her the story about my strange conversation with the prince inside the city gates?

Since my realizations overnight, any thought of the royals filled me with a heady mix of anxiety and excitement, but I kept my face still. It was complete truth that I didn't know the first thing about helpful contacts for a fledgling merchant.

"Oh well." Mariam's momentary disappointment didn't last long. "Ali!" she called. "The scales are here!"

She disappeared out the back door of the small house, but I stayed in place, considering our conversation. My realizations of the night before had opened up more than one part of my thinking. I had stayed with Nyla in an effort to cling to my old life. But Rek knew of my connection to Ali now, so even that poor reasoning no longer precluded me from accepting Mariam's offer of employment.

But if I left Nyla to work for Mariam, would other people think like Mariam—that I had been holding back from Nyla and was now helping my friend?

The thought left a sour taste in my mouth. As much as I disliked Nyla and Kasim, I had always taken pride in my work, doing it to the best of my ability. I didn't do it to honor them but for my own sake. It was what my father had taught me, and I credited my approach with buying me respect among the traders in the market and the staff of the other merchant families. I hated to think of that being sullied.

The door behind me opened, and I shook myself out of my thoughts and turned with a smile. An elderly lady—Mariam's sole servant who had followed her from her parents' household— stood in the doorway with a shocked expression.

I stepped toward her, keeping my smile in place. Agnes must still be dazed at the dramatic upheaval in the family's fortune, especially given its source.

But her words had nothing to do with the gold.

"Zaria, there's someone here to see you."

"Someone to see me?" I stared at her. "Here? But…who?"

Had Nyla sent someone chasing after me? Another servant from her house wouldn't be hanging back in the courtyard and sending a formal message with Agnes, though, as if I were a grand lady receiving visitors.

Agnes didn't answer, just shaking her head, the dazed look still in place. I hurried around her and pushed open the door, giving me a clear view of the small courtyard between the building and the gate.

I stopped halfway out the door, staring at the familiar figure standing calmly in front of me.

"It's Prince Tarek," Agnes said superfluously from behind me, having apparently overcome her shock.

"Yes," I said, my eyes locking with Rek's. "I can see that."

"So you do work here." Disappointment lingered in Rek's tone.

Yesterday, I would have attributed it to his distaste at associating with a servant. Today, everything seemed different and uncertain.

"Actually, no." I kept my voice level.

His expression changed to confusion, his glance flicking from me to the building behind me. I glanced back myself and saw Agnes had left—probably to inform the rest of the household of their shocking visitor. So much for my telling Mariam I had no royal connections.

I looked back at Rek. "I can understand why it's a bit confusing, but I actually work in Ali's brother's household. They sometimes release me to help Ali, which is why I was with him yesterday and why I'm here now."

"Oh." Rek was silent for a moment. "Then I'm glad I found you." Another pause. "What is Ali's brother's name?"

My heart leaped despite myself. Did that mean he intended to come looking for me again? I took several steps forward, bringing me to a more comfortable distance for a conversation.

"It's Kasim. I work for his wife, Nyla."

"I've heard their names. They're among the wealthier of the city's merchants and must have a large household. I'm surprised this Nyla sends you to help with woodcutting."

I grimaced. "Only when she's particularly irritated with me."

A crease appeared in his brow, so I hurried to add, "Not that I mind. The joke's on her, really, because I enjoy the occasional break beneath the trees."

His expression lightened. "You always did love the palace gardens."

A stab of pain hit me at the reminder of happier times, but I kept the emotion from my face. It wasn't Rek's fault my father had died and my life had changed—and I no longer believed it was his fault I'd lost my friends, either.

"You seemed surprised to see me in Karema yesterday." Beneath my calm exterior, my heart beat quickly as I waited for his response.

"Of course," he said. "We didn't know you were back in the city, let alone living here now." Unspoken behind his words was the accusation: *You didn't come see us.*

"I never left the city," I said softly. "I've been working for Nyla ever since my father died."

"What?" The startled word burst out of him, and he took a hurried step toward me. "Working right here in the capital the whole time? Impossible! You went to relatives in Ardasira."

"Ardasira?" Now it was my turn to be startled. "But I don't have any relatives there. I don't have any close relatives left at all, as far as I'm aware. But the ones I did have were all Kuralani."

Anger flared in his face for the first time in the conversation, but it didn't hurt like it had yesterday.

"You've been right here, so close, all this time? How is that possible? Why did you never come to visit?"

I gave him a pointed look. "I'm a servant now, Prince Tarek.

Do you think servants can just stroll into the palace and ask to take tea with the princess?"

A flash of embarrassment crossed his face, the emotion rocking me. All this time I had thought the whole lot of them—but especially Rek—were embarrassed at my new position in society. But from his reaction, my status wasn't on his mind at all. He appeared to have forgotten about it completely in the course of two minutes' conversation. I had wronged him. I had wronged all of them.

"I'm sorry," I said softly. "I did try to come once, but I was turned away at the gates. Perhaps I should have tried writing instead. I just thought…" I paused, wishing I had a better excuse. "Everything had changed, and I thought if you wanted to see me, you would come to me." I made a face. "Of course, that was when I believed you knew where I was."

"You mean you thought we'd dropped you because you were no longer the daughter of a vizier?" The hurt in Rek's eyes pierced me, especially since it was deserved.

"At first I thought it was your parents," I said hurriedly. "I know none of you were in control of your own movements before you came of age."

One of his eyebrows quirked upward. "But I came of age not long after you left. So then you thought it was me keeping the others from resuming contact."

I winced. He was too insightful. Even after all this time, he knew me too well.

"I'm sorry," I said again.

Rek shook his head, but the old knowledge went both ways. I could read his eyes as the hurt softened and faded from them.

"This is an unexpected visit," said a new voice.

I spun around, suddenly realizing how close Rek and I had gotten. I took a hurried step back, keeping my gaze on Navid.

"Prince Tarek is just here to—" I broke off, suddenly realizing

I didn't know why Rek had come. I didn't dare assume it was purely because of our old friendship.

My eyes flicked to the prince, but he was focused on Navid, his gaze assessing.

"A little late, aren't you?" Navid crossed his arms. "By three years or so."

I stared at him, astonished. Navid was the only other friend I had confided in, knowing more about my history than Kali, but unlike the miller's daughter, he had always seemed to accept the reality of the situation. I had never heard him express anger at the royals before. What could have possessed him to talk to the crown prince in such an antagonistic way? The last thing his family needed was to invite extra scrutiny right now.

"We've just discovered that was all a misunderstanding," I said in repressive tones, trying to give him a warning with my eyes.

He didn't uncross his arms, however, and Rek had developed a similarly stiff stance, his eyes only flicking to me briefly before focusing back on Navid.

"That's a big misunderstanding," Navid said, although his tone did soften a little.

"Yes." I nodded. "We only discovered the truth because we happened to see each other in the forest yesterday."

"The forest?" Navid's shocked face made me groan internally.

Hadn't Ali told his son the whole story of how we encountered the thieves? Either way, Navid was going to have to work on his acting if he wanted to pull off a deception on the whole city.

I glared a further warning at him before turning to Rek.

"This is Navid, Ali's son. He's a good friend of mine."

I said it to try to ease the tension between the two men, but Rek's face only tightened, his eyes raking over Navid's tall frame.

I bit my lip. Had he misinterpreted my words? I stayed silent, unwilling to correct any possible misconception. Any innocuous explanation for Navid's behavior was far better than the least hint that his family had something to hide.

But neither could I let the two of them go on, sizing each other up. "Prince Tarek—" I began, only for him to cut me off.

"Rek." The correction was short and clipped, at odds with the friendly sentiment, and his eyes remained on Navid.

I raised an eyebrow, but even without turning to see it, he apparently heard his own tone because he threw me an apologetic look.

"Just like always, of course." This time the words sounded welcoming.

"Three years have passed," I said, not sure why I was resisting.

"What are three years compared to a lifetime of friendship?"

Warmth filled me, although Navid looked far less impressed by the prince's words. I tried to suppress my emotions and focus on coming up with a new topic of conversation that would jolt Navid out of his unhelpful attitude.

But just as I was about to make another attempt to speak, the door in the wall behind Rek squeaked open. All three of us turned to look at the new arrival, our faces showing varying levels of the same shock.

"Adara!" It was Rek who spoke. "What are you doing here?"

"I think that's my line, brother. What can possibly have brought you—" Adara's cool, polished voice cut off in a sharp gasp. "Zaria!"

She swiveled between me and her brother, eyes wide and all trace of the elegant young lady gone, replaced by the animated girl I grew up with.

"This is why you snuck away from the palace this morning?" she demanded of her brother.

"I didn't sneak anywhere," Rek said in dignified tones.

She rolled her eyes. "Close enough."

"And what, to ask again, are *you* doing here?" He gave her a glare similar to the one I had just been directing at Navid.

She just laughed. "Obviously I had to know what lead you were pursuing that you didn't want the guards involved in, so I followed you. But never mind that now! I can't believe it. Zaria is back! Why didn't you tell me?"

Her eyes lingered on me, her expression confused. She looked half delighted to see me again, and half hurt and bewildered. I understood the feeling since I had felt the same confusing mix of emotions in the forest only a day ago.

"Actually, I never left," I said. "I don't have relatives in Ardasira—I've been here the whole time."

"We were waiting all that time for her to write," Rek added, "while she was waiting for us to visit—thinking we'd abandoned her now she's a servant."

"A servant!" Adara's hands flew to her mouth, her bright, expressive eyes full of horror. "Oh no! And here in Karema this whole time? But surely…"

Her response seemed to confirm my old fears, but now that she was in front of me again, they all seemed like nonsense. Of course my oldest and closest friend was upset on my behalf, not her own.

"I'm all right," I said. "I'm just so sorry. I should have known you wouldn't…I should have tried harder to…"

"But what could you have done?" She turned a reproachful look on Rek. "You know how closely father kept us guarded back then. You should have looked harder."

"Me?" Rek frowned. "How is this suddenly my fault? You know I looked—but I was looking in Ardasira. I was never going to find her there when she was here the whole time."

Rek had looked for me? Of course he couldn't have gone to Ardasira himself, but even the thought of him making inquiries about me brought back the previous warmth. I had never been abandoned at all. At least not by them.

Looking away, I blinked moisture from my eyes, my gaze

falling on Navid. His arms had dropped to his side, all hostility gone from his face. He looked more dazed than anything, his eyes fixed on Adara.

I turned back to her, trying to view the princess through his eyes. Her long, sheer chemise was silk with golden embroidery around the neckline, and her ankle-length outer robe fell in soft, expensive folds. Combined with the thin golden chains that wound through the piles of dark hair on her head, she looked the picture of a beautiful, unapproachable royal.

But her face was animated, emotions flitting rapidly across it as she sparred with her brother. Her manner softened the picture, transforming her classical beauty into something more approachable and appealing.

I looked back at Navid, a sinking feeling in my stomach. I had been the inadvertent cause of this meeting, and I only hoped it wasn't going to bring my friend pain. I couldn't blame him for being struck by her, but he would do well to overcome the emotion as quickly as possible.

I cleared my throat, bringing everyone's attention back to me. "Of course it's not Rek's fault. I should have tried harder. But wishing can't change the past. I'm just so glad to see you now."

Adara laughed, a bright, bubbling sound, and rushed forward to throw her arms around me. "That's my Zaria! Always so practical."

Some combination of her words and manner jolted my memory, and I realized how similar she was to Kali. Was that why I had found the miller's daughter so instantly likable?

"Someone has to be practical," Rek muttered. "It certainly isn't one of your qualities."

Adara gave him a mock glare, but she couldn't keep the smile off her face.

"I still don't understand," she said plaintively. "How could this have happened? I'm sure they said…"

"I'm so sorry, I've been remiss," Navid said suddenly, breaking into the conversation. "Please, come inside. Let me offer you some refreshments."

Adara turned a beaming smile on him that made me groan inside. Couldn't she look dour and disapproving, just this once?

To my chagrin, her face only brightened as she took Navid in for the first time. It was just like her not to have noticed him in her shock and excitement at seeing me.

"Actually," Rek said quickly, "it's better if we keep this as brief as possible and are seen by as few people as possible. Especially now my sister is here, we really should be getting back to the palace."

Adara turned a frown on him while I glanced at the house's windows. Navid must have convinced his parents to stay back while he came to investigate, but I would be astonished if they weren't already watching us from within the house. Unless they were too distracted by all that gold they were supposed to be counting...

"Ooh!" Adara pressed her hands together, in response to something Rek said. "Don't tell me you were following a lead, then?" Her excitement dimmed, her lips curving down. "But Zaria couldn't possibly be involved with that gang!"

"The thieves?" I asked, all thought of Navid's family forgotten. "Is that what brought you here, Rek?"

I carefully refrained from looking in Navid's direction, hoping he was doing a better job of looking nonchalant than he had earlier.

"Of course I don't think you're involved with them," Rek assured me. "But you were in the forest yesterday, and from what that woodcutter said, you saw something." He grimaced. "I know it's a stretch, but honestly I'm ready to follow any potential information, no matter how slim the chance of value, at this point."

"Rek is determined to prove himself to Father," Adara said conversationally.

"Adara!" Rek hissed.

She ignored him. "He wants to lead a delegation across the desert to the Four Kingdoms, but first he has to convince Father he's capable. And of course we have to find the traitor before we can do anything else."

CHAPTER 8

"Traitor?" I looked between Adara and Rek in bewilderment.

"Adara!" Rek repeated in an even sterner tone.

"It's Zaria!" she said. "We can trust Zaria."

Rek threw a significant look toward Navid.

Adara smiled at Navid sweetly. "Navid is a good friend of Zaria's, so I'm sure we can trust him, too."

Rek groaned. "And this is why Father doesn't put you in charge of investigations."

Adara just laughed. She had never been one to be offended by the words of others—especially her brothers.

I couldn't help smiling at the familiar dynamic between the siblings. Apparently growing up hadn't changed Adara much.

But beneath the surface, my mind was roiling. Adara's cryptic comments sounded serious. If there was more going on here than a gang of thieves, I couldn't possibly justify keeping their hideout secret from the royals.

"What traitor?" I asked, my eyes on Rek. "You can't mean the thieves. They're criminals, certainly, but I wouldn't classify them as traitors."

He hesitated for a moment, his eyes straying to Navid again, and then he sighed. "I might as well tell you since Adara is clearly going to. We have reason to believe someone in the palace is working with the gang—directing their activities."

My eyebrows shot up. "Someone in the palace?"

That was bad, but it still didn't sound like it qualified as treason. I waited, guessing there was more to the story.

"Obviously we don't want this information becoming public, but Father had organized for a delegation from Lanover to cross the desert for a visit."

"Lanover?" Navid's eyes widened. "One of the Four Kingdoms? I know Kuralan has been desperate to make connections with the new kingdoms given Ardasira is so much ahead of us there." He lowered his voice to a mutter. "We certainly have more need of the economic assistance than they do."

"Indeed," Rek said, a frosty edge to the word. "My father had been working toward the goal for some time."

"He was totally paranoid about it," Adara interjected. "He didn't want anything to go wrong, or for there to be any disruption to their journey, so he kept the whole thing under strictest secrecy. He was going to announce it once they arrived here, at the capital, and then there would have been a series of events and celebrations to make the most of it."

"So what happened?" I asked, my stomach sinking.

"Their desert crossing initially brought them to Ardasira, and they traveled north by road from there," Rek said grimly. "Almost as soon as they crossed the border into Kuralan, they were attacked by the gang of thieves. Father had sent a squad of our guards to meet them at the border, to bolster the numbers of their own guards, so the actual delegation escaped. However, a number of guards—both ours and theirs—were killed. The delegation formed the impression Kuralan was a lawless, dangerous place and turned straight back to Ardasira."

"Oh no!" I swallowed, my eyes widening.

That story must have spread all over the Four Kingdoms by now. This could destroy all Kuralan's hopes of future wealth through trade with the new kingdoms. We'd had nearly a decade of poor harvests now, and people had been pinning their hopes on the desert crossing newly rediscovered by Ardasira and on the prosperous kingdoms beyond.

I exchanged a glance with Navid. I would never betray Rek and Adara's confidence. But Rek could rest easy in Navid's discretion as well—if the story became widely known here in Karema, it would bring far too much unwanted attention to Mariam's planned cover story.

"Could it be coincidence?" Navid asked with a frown. "That gang has been terrorizing the roads on and off for decades."

The lines on Rek's face deepened. "My family is well aware of their depredations, and the guards have been under instruction to do all they can to capture them for years. More than once, we thought we had them only for the gang to disappear."

"I meant no criticism of your family," Navid said quickly. "I'm just trying to consider all the possibilities."

I knew I should say something to smooth the moment over, but I was too busy thinking. The thieves disappearing sounded ominously familiar. I was going to have to tell Rek what I knew. But I would protect Navid and his family if I could.

"It was an ambush," Adara said sadly. "Several merchant caravans passed through untouched—and they had less protection than the delegation. There's no question it was targeted."

"Which means someone in the palace had to have directed them to make the attack," Rek said. "No one else knew the delegation was coming, let alone the exact timing and route. Father is overseeing the investigation on the palace end himself, but he has permitted me to go after the gang. If we can finally capture them, we can learn from them who they're working with."

"It's an impossible task," Adara said matter-of-factly. "No

one's caught the gang in decades. But of course Rek is determined to succeed." She sent him an affectionate smile.

"Of course I'll do my duty by my kingdom to the best of my ability," Rek said stiffly.

Adara rolled her eyes. "Of course it has nothing to do with impressing Father sufficiently for him to give you command of the delegation he wants to send to Lanover to repair relations."

"The delegation can't go until the traitor—and the gang—are caught," Rek said. "We have to be able to show we've dealt with the problem decisively if we're to lure them back."

"Have you considered Azzam?" I muttered under my breath, but Adara caught the words.

"Azzam?" She stared at me. "He's the one who told me you'd gone to Ardasira! What a snake! He said he didn't know the name of your family, but he was sure you'd write as soon as you had the chance. I've hated him ever since," she added vehemently. "Even before I knew it was a lie, I thought him unfeeling for sending you off without even a goodbye. And now…you're probably right! He must be the traitor."

"Azzam?" Rek frowned, something flashing in his eyes. "I didn't know he was the one to tell you about Zaria leaving. I thought it was one of the officials—the one who resigned around that time—not a vizier." His frown deepened. "My efforts to track her down would have been easier if I'd known the person involved in her departure was still at the palace!"

"Sorry, I thought I told you." Adara sounded guilty. It was just like her to be so scatterbrained, though.

Rek was silent for a moment. "It's strange behavior, and I'll certainly be holding Azzam accountable for his actions, but it's a big leap from that to treason." His attention had returned to the more important matter on his mind.

"No, it's not!" A mulish look crept over Adara's face. "He lied to us! How can we trust him now?"

"We can't, of course," Rek said. "I'm not minimizing what he did. I'll see him out of the palace, if I can manage it. But we have to take the investigation against the traitor seriously. We need actual evidence because if we make a mistake and leave the real culprit free to act, it could be fatal."

A vindictive part of me cheered at the thought of Azzam being the one thrown from the palace, but a more cautious part prevailed. "Please don't send Azzam away in disgrace on my behalf."

"He sent you out here to be a servant for *three years*," Adara cried. "We only found you again by accident. Of course we should get rid of him."

Rek met my eyes, a serious look in his. "I understand your concern, Zaria. And I swear I'll do everything I can to ensure he can't come after you—given what he's done to you previously it's a valid fear. But we can't just let it go. He acted without authorization and then lied to us about it. How could we trust him as a vizier going forward?"

"Of course you couldn't," I said and hesitated. "But that is assuming…I mean, there are other…possibilities." I wasn't sure how to discreetly phrase my thoughts, but I had long assumed his parents wished to keep us apart due to my loss of status, and it was still possible that was true.

For a moment Rek just frowned at me, and then understanding crossed his face. He stepped closer, dropping his voice low so the others couldn't hear.

"You fear Azzam was not acting without authorization, but under the command of my parents. It would make more sense of his actions, but I can't believe it to be true. They always liked you."

I wrinkled my nose. "Your mother liked me."

He gave a tight smile. "You know what my father is like. He's too focused on ruling the kingdom to like even his own children."

"That's not true," I said swiftly. "He has always been proud of you. It's obvious to anyone who sees the two of you together."

Rek sighed. "Proud, perhaps, but that is not quite…" He shook his head. "That's beside the point. I don't think it likely that Father commanded such an outrageous thing against the child of one of his viziers. I know he valued your father and considered him one of the most promising of the junior viziers. But I won't act rashly. I'll investigate before I take any action."

I nodded, relieved. As much as I didn't want Azzam coming after me, even less did I want to attract the ire of the sultan.

"Thank you," I said. "And it might be for the best to keep him close, just in case he is the traitor, after all. As you said, you need proof, and that will be easier to get if you haven't evicted him in disgrace."

"Very wise." He smiled down at me. "As your recommendations always were."

Adara, who had taken our exchange as an opportunity for her own private conversation with Navid, approached in time to hear Rek's final words. She let out an unladylike snort. "Oh really? You didn't think so highly of her suggestion that time the twins convinced us to break into the royal treasury, and the guards caught us, and Zaria said you should—"

"Adara!" I cried. "I was seven years old!"

"I think I need to hear the full version of that story." Navid trailed behind Adara, his eyes only for her.

Rek looked at him with misgiving. "I think we need to be returning to the palace." Adara opened her mouth to protest, and he fixed her with a stern look. "Now."

Adara sighed. "I suppose you're right."

"Are you really allowed to wander wherever you like now that you're of age?" I asked her in wonder. "It seems hard to believe after how cloistered you all were as children. It was hard enough just to get permission for us to go riding in a large group with a whole squad of guards in tow."

"Isn't it delightful?" Adara cried. "All I have to do now is take my maid and two guards—and let the guard captain know where I'm going."

"Funny, I don't see a maid and two guards now," Rek said with false surprise.

She laughed. "My maid is waiting outside, thank you very much. Obviously I couldn't tell the captain where I was going because I didn't know myself. And I didn't need guards because I kept in sight of you the whole time."

"Although I didn't even know you were there," Rek said. "But I suppose your unwavering faith in my ability to protect you despite this impediment is meant as a compliment."

"Naturally." She gave him a broad smile.

He sighed and gestured for her to precede him to the gate. Instead of doing so, she turned to offer her hand in farewell to Navid, her golden cheeks turning faintly rosy as he bowed gallantly over it.

Rek stepped forward, as if he meant to break up the scene, but I caught at his arm, speaking in a low voice.

"I need to speak to you for a moment."

Rek looked reluctantly toward his sister, and my grip tightened. "It's important."

His gaze snapped back to me, his brows lowering. Stepping swiftly to one side, near the wall, he towed me with him.

Navid's attention appeared to be fully on Adara as he murmured something that made her giggle, but I caught the brief moment his eyes flickered to us. There was concern beneath his smiling expression, but he didn't relinquish the opportunity my actions had provided.

"I did see something," I said in a whisper. "In the forest, just after we met."

Rek's attention was focused now, the intensity of it nearly making me lose my train of thought.

"The man we were chasing was a decoy," he said, stating it as fact. "I was almost certain of it after he escaped us. We were supposed to be chasing a legendary gang of forty thieves, but forty people couldn't move that fast or that nimbly."

I nodded. "The rest of them were moving in the opposite direction, toward me. I hid in a bush and heard them talking. He was definitely a decoy."

"Did they say something that might lead us to their whereabouts?" Rek was now the one gripping me, and I tried not to be distracted by his hand on my arm. "Or did you get a good look at them? Did any of them have any distinguishing features?"

I took a deep breath, afraid of what my next words might unleash. "Actually, it was bigger than any of that. It was completely…fantastical."

I paused, worried about the unbelievable nature of what I was about to impart. He responded to my expression by taking my remaining arm in his other hand, giving me the impression that for that moment, I was his entire world.

"Whatever you have to tell me, whatever you saw—you know I'll believe you, Zaria. I was angry and confused when I first saw you yesterday, but I only have to look at you to see you're the same person you always were."

I nodded, overwhelmed at his words but determined to get the confession over with.

"I saw them go into their hideout. I know where their headquarters are—where they hide the gold they steal."

Rek's jaw dropped. Whatever he'd thought me about to say, this was more than he'd dared hope for.

"And you could lead me there?" he asked eagerly.

"Yes, I think so."

I had taken careful note of our surroundings, and the route we took back to the road. Not that I had planned or wanted to go back to the cave, but it had seemed prudent.

I swallowed. "But that's not all."

"Not all?" Rek looked back down at me with a laugh in his

eyes. "Don't tell me you singlehandedly detained them all, and I'll find them trussed up in a row, waiting for arrest?"

I chuckled reluctantly. "I'm afraid not. I cowered in the bushes until they left. But after that, I went inside and…This is the unbelievable bit. The reason they kept managing to elude pursuers inside the forest is that they're using an enchanted cave with a hidden entrance. And inside the cave…" I shook my head. "Even a lifetime of theft couldn't have filled that cave. As soon as I saw it, I knew…Rek, somehow they found the missing second treasure cave of legend. That's why the entrance is hidden. That's why they can disappear, literally into thin air."

"You found the treasure cave?" Rek whispered. "And it's also the thieves' hideout?"

"What!?!" Adara shrieked from over his shoulder, and I jumped guiltily. I'd been too distracted by Rek to notice her approach.

He whirled around, frustration clear in the lines of his body. He hadn't been planning to share this new piece of information with his sister.

"Zaria?" Navid asked in a strangled voice.

I shrugged apologetically at him, thankful neither of the royals were taking any notice of us. I had carefully left Ali out of my story, making it sound like I had run into the robbers almost immediately after seeing Rek. Hopefully if they noticed Navid's response, they would think he was upset at my not telling him about it.

"No one can know about this, Adara," Rek said seriously. "No one."

She looked at me. "Was the treasure amazing? Was it as big as the legends say?"

I nodded, and she squealed, jumping up and down and clapping her hands.

"This is so much better than I could possibly have imagined! Did you take some? Can I see it?"

"Of course I didn't take any!" I said. "For all I know, it might be guarded by some terrible enchantment."

Rek looked back at me, his forehead creased with concern. "Did you see any sign of an enchantment?"

I shook my head reluctantly. "No, but that doesn't mean one wasn't there." I paused, prodded by my conscience. "I did actually take a single gold coin. It's back at home, hidden under my bed. I could go and fetch it, if you—"

"You don't need to prove it, Zaria!" Adara cried. "Of course we believe you. You were always the most honest of us as children." She wrinkled her nose. "Except perhaps for boring Rek, here. And besides, who would make up such an outrageous tale?"

"Finding that treasure cave could change everything." Rek's eyes glowed. "It would put us on much more equal footing with Ardasira for a start and give us something immensely valuable to offer the Four Kingdoms. Even without the gang, this discovery—"

"*If*," I interrupted firmly, "it doesn't have some deadly enchantment on it. I wouldn't go building castles in the sky quite yet."

"Always so sensible, Zaria," Adara murmured, but she slipped an affectionate arm around my waist.

The contact loosened a tight knot deep inside me, and I had to restrain myself from throwing both arms around her and squeezing tight. Even with all my new friends, I had missed my old one desperately.

"Zaria is right," Rek said. "The treasure in the cave has been there for centuries. It's not going anywhere right now."

Navid winced slightly, and I kicked his ankle.

"It shouldn't be our first priority," Rek continued. "We can use this discovery to catch the gang and uncover the traitor. Once that's managed, Father and his experts can investigate more closely and determine if there are any enchantments."

"Ooh!" Adara sounded eager enough to make me eye her with

misgiving. "So you're not going to tell Father straight away? Bad crown prince!"

"Father has entrusted the investigation into the gang to me," Rek said with dignity. "For now that's all this is. After we have them in hand, of course we'll tell him about the cave and leave it to him to sort out."

Adara gave a little crow, glancing at me. "Didn't I tell you he was desperate to be the one to uncover the traitor?" She looked at Rek. "Or are you afraid Father will decide the gold is more important and seize the cave before you have your chance to catch the gang?"

Rek was silent, making me think both were true. Despite my misgivings about what I was potentially being dragged into, I couldn't help being pleased that not all of the adventure loving boy had been swallowed up in the dutiful, responsible young man.

"So what's the plan, then?" Navid looked between me and Rek. "Should the three of us lie in wait in the cave? I suppose we'd better bring some guards, given there are forty of them. Or will it just be an information-gathering mission to begin with? If we can identify the thieves, we wouldn't have to arrest them on the spot."

"Excuse me!" Adara put her hands on her hips. "You aren't leaving me behind!"

Navid and Rek turned identical horrified expressions on her. I struggled to keep my lips straight. I knew Adara well enough to know they were fighting a losing battle.

"Of course you can't come, Adara," Rek said. "This could be incredibly dangerous."

She stared him down. "Then why are you going? *You're* the crown prince."

"I'm also in charge of this investigation, and something of this sensitivity can't be entrusted to anyone else."

"I'm coming," she said in a note of finality. "If something

happens to us, they always have the twins. They'll have to rule the kingdom after Father."

Rek and I both shuddered, the similarity of our reaction provoking a reluctant smile from him.

"I assume the twins haven't changed much?" I asked.

"Not a whit," he replied.

"Well, maybe a little," Adara said fairly. "But it would be better for the kingdom if we keep Rek alive. I think we should bring some guards at least."

I nodded my agreement, glad my friend had developed a little common sense and caution.

"Of course," Rek said. "There are a small number I can trust. We can hide in the cave and get the information we need." He looked at me. "I assume there are places we could hide?"

I nodded, a little reluctantly. "The cave is full of all manner of items. But, of course, I have no idea what the gang does in there. It's possible they search it thoroughly each time."

"That seems unlikely. If the gold is still there, they'll think their hideout secure," Rek said. "But we'll leave one of the guards outside—up a tree or something. If we don't emerge, he can carry word to Father."

"I don't know how long it will be before they return," I said, feeling like a killjoy. "We can't camp out in the cave for days."

Adara looked horrified. "No, thank you!"

"My network will inform me when they're next active in the area," Rek said. "From what you've said, Zaria, they hide their gold in the cave. Once they've robbed again, we'll know they're heading there. We just have to be ready to get there first."

"That's one of the points that's been bothering me," I murmured. "Why store their gold in a cave already overflowing with it? Why bother robbing at all?"

Rek frowned, his arrested expression showing he was also struck by the incongruity of it.

"There's something bigger going on here," he said. "And it

must have to do with the traitor. We need answers, and this is how we're going to get them."

"Are you sure?" I looked at Adara with concern.

He sighed, dropping his voice to answer. "I'm not saying they're the companions I would have chosen…" His eyes lingered on Navid rather than Adara. "But there's not just one traitor to worry about. The way the gang has been slipping past my squad is highly suspicious. At this point, I don't trust anyone other than the few guards I know well. We need to uproot the traitors in our midst before we bring more people into this."

He looked at me in concern. "You don't have to be a part of it if you don't want to, though. I need you to show me the spot, but you don't have to—"

"No." I shook my head firmly. "I'm definitely coming." I wasn't abandoning Adara and Rek to face the thieves alone.

"In that case," Rek said, with a conspiratorial grin that reminded me of his youthful self, "be ready for my message."

CHAPTER 9

"You told them about the cave." Navid's words sounded accusing, but they didn't hold any heat.

The royals had left, but the two of us still lingered in the courtyard.

"I had to," I said, refusing to feel guilty. "It was bad enough when it was just the thieves, but now there's treachery involved… I couldn't delay it. This might be the only way to catch them."

Navid sighed. "Yes, you're right, of course. And I don't regret…"

He let the words trail away, but I gave him a knowing look.

"You don't regret a chance to spend more time with the royals, lover boy?"

He flushed. "I don't know what you're talking about. But, of course, I'll make the most of any potential royal connections I can build. The association could prove invaluable for my new business."

I frowned. "About that…"

He nodded. "I know. For now, at least, we need to keep the whole thing very quiet. Do you think anyone saw them coming in here?"

"We can only hope not. I assume your parents can be trusted not to say anything—especially with what's currently hidden in this house. What about Agnes, though? Not that she seems like a chatty one."

Navid laughed. "Not at all. I can't remember the last time I saw her talking to anyone outside the family without an air of great suspicion. She doesn't even trust the baker who she's visited every day of my life to buy our bread."

Now that Rek and Adara were gone, the whole situation seemed less straightforward than it had when we were together.

"I'm not sure what I'm going to do when Rek sends his message. I should have thought of it straight away, but—how am I going to explain my need to suddenly dash off to Nyla? Can you imagine how she'll react if I attempt to mysteriously disappear without warning?"

Navid grimaced. "All too well."

"I suppose I should be going back now." I sighed. "If I'm going to have to disappear at some point, I shouldn't antagonize Nyla now. Given your parents' ruse about having guests, she'll know your father didn't go woodcutting today."

Navid gave me a sympathetic look. "Are you sure you don't at least want to stay for a meal?"

"I'd better not."

I turned toward the gate, but the sound of my name made me turn back. Agnes shuffled out of the house, a bright spark in her eyes and something in her hands.

"Here you are." She held out the scales. "Mariam is finished with them and says to return them with her gratitude."

I took them, but my focus remained on her face. Had she been the one watching from the windows? She certainly looked excited. I didn't think she could have heard our words, but even so, a visit from the prince and princess was a momentous happening. Could she really be trusted to keep the events of the morning quiet?

Navid noticed my lingering interest and understood at once.

"You don't need to be concerned about Agnes. She's as loyal as they come."

Agnes drew herself up. "I'll have you know I was loyal before either of you took your first breath. The cheek!"

I bobbed my head in respect. "Many apologies, Agnes. I never intended to doubt your loyalty."

Her eyes narrowed, and she shook her head. "You young people," she muttered. "All the same." Turning, she hurried back into the house.

I turned a concerned eye on Navid. "Is she offended? Should I go and talk to her? I didn't mean to—"

His chuckle made me go silent. "You don't need to worry about Agnes. She's been bemoaning the shocking behavior of *young people* since before we were born as well. It's one of her greatest joys in life."

I grinned. "Your mother is lucky to have her."

He nodded, a more serious expression on his face. "We're all well aware of it. She's treated like a grandmother more than a servant. She's stuck with us for so long that she's family now."

"As it should be." I tucked the scales under my arm. "But I really have to get moving."

I took the long way back through the streets, avoiding the market, because I didn't want to face questions about Ali and Mariam's supposed visitors while my head was in such a whirl. I knew I should be thinking of an excuse for my upcoming disappearance, but I couldn't help reliving the conversation in the courtyard instead. Adara and the twins—and even Rek—had never abandoned me at all! We were friends again!

In a strange way, I felt as if I were getting part of my father back. The palace and my friends there had been the backdrop of my life with him. And while I could never feel his strong arms around me again or hear his even voice, the part of my life that had included him no longer felt so distant.

A chiding voice reminded me that I should be strong enough by now not to care—strong enough to let go—but it wasn't able to stop the waves of joy that washed over me.

But every time I threatened to get too giddy, other thoughts intruded. Gangs of thieves, traitors, and attacked foreign convoys were a great deal less delightful than the return of old friends. And even worse was the thought that Adara and Rek wanted me to lead them into danger.

Adara had never had any interest in learning to fight—except for a brief period when she was fifteen and insisted we work with the palace knife master. And even that occasion had only been because she wanted our dancing master to teach us a knife dance she had seen a visiting performer display. What would happen to her if the thieves found us in that cave?

I shook my head at my foolishness. There were forty of the thieves. Even Rek, with all his sword training, would have no hope of escape if we were discovered in the secret cave.

I could refuse to take them, but I'd seen the way Navid was looking at Adara, and I knew how good she was at wrapping people around her finger. If I refused, the odds were good that Navid would tell the princess that his father also knew the cave's location. Ali would never disobey a royal order, and all I would achieve would be dragging Navid's family into the mess.

Rek and Adara might be old friends, but they were also royalty and I was a servant. If they were determined to do this, I couldn't stop them.

I sighed. All four royal children had a streak of recklessness that must have come from Sultana Rabia because it certainly hadn't come from Sultan Khalil.

My thoughts were still churning between the good and the bad when I opened the familiar gate at home and slipped into the courtyard. Without conscious thought, I turned toward the kitchen entrance, crossing the large open space with quick strides.

"Zaria!" The loud call from the main doorway made me halt abruptly.

Turning slowly, I faced Nyla, who remained in place just inside the door. She beckoned imperiously, and reluctantly I began to walk slowly toward her.

How had she appeared so quickly? Had she been watching for me from a front window? With a horrible, sinking feeling I remembered our last conversation and her demand that I discover what Mariam was weighing. Everything that had happened since had driven it from my mind completely. But the unexpectedness of the morning was no excuse. I'd left myself totally unprepared to face the inquisition that would now be coming.

When I neared her, Nyla turned and marched inside the front receiving room. I trailed behind, trying not to look as dismayed as I felt.

But as soon as we were both inside, she surprised me by not launching into speech. Instead she held out her hand, an unsettling gleam in her eye. I stared at it, uncomprehending.

"The scales, girl!" she cried, casting a look upward as if she couldn't believe my denseness.

"Oh." I started, looking down at the object under my arm. Although I'd been clutching it all the way home, I'd completely forgotten it was there.

I held it out, and she snatched it from my hands, turning it over eagerly. I watched her in confusion until she let out an outraged gasp.

"What!?" she cried. "Impossible!" For a moment she leaned forward, seeming to pry at something I couldn't see, and then she held up a sparkling golden coin.

I stared at it, horrified. How could that possibly still be there?

It shone in a shaft of sunlight, as if taunting me. How had I missed it? But thinking back, I hadn't really looked at the scales at all. I'd been too distracted. And from the look of her, Agnes had been the same.

I could only assume Mariam and Ali had rushed through the process of weighing the gold, conscious of the royal visitors in their courtyard. They obviously hadn't been paying close attention either.

But that still didn't explain how it had become wedged in the scales in the first place.

"I knew something strange was going on," Nyla said, unprompted. "What could Mariam want to weigh with such large scales? That family is so poverty stricken it's an embarrassment to everyone who knows them."

Had Nyla somehow caused the coin to become stuck? Now that I was paying attention, my usually excellent memory leaped to the fore again. I had run into Nyla in the courtyard on my way out, and she had asked to see what I was carrying. She had even examined the scales.

"What did you do to the scales?" I asked, a little impressed in spite of myself.

"Quick thinking, Zaria." She looked down her nose at me. "You should try it sometime."

I suppressed my natural reaction and waited. Nyla could never resist boasting.

Sure enough, after only the briefest of pauses she spoke again. "I was eating bread and honey when I saw you slinking off this morning through the courtyard."

So she *was* watching for me out the front windows. Of course she was.

"You're not very observant," she continued, "so you probably didn't notice that I still had some bread in my hand."

I wanted to roll my eyes, but for once her comment was partially earned. I'd been so frustrated at myself for sleeping late, and so eager to escape the conversation with Nyla, that I hadn't been paying attention to what she did while holding the scales.

"You put honey on the scales?" I asked.

"You didn't think I trusted *you* to find out what was going on with Mariam, did you?" she asked with a sniff.

When I didn't reply, she looked down at the coin in her hand. "This must be some trick, though! It must! Ali and Mariam can't possibly have so many gold coins they have to weigh them instead of counting them. The whole idea is ludicrous."

She fixed me with a piercing glare, her eyes slowly narrowing. "What do you know of this? Tell me at once! How much was there, really?"

"I didn't see Mariam weighing anything," I said truthfully. "I was in the courtyard the whole time."

I expected Nyla to question this, pressing me hard, but she just rocked back with a dissatisfied expression marring her otherwise elegant features.

"Of course Mariam wouldn't want one of my servants getting a glimpse of her illicit dealings."

"Illicit dealings?" I protested. "Surely there's nothing like that going on. I heard…Mariam said something about visitors…"

"Ah yes, I heard that rumor." Nyla's sour expression grew. "You would think if Mariam had relatives staying, she would bring them to meet her Karema relatives. But, no. She's obviously too busy *weighing* their gold."

For a moment she just stood there, tapping her hand against her leg as she considered something, my presence apparently forgotten.

"Kasim is out—as he always is when he's needed," she said, as if to herself. "But he'll be home at some point. He might love those foolish books of his, but he won't get so distracted he misses a meal." She straightened. "As soon as he comes home, I'll send him over to Ali. Yes, that's the best plan. Ali can't turn away his own brother. Kasim can meet these relatives and find out exactly what's going on."

She looked down at the coin, turning it over in her palm.

Since she seemed to have forgotten my existence, I edged slowly backward toward the door. When she made no comment or any indication of noticing, I slipped out into the corridor.

My thoughts were whirling again, so I did the first thing that came to mind and headed for the kitchen. The large room was even busier than usual, with people bustling to and fro, but Yara still spotted me immediately.

"Zaria! You're back. And you don't need to tell me you haven't eaten, I can already tell by looking at you."

I shook my head, slipping onto a stool at the big table. "How do you do that?"

"I've been alive a lot longer than you, my girl, and seen more hungry people than you can count."

A plate appeared in front of me, and I began to ravenously eat. When I'd assuaged my first hunger, I took a longer look around the kitchen.

"It seems unusually busy," I said cautiously. "There isn't a party planned for tonight, is there?"

Yara called to a young boy, halting him just before he grabbed a cooling pie.

"No, thank goodness. But we heard the news that Mariam has guests. We're cooking extra to send to her, like we always do. Not that she..." As her voice descended into grumbles, I spoke quickly.

"She sent back your scales with a message of gratitude. But Nyla caught me on the way in and took them. I suspect you'll find them abandoned in the front receiving room."

Yara's demeanor instantly changed. "Extra work or not, it's a pleasure to help out someone as gracious and appreciative as Mariam. They're certainly not qualities you'll find around here." She gave a sniff that was humorously reminiscent of Nyla herself and bustled away again.

I hid my grin as I returned to my food. Whatever tones Yara might adopt, and whatever complaints she issued, her actions spoke the truth. As soon as she heard Mariam had guests, she had begun preparing food to send over. She had an unwaveringly kind heart beneath her wild mood swings.

A sudden thought hit me. "I suppose that means you'll be sending someone over with the food shortly?" I asked.

"Of course." She gave me a look of fond exasperation. "The food won't fly there on its own."

"Could you make sure they pass on a message for me?" I asked. "To Ali and Navid—both of them, mind!"

Yara gave me an odd look but nodded. "They can do that easily enough. What is it?"

"Just let them know that Nyla intends to send Kasim over later today to inquire about their visitors and their apparent change in fortune."

"Change in fortune?" Yara's eyes brightened at the hint of gossip. "Is Mariam's family going to help them out, then?"

I shrugged. "Just make sure they give that exact message."

Yara rolled her eyes upward. "I love you dearly, Zaria, but you're no good for a comfortable chat."

I grinned at her. "Apologies, Yara. You'll have to wait until Rowan is off duty. I know perfectly well that beneath his stolid exterior, he loves gossip almost as much as you do."

"The cheek!" said Yara, but she was also grinning. "I'll send him with the food and your message himself, which will serve you right."

My grin broadened. "Perfect. You're a true gem, as always, Yara. Rowan can be trusted to get the message right."

I departed the busy hum of the kitchen with a soft sigh of relief. Thank goodness I didn't need to find an excuse to immediately dash back to Ali's house. With Rowan warning them of Kasim's imminent arrival, I'd done all I could to ease them over that hurdle.

Not that a period of calm reflection brought much relief. I had seen too often that Kasim's blustering personality could overwhelm Ali. Mariam was made of sterner stuff, and Navid was impervious to his uncle's combination of foolishness and force. But I couldn't be sure the two of them would manage to make Ali hold his ground.

There was nothing I could do about it, however. I would be far better off working out how I was going to explain my need to drop everything and run off at an unknown future point. I had instructed Rek to send his message to Rowan, so I was confident it would get through to me. At worst, I could simply bolt without an explanation, but there'd be a lot of unpleasantness on my return if I did that.

I was still considering the matter when I went to sleep. Knowing Kasim had left for his brother's immediately after the evening meal and still hadn't returned, I had expected to find sleep difficult. But after the emotional surprises of the day, I nodded off almost instantly.

It felt only moments later that I was being shaken gently awake.

"Zaria!" a familiar voice said in an urgent whisper. "Zaria!"

I sat up, nearly colliding with Yara's head as she bent over me.

"What is it? What's happened?" I looked urgently around, a string of confused, nonsensical scenarios streaming through my mind.

"Rowan sent me," Yara said, the gleam of excitement visible behind her serious expression. "A message arrived for you from the palace."

"A message?" I gasped. "From Rek? Already?"

One of her eyebrows rose. "Prince Tarek, yes," she said, with emphasis on his full name.

Her curiosity was fanning higher, but I was too shocked to think about all the questions she was going to have after this.

"It's too soon, surely?"

"I'm not sure what you're talking about, but I'm to tell you to meet at the south gate. Immediately."

She looked at me expectantly, but I offered no explanation. Leaping from bed, I pulled on the closest clothes to hand, choosing my sturdiest shoes.

Unable to contain herself any longer, Yara burst into further speech. "Zaria, why is the crown prince sending you urgent messages to meet him in the middle of the night?"

"I can't explain now," I said, taking the easy way out. "You heard the message. I have to go immediately."

I slipped a single item from the tiny side table by my bed into my pocket. The gold coin was sitting out because I had been examining it again before falling asleep, and seeing it reminded me of my desire to return it. With treachery involved, I wanted even less to do with this treasure than before.

Planting a kiss on Yara's cheek, I brushed past her and out into the corridor. All the hours I'd spent worrying about finding an excuse to leave had been unnecessary. I could have saved myself the trouble if I'd only known the summons would come at night.

Rowan waited for me at the entrance to the stables. He led me swiftly past the sleeping horses, not pestering me with questions, just holding open the small door that gave access to the alley that ran down the side of the house. He used it for the delivery of supplies for the stables, and it was the entrance I had directed Rek's messenger to use.

Only at the door itself did he hesitate. "Stay safe, Zaria," he murmured in a gruff voice. "Don't go getting yourself into trouble."

I gave him an airy smile that ignored my own deep concerns. "I promise I'll do my best, Rowan. Thank you for sending Yara to wake me."

He chuckled. "She'd have stopped baking me treats if I left her out of something as dramatic as this."

I laughed. "You know she dotes on you and would never stop baking you your favorite buns."

"Nonsense. You'd better be getting on now." He held the door wider.

I nodded once and fled into the dark, silent streets. The call had come faster than I expected, but I couldn't refuse it. All I could do was hope that I managed to escape the snares of a magic treasure cave for the second time in as many days.

PART II
THE PRINCE AND THE THIEVES

CHAPTER 10

I arrived at the south gate out of breath. The streets had seemed to stretch on forever, far longer than when I walked this way with Ali and his donkeys.

"Zaria!" Adara's voice sounded far more excited than the dangerous mission warranted.

I waved my hand in the direction of her mount, too busy catching my breath to reply. Navid had beaten me, since his house was closer to the city's edge than Kasim's, and I eyed him with concern.

I pulled him slightly away from the royals, lowering my voice. "Kasim?"

His face tightened. "He knew about the gold," he murmured back, equally quietly. "Something about a trick with the scales."

I winced. "I'm sorry about that. I had no idea."

"He seemed convinced we'd stolen it, and it was hard to persuade him otherwise when we couldn't produce any relatives." He sighed. "After that he insisted on carrying Father off to discuss affairs *brother to brother*. I'm fairly sure his intention is to force Father to split the gold with him in exchange for his silence, but then the messenger arrived, so I had to leave."

We both looked toward Rek, who was watching us from atop his dark chestnut mare with narrowed eyes and a brooding expression.

"Apologies, Your Highness," Navid said quickly, in a louder voice. "A family affair."

"Just Rek is fine. Since we're all about to risk our lives together."

I was sure there was a pointed message in there, but he couldn't entirely hide the underlying excitement. He was nearly as bad as Adara.

"I almost didn't recognize you without that impressive white stallion," I said.

A cloud shifted, sending a spear of moonlight down to light his grin. "We wanted less conspicuous mounts for this business."

"I'm surprised we're riding at all." I frowned. "I don't think we'll be able to conceal the horses inside the cave. Are you thinking of waiting outside to catch the thieves when they arrive after all?"

He shook his head quickly. "We'll tether them some distance from the entrance, but we want to move quickly now."

I considered arguing that it would be a safer plan to wait outside the cave, but I knew Rek wanted to overhear significant conversation among the thieves, and that was unlikely to happen outside. And I suspected both he and Adara would refuse to come so far on such a venture only to leave tamely without entering the hidden treasure cave.

I saved my breath.

A plain faced man, who looked to be in his thirties, stepped forward and silently held out the reins of another dark-colored mare. I took the reins with a leap of excitement as Rek introduced the guard as Samuel and a second one behind him as Benjamin.

It had been years since I had ridden, but I had no hesitation or nerves as I let Samuel boost me into the saddle. I had missed riding through the trees on the back of a finely bred horse, and even the terrifying plan before us couldn't prevent a spark of pleasure at doing so again.

Benjamin separated from the group, crossing the rest of the way to the gate and engaging in a quiet conversation with one of the guards there. Within moments, the gate had been swung open enough to let us all file through before it thudded shut again.

"My cousin," Benjamin said in response to inquiring looks from both me and Navid. "He won't cause us any trouble."

Neither of us replied because Rek urged his horse forward, picking up speed, and the rest of us hurried to follow. I directed my mare to the front of the small pack, gesturing at the trees to our left.

"We need to go east. Close to where we ran into each other, but a bit further south."

Rek nodded. "I can get us to the spot where we crossed paths. You can lead the way from there?"

I agreed, and we settled into a comfortable pace, riding abreast.

"Your message came much faster than I expected," I said. "I thought the thieves intended to leave this area for a while."

"Perhaps they ran across a caravan that looked too juicy a target to ignore," he said. "All I know is the report of the robbery came in as I was about to head for bed for the night. Captain Jerome knows I want all information on the gang delivered to me immediately, so the message came straight to me."

I nodded. Jerome must be the guard captain I had seen in the woods with Rek.

Any further conversation became impossible as Rek led us off the road. Once in the forest, the trees forced us to ride single file. Beneath the canopy of leaves, the moonlight became patchy, and both Samuel and Benjamin lit lanterns which they held aloft to give just enough light for the six of us.

I could understand Rek not wanting to advertise our presence too widely through the forest—I just hoped none of the horses put a foot wrong and came up lame in the gloom. But without knowing how swiftly the thieves were moving, we had no way to know how much time we had.

"Is it possible they'll have beaten us there?" Adara asked in a breathy voice, obviously thinking the same thing I was.

"Unlikely in the extreme," Benjamin said shortly. "The message reached the palace via the royal messenger system. Our couriers move far faster than ordinary travelers, and especially compared to a large group. With no one on their tail, the thieves won't push themselves to the sort of extreme speed that draws attention."

I nodded, trying to reassure myself with his words, but in truth, I couldn't help wondering if it would be better if they did beat us there. As long as we had some sign to give us warning, it would mean an excuse not to enter the cave.

No such sign appeared, however, despite it taking me longer to find the right spot than I would have liked. In the darkness, the forest looked different, and I almost missed the unnaturally round clearing.

The other five looked around with interest, but none of them expressed the doubt they must be feeling at seeing an ordinary stretch of forest. I dismounted and stood in front of the hidden cave entrance.

In spite of my resolution to save my breath, I couldn't help asking once.

"Are you sure you want to do this?" My question was directed toward Rek, but my eyes strayed to Adara.

He also looked at his sister before glancing inquiringly at Samuel.

"There's no sign of anyone having been in this area tonight, sir," he said. "These tracks are older than that."

Rek nodded and turned back to me. "They're not in there yet, so we can have a quick look, at least. If there aren't sufficient hiding spaces, we'll come straight back out."

That meant the faster I moved, the better. I turned back to face the empty air.

"Open sesame."

"Seriously?" Adara asked with a giggle. "That's what opens the cave?"

Before anyone could answer, the grinding noise of moving stone drowned out further conversation. Rek, Adara, and Navid were transfixed by the opening that was slowly appearing, but I caught a concerned look pass between Samuel and Benjamin. If the thieves were close, they'd surely hear the noise.

Impatience seized me, and I swung down out of the saddle. The others followed my lead, all of us turning our reins over to Benjamin.

"Remember, your role is only to watch and report back to my father if things go wrong," Rek told him sternly. "Don't try anything heroic. One more sword will do us little good against forty."

"Your Highness, I really don't think this is—"

"Your objections have been noted," Rek said in authoritative tones, rendering his guard silent. "I mean that literally," he added, softening the words with a smile. "I've left a letter in my room explaining that both you and Samuel strongly objected to either myself or Adara being part of this night's work, and that you only complied under royal command. If anything happens to the rest of us, you won't be blamed."

"We'll see about that," Benjamin muttered as he collected the final reins. But it was clear from his expression when he looked at Rek that he was only allowed such informal asides because of his extreme loyalty. I could see now why Rek had wanted only his most trusted men to join us.

We took both lanterns with us, Benjamin seeming content to rely on the horses' instincts and the patchy moonlight. The others spoke in whispers as we moved along the rocky tunnel, questioning the blank stone ahead of us.

"There's a bend in the corridor," I explained. "The cave is just beyond it."

We turned the corner in a huddled group, so close together that Navid almost collided with Adara when she stopped abruptly. I had thought myself inured to the wonders inside the cave by my previous exposure, but it still made me catch my breath. In the span of less than two days I had already forgotten how much of it there was, the overwhelming reality robbing me of coherent thought for a moment.

I recovered faster than the others, however, and turned to examine their expressions, even as I issued the command to close the cave behind us. There was something entertaining about the matching expressions of slack-jawed shock and amazement.

"It's…bigger than I expected," Rek said after a moment.

"So you see the problem," I agreed, and he gave me a sharp look.

"How could any thieves—even forty of them—need more than this?" he said slowly, and I nodded.

"There's something going on here we don't understand," I said. "I'm sure of it."

"That's why we're here, isn't it?" Navid asked, finally coming out of his stupor. "To find out what's going on?"

Reluctantly, I nodded.

"Surely there's somewhere to hide in all of this." Adara put her hands on her hips and examined the chests of gold, rolled carpets, bags of jewels, and piles of material with a tilted head and assessing eye. "We'd be better off in the far back, of course. The lantern light barely reaches there. But would we be able to hear anything?"

"We should spread out," Samuel said. "If one of us is discovered, it doesn't necessarily follow that they'll search the whole cave. They may well expect a group of people to be hiding together." He looked around at us with a worried eye. "If any of us is found, we must pretend to be here alone."

"Adara, I want you right at the back of the cave," Rek said immediately.

"Not alone, though!" She shivered dramatically.

Rek looked in my direction, so I spoke quickly.

"Navid can hide near you."

If we were really going to do this, I wasn't cowering in the back of the cave, out of earshot, while Rek faced the danger closer in. Navid looked like he was equally reluctant to hang back, but one glance at Adara was enough to silence whatever protest he'd been about to make.

I smiled to myself. His foolish infatuation was good for something at least.

Samuel issued crisp orders for us all to find a hiding place. "And don't go leaving a foot or arm hanging out," he added, which made Adara giggle. "As soon as everyone is concealed, we'll extinguish these lamps and wait."

"It might be a long wait," Rek warned, his eyes on his sister. "So don't get bored and leave your hiding place. You know if you do that it will be just the moment the thieves arrive."

She rolled her eyes and set out for the back of the cave, Navid trailing behind her. The rest of us spread out as well, but I noticed even Samuel moved slowly, despite his brisk words. Our good sense might tell us there was a need to move quickly, but it was impossible not to get distracted by the extravagance of the wealth around us.

I tried several different spots about halfway back before settling on a spot against the left wall. A whole collection of rolled carpets had been placed there, leaning against the rough rock. They created a small, triangular gap behind them that was just big enough for me to squeeze into. Sitting with my back against the rock, I could see out between two of the carpets, but I was well out of the gleam of light from our lanterns and suspected I would be from those of the thieves as well.

As soon as I was properly settled, it hit me that this could be a very long and boring wait. And one made worse by my anxiety over all the many things that could go wrong. Maybe if I'd thought harder, I could have come up with an argument to convince Rek and Adara not to risk themselves so rashly.

But I only had to think back over ten years of close friendship to reject that thought. Adara had been raised alongside the twins —always striving to prove she could keep up with her brothers. And although Rek had seemed to turn serious and responsible as he neared eighteen, it was now obvious that the old captain of our mischievous adventures still lurked beneath his crown prince exterior. Only Sultan Khalil himself could have turned them back, and Rek had carefully arranged matters so no word of his plans reached his father's ears.

I gave up thinking about futile, impossible courses of action and focused on breathing quietly instead. Once the cave was filled with forty other people, it seemed unlikely that the sound of our breathing would cause a problem, but in the silence and darkness that had now fallen, every breath seemed terrifyingly loud.

I was still working on the silent breathing when a distant grinding made me start enough to rock one of the carpets. I steadied it, my heart beating fast. We had thought ourselves in for a long, boring wait, but we must have been only just ahead of the thieves in the forest.

Had they heard us opening the cave? It had sounded loud from above ground, but perhaps the trees kept the sound from spreading too far.

I strained, trying to hear the clop of forty horses, trained to endure the cold, dark tunnel. But it took longer than I expected to hear any further noises, and when I did hear hoofbeats, they sounded off somehow, as if their strides were too short.

Despite my resolution to hang back, I leaned forward, pressing my eye against the tiny gap in front of me. Light had appeared around the turn in the tunnel, and the first thief should come into sight at any moment.

A loud, ragged gasp echoed across the cave as a lone person appeared around the bend. He stopped, only to be butted in the rear by a rectangular, gray head. The donkey brayed loudly, and the man moved to one side, letting the animal pass. The lantern attached to the donkey's harness shone full on his face, and I barely suppressed my own gasp. Kasim.

CHAPTER 11

lthough Kasim was frozen, the lead donkey had continued moving forward, a string of nine more following behind. Each carried two baskets. I shook my head at the greed and temerity.

Navid had thought his rich uncle meant to force his poor father to split the gold he had brought home. But the selfish man had wanted more than that. Once he had Ali alone, he'd obviously forced him into telling the truth about where the wealth came from.

I waited for Ali to appear around the cave entrance, but he didn't come. Instead Kasim peered at a paper in his hand before uttering the words to close the cave entrance behind him. He must have convinced Ali to tell him the location of the cave and give him the instructions for opening it. I was at least glad Ali wasn't in the middle of this dangerous situation.

Of course, Kasim alone might be enough to wreck everything. How far away were the thieves? And what would they do if they arrived and found Kasim loading gold into his baskets? He'd brought *ten* donkeys and no one to help load them. He obviously didn't intend to trust anyone with details of the cave.

I muttered some strongly worded insults under my breath. There could be no worse time for Kasim's mix of greed and foolishness to come to the fore. He hadn't even waited for it to be light to rush over here.

I half-expected Rek to appear from hiding and order Kasim away. But the cave stayed silent except for Kasim's exclamations of disbelief. I wasn't certain where the others were concealed and how many of them could even see Kasim. They might think it was one of the thieves who had arrived.

He leaped on a nearby bag of jewels, heaving it into one of the baskets of the closest donkey. Next he reached for a small chest, panting and puffing as he hefted it up. He nearly tipped over backward trying to lift it high enough to ease over the edge of the basket.

I groaned. It was going to take an agonizingly long time for him to fill all the baskets. And the thieves could arrive at any moment.

Again I waited for Rek, or perhaps Samuel to appear. There was a good chance Adara and Navid lacked a clear view of what was happening, so they wouldn't risk emerging while there was someone else in the cave. But surely Rek had chosen a position that gave him a clear view of the entrance. And he would be even more concerned than I was about Kasim ruining our whole plan.

Of course, he might not recognize who Kasim was, but he would surely be able to tell he wasn't one of the gang. The man's reaction to the cave had made that clear. Still, Rek might not want to risk giving away our presence, and even knowing Kasim's identity, I couldn't blame him. The merchant definitely couldn't be trusted to keep silent about anything that didn't directly benefit him. He would certainly be unmoved by thoughts of the good of the kingdom.

Rek had thought we had a solid window of time before the thieves appeared. Perhaps the best plan was to do nothing. Kasim might well finish loading up and leave the cave before the thieves ever arrived.

We would still have the aftereffects of his presence to contend with, though, since he was making no effort to hide his pilfering. When the thieves did arrive, they'd be sure to notice someone else had been in here.

Then again, if they believed the person was gone, it might actually work to our advantage, provoking more interesting conversation than they might have unprompted. Of course, if they got nervous and searched the cave in case the intruder still lingered...

I shook my head. Surely they wouldn't suspect someone of robbing them and then hiding away in the back of the cave. From their perspective, the theft could have happened any time between their last visit and now.

If only Kasim would load the donkeys faster...

It seemed to take half the night, but at last Kasim filled the final basket. The poor donkeys were braying and flicking their tails, more than sick of the dark cave, but Kasim ignored them. He had been muttering happily to himself for some time, and he now stood back and rubbed his hands together. I could almost see him plotting to come back as soon as possible. Was there no end to the man's greed?

Finally, finally, he turned the lead donkey back toward the entrance, and the lights of the donkey string disappeared around the corner. But no grinding sound came. I waited and waited some more. Still it didn't come.

What was Kasim playing at?

Hurried footfalls sounded, and the merchant appeared. All his earlier pleasure was gone, his expression strained, and his face lined in the light of the lantern he carried.

He strode up and down, peering at the ground as if searching for something small as he retraced his steps.

"Over here. It must be over here," he muttered as he moved

closer to my position. "I had it in my pocket, I'm sure of it. Perhaps when I bent down to…"

He bent again, peering behind a nearby chest. It would be terrible luck if he stumbled on one of us in his search. What could he be looking for?

"Think, Kasim, think." He straightened and pressed his hand to his forehead. "You wrote it down yourself, you must remember the words. Open Barley? No, you already tried that one. But it was some sort of grain, I'm sure of it. Open Wheat?"

Unbelievable! He'd forgotten the words to open the cave entrance again. And lost the piece of paper he had written them on. How could anyone forget something both so short and so nonsensically silly?

But as he spun briefly toward me, I caught the gleam of desperation in his eye—so like the earlier gleam of avarice. Ali had spoken of being gold-struck on sight of the cave, and obviously his brother had been even more greatly affected.

After a long moment of stillness, Kasim turned back to the tunnel and disappeared from sight again, still muttering. If he tried every grain he could think of, would he eventually stumble on the correct words?

Reluctantly I admitted to myself that we couldn't afford to wait for however long that might take. Kasim had trapped himself in a fatal situation entirely through his own actions, but I couldn't leave him to his fate—both for his sake and for ours. As much as I disliked the man, I couldn't sit back and watch him killed when I had the means to assist him.

I shifted onto my knees, my muscles and joints protesting the long period of immobility. But just as I began to move aside one of the carpets to make room for me to crawl out, the cave filled with the sound of moving rock.

I sighed with relief and pulled the carpet back into position. Kasim had finally remembered the correct phase.

The rock stopped moving, and I waited anxiously to hear it

close again. Within minutes Kasim would be gone from the delicate situation. But instead of the distant braying and hoofbeats of donkeys, a muted scream of terror reached my ears.

I straightened, my breath catching as I peered from my hiding place. Running steps sounded, and Kasim burst back around the bend in the tunnel, his face desperate. He looked one way and then another before taking several steps forward, only to freeze again. He looked as if he were trying to choose a hiding place and failing.

Cold rushed through me. I had assumed the rock opened because Kasim had stumbled on the correct phrase. Instead, something far more terrible had happened. The cave had been opened from the outside.

Other cries, harsh and full of outrage, sounded. The donkeys had started braying at last, but the sound of their hoofs was growing louder, not softer, as if someone was leading them back into the cave.

The first of a line of horses turned in. The face of the man riding it was set in lines of anger, and I recognized him from my one other encounter with the gang. Their captain.

"Who dares to enter our cave?" he snapped, peering down at Kasim, still frozen near the entrance. "Who dares to steal from us?"

Kasim opened his mouth, but the words that came out were gibberish.

The robber captain swung down off his horse as did the others behind him, coming to stand at his back.

"How did he get in here, Esai?" asked the one closest to him in more measured tones. "How did he find it? That's the important question."

I didn't recognize the second man, although he had distinctive, arched eyebrows. Was he the missing Davis who had led Rek and his guards away?

Kasim moaned.

"We're not going to get any sense out of him," said a burly man in disgust.

I recognized his voice more than his appearance. This was the man who had challenged the captain last time, only to back down again. His appearance suggested he was stronger on temper than intelligence.

"It would appear not," said the captain in a tone of cold disgust.

My mind raced. Of course they needed to get information out of Kasim, that much was obvious. For once, his foolishness might work to our advantage. It would be a while before he was in a fit state to answer questions which gave me time to think of a way to get him out of the situation.

I gritted my teeth, trying to think what could be done, while the captain—Esai—turned to look back toward the tunnel where one of the other thieves was now leading the donkeys back in.

"No one steals from us and lives," he said, gazing at the baskets full of gold and jewels.

I squeezed my eyes shut at the threat, pleading with my brain to work faster. Would they keep him stashed in the cave or take him out into the forest, thinking to get clearer answers from him out there?

The ominous sound of ringing steel made my eyes flash open. I shot onto my knees, acting on instinct rather than logic as I reached for the carpet in front of me. But before I could push it aside, a sickening sound made me freeze. Almost reluctantly, I pressed my eye back to the gap.

The burly thief stood two strides in front of his previous location, the sword in his hand now dripping red. My stomach flipped, and I had to fight to keep it from rejecting my last meal as my eyes traveled to Kasim's still form, lying on the floor in a rapidly spreading pool of blood.

CHAPTER 12

The captain turned, obviously just as caught off guard by the actions of his lieutenant as I was.

"What have you done?" he barked.

"You said he couldn't live." The burly thief started to clean his sword.

"I didn't mean you should kill him instantly," Esai said with a growl. "Now how will we learn how he discovered this cave? Or who else he has told about it."

The killer shrugged. "He must have seen us last time we were here. Perhaps he was hiding up a tree or something. It's the only way he could have known. And he was alone here in the middle of the night with ten donkeys." He glanced back at them in disgust. "Obviously he wanted to keep the discovery all to himself."

"All those things may be true," Esai said coldly, "but we cannot afford to assume they are. We must find out who this man was and who he has told about our cave. All of which would have been easier to do if he was alive."

My stomach turned again although I was carefully averting my eyes from Kasim's body. So he really was dead. It was hard to fathom. His death alone would mean complete upheaval for our entire household. But the manner of his demise, coupled with the captain's words, made it sound as if every one of us was in great danger.

"We cannot risk not investigating," Davis said, backing up the captain. "Just look at those baskets! Look how much he was going to take. It would have meant complete disaster."

"Had he already taken previous loads away?" another of the thieves asked, sounding more concerned than the possibility warranted, given how much still remained. "He may have ruined everything already."

Esai laid a hand on the closest basket. "No, I think we can be sure that has not happened. If it had, at least some of our retired members would have converged on the cave by now—my father at their head."

Several of the older looking thieves looked queasy at his suggestion, leaving the strong impression Esai's father was a man more feared than respected among them.

It sounded as if Esai had inherited command of this gang from his father. Had it really been going for so long? There were always reports of bandits on the roads, but I had never suspected it of being a single gang, uncaught for decades.

I glanced around at the chests of overflowing gold. If they never spent the riches they stole, it would make it a lot easier to avoid capture. But I still couldn't work out what the point of it was if they never enjoyed their ill-gotten wealth.

And why would Kasim raiding the cave bring back the retired thieves? Did it have something to do with the enchantment? Would they be magically notified of any breach on their stronghold?

But that couldn't be the case, or they would have come after Ali's thievery two days ago. My head whirled trying to make sense of it, and all the while, in a distant part of my brain, I was still screaming with horror at seeing my employer murdered in front of me.

"If we had continued down south for the next few months, like our original plan, we would have missed him entirely," Davis said, sounding sickened.

"We would have heard about it, as I said." Esai spoke shortly, still out of temper.

One of the other thieves swore. "If it wasn't for that cursed enchantment, we wouldn't be stuck coming back here so often. And we wouldn't have to worry about people like him." He pointed at Kasim's body.

The captain gave him a cold look. "Are you perhaps suggesting we should abandon this cave and the traditions of our fathers?"

"No, no, of course not," the man said hastily. "It's just impossible not to think about how much simpler matters would be if we just spent our—"

"Perhaps you know of other gangs with a record like ours?" Esai asked, sounding dangerous now. "A gang that has operated for decades without a single member being apprehended? You knew what you were signing up for when you joined, and you knew that there are only two ways out—like Joseph here..." He pointed at a thief who stood slightly to the side of the group, a few gray strands in his otherwise black hair. "Or like that." He pointed at Kasim.

The burly thief stepped forward, his hand on the hilt of his now clean and sheathed sword. The grumbling thief took a hasty step backward.

"Hold on, I'm not saying nothing about leaving. Nothing like that. But a man can wish things were simpler, can't he?"

"I prefer not to waste my time on imaginings." Esai turned away from him in a clear dismissal.

At a hand gesture from him, twenty thieves sprang forward to each take a basket from one of the donkeys. I expected them to begin returning the gold and jewels to their original places, but they merely tossed the baskets toward the edges of the cave, seeming not to care where they landed.

The gold clinked and clanged, many of the coins bouncing out and rolling in all directions. The thieves ignored the mess, except for one who looked down at Kasim's body in distaste.

"And what about this one? What do we do with him?"

"Leave him there," Esai said, "as a warning. If anyone else does know the secret of the cave, let them discover what happens to those who try to rob us."

The man made a face but didn't protest, and I understood his disgust. If they meant to come back any time soon, they might not like what they found.

"When we robbed that caravan and headed here to deposit the gold, you said it was enough to move forward my retirement," Joseph, the man with gray in his hair, said abruptly. "Has that changed?"

Esai hesitated, and I could see the reluctance flickering in his eyes as the lamplight hit them. But he glanced around at the rest of his men and shook his head.

"The treasure has been fed, and this thief didn't make it out of the cave, so matters remain the same. Thirty-nine of us should be enough to track down this man's identity and ensure the silence of those closest to him."

Icy fear trickled through me. Nyla was one of the people I liked least in the world, but I still didn't want to see her murdered in her bed. And as for the rest of the servants…

"Choose your earnings," the captain said to Joseph, his voice heavy as if the words had some long-standing custom behind them.

The gray-haired man gave him a half bow and moved off toward the back of the cave. I gulped, a more immediate worry overtaking me as he poked around among the treasures in the further reaches. I no longer had to wonder what would happen if he stumbled on the hiding place of one of the others. I pictured Adara lying beside Kasim and was nearly sick again.

But as the minutes stretched on, there was no shout of discovery or cry of fear. Another thief led forward one of the horses, and the man began to fill both the saddlebags while a third thief counted portentously.

When he reached ninety-nine, the gray-haired thief unrolled a thick piece of material and regarded it for a long moment. I couldn't get a clear view from my hiding place, but it looked like a tapestry.

Eventually the man nodded, rolled it back up, and laid it across the back of his horse, securing it behind his saddle. He led his mount back to the rest of the thieves near the entrance, many of whom gave him openly envious looks.

"You have played your part and now receive your reward," the captain said in the same ringing voice.

"I take the secret of our brotherhood to my grave," the thief replied, giving the same half bow again.

He clambered up onto the back of his now heavily laden horse, and the others seemed to take it as a signal. Within moments they were all mounted, except for one who took charge of the string of donkeys.

As the thieves started back out of the cave, Esai and Davis lingered behind, bringing up the rear of the group. As they started toward the tunnel, I heard Esai say something about going into the city. But though I strained to hear more, they moved too quickly, passing out of hearing before I could catch any specifics.

For a wild moment, I considered trying to sneak after them, but the grinding noise of the cave entrance began, and I knew I wouldn't be able to hear anything regardless. When the noise finished, I waited impatiently for it to begin again, signaling the gang had all departed and were closing the entrance behind them.

Although it couldn't have been long in reality, it seemed to take an inordinately long time before complete silence fell. The silence stretched out for a full minute. None of my companions moved or spoke, and I could only assume they were doing the same as me—straining their ears as they waited nervously for the grinding to resume. If any of the thieves came back, or realized they'd forgotten something, or…

Eventually the silence became too much to bear, and I kicked the carpet in front of me with unnecessary force. It fell forward with a thump that echoed across the cave.

I stood, stretching carefully as my body screamed at me in protest for having kept my curled position for so long. A light flickered, illuminating the cavern, and Rek appeared. He hurried toward me, and I went forward to meet him in the middle.

I swerved around Kasim's body, carefully averting my face. Rek, however, was looking down at him, a mixture of frustration and sorrow on his face.

"I don't suppose you know who that was or what he was doing here?" he asked.

"That was Kasim," I said shortly.

"Kasim?" He looked up at me in surprise. "You mean the man you work for? But he's Navid's uncle." He looked toward the back of the cave where Adara and Navid had just appeared.

"There wasn't a lot of affection between them, but…" I hurried toward Navid. "I'm so sorry," I said to him. "I was going to come out—to try to help him—but it all happened so quickly."

Navid frowned, obviously confused. He took a step around me, peering toward what held Rek's attention. For a blank moment, he just stared at his uncle's body, and then he swallowed convulsively.

"Is that…?"

"Yes," I said softly. "He must have convinced your father to tell him about the cave, gone to get the donkeys, and then come straight here. Only then he couldn't remember the words he needed to reopen the entrance." I shook my head. "Given how quickly everything happened, I suspect he would have run into the thieves outside even if he had managed to get it open."

"I didn't pick my hiding place very well." Navid sounded slightly sick. "I couldn't properly see or hear anything at the front of the cave." A fleeting glance toward Adara told me what he'd been thinking of when he chose his position.

"I couldn't work out what was going on, either," Adara said in a small, sad voice. "I had no idea…" She trailed off, her brow furrowed, her concerned eyes on Navid.

"If he hadn't been so greedy, this would never have happened," Navid said harshly. "He must have bullied Father into telling him the truth and giving him all the details, but what did he even need more gold for? He was already rich!"

"Some people can never have enough." Adara slipped her hand into his, giving it a comforting squeeze.

Rek cleared his throat significantly, and she flushed slightly and pulled her hand away. Rek's disapproving gaze lingered on Navid, however, making me uneasy. Navid must have forgotten that we'd left his father out of the story we gave the royals. But when Rek spoke, he didn't mention Ali.

"As sorry as I am about your uncle, Navid, I'm even more concerned about the effect this could have on the whole kingdom. I got a good look at most of the thieves, but beyond that, we heard little information of use. They mentioned nothing about a second base, and now it sounds like they mean to move to another part of the kingdom for several months."

"No," Samuel corrected him with a furrowed brow. "They *were* going south. It sounded to me like they now mean to stay here and investigate this uncle of Navid." He nodded toward Kasim's body.

"Yes, that's what it sounded like to me, too," I said.

An intense look came into Rek's eyes, as if he were calculating something. "You were both slightly closer than me, so you'll have heard better. My long legs made finding a place difficult. If the thieves intend to investigate inside the capital, that's a real opportunity for us. They normally avoid large cities and stick to the roads." His brow clouded. "But you work in Kasim's household, Zaria. You could be in danger."

I shrugged, trying to downplay my own concern. "I'm a nameless, faceless servant girl—one of many. I've seen the thieves twice now, but they've never seen me. I shouldn't think I'm in any especial danger. Navid is more likely to be in trouble than me."

"I'm not worried about that," Navid said instantly. "Catching this gang is worth a little risk."

Rek nodded solemnly. "You have personal reason to want them brought to justice, so I shan't try to deny you have a right to get involved."

Navid thanked him, but a glance my way showed his feelings were more complicated than he was letting on. He wouldn't miss Kasim at all, and he probably felt guilt at being assigned the role of grieving relative.

A stab of true sorrow hit me. Who would miss Kasim as a person rather than a provider of employment? Would anyone? Certainly Nyla wouldn't.

How truly sad to live a life surrounded by people but connected to no one by either love or respect. It put my own desire to cling to those I had loved in perspective.

"I'm sure the thieves were talking about the enchantment as well," I said, steering my thoughts back to more immediate matters. "But I can't quite put it together. None of it made sense without more information."

I worried at the tantalizing threads in my mind, going over the different comments they'd made. Strangest of all had been their odd behavior around the retiring thief and his saddlebags of treasure.

I turned to Adara and Navid. "I couldn't hear or see much

from the front, but could you see that thief who went right to the back and was taking treasure instead of leaving it?"

"We saw him." Adara grimaced. "I've never been so terrified in my life. I thought he was going to find one of us for sure."

"Does that mean you're willing to step back from all this now?" Rek asked instantly.

She gave him an exasperated look. "Of course not."

He sighed, clearly disappointed.

I ignored their bickering, still trying to make sense of the tangle in my mind. "Could you see what sort of things he was taking? It didn't look like gold coins to me."

"No," Navid agreed, his face thoughtful. "I didn't see him take a single coin. He seemed to be focused on more unique items. I remember him choosing a large gold goblet and an elaborate gold necklace set with enormous rubies."

"And he took that set of gorgeous painted vases we were admiring," Adara added. "I've never seen anything like them. And that tapestry, of course."

"Do you think you'd recognize those vases again if you saw one of them?" Rek asked.

"Definitely." Adara nodded.

"That's something, then." Rek was sounding more and more cheerful. "We can send out word in case anything like them turns up for sale in any of the cities. If you can confirm it's one of the vases from this cave, we might be able to trace the man selling it."

I tuned him out, still focused on my own thoughts. But Samuel's voice jerked me out of my abstraction.

"We should be moving," he said. "Now that the thieves have come and gone, Benjamin will be getting jumpy if we don't appear soon. We don't want him riding back to the palace to report our deaths."

"Yes, there's nothing to be gained staying here any longer." Rek eyed the closest chest of gold doubtfully. "Should we take anything? As proof of the cave, I mean? We obviously won't be staggering out of here with chests full of gold."

"I wouldn't recommend it," I said. "Not while we still don't understand the enchantment. In fact, I brought my own coin to return."

I thrust my hand into my pocket, seeking the small circle of metal. Instead of cool gold, however, my reaching fingertips hit only material. I frowned and dug around harder. But while my pocket seemed to be unusually gritty, there was no sign of any object in it at all.

I frowned back toward my hiding space. Had it fallen out while I was twisting around in there? I stepped toward the carpets, pulling my hand out of my pocket as I went.

The flickering flame of the closest lantern flashed across my fingers as I moved, and I stopped in surprise, staring at them. For a second, my hand had seemed to gleam golden. I peered more closely and saw my fingers were coated in a fine layer of dust that appeared gold in the orange light.

And my pocket had seemed unusually dusty…

All the strands came together in my mind, and I whirled back to the others, my voice sharp.

"We need to get out of here right now!"

CHAPTER 13

"*E*xplain it to me again?" Rek asked. "I want to be sure I fully understand your theory."

"Of course." I hoped my voice betrayed none of my inner turmoil.

As the smallest of our party, it was perfectly natural that I should have been the one chosen to ride double, leaving my horse free to carry the tragic burden of Kasim's body. However, logic dictated that I should have doubled with the second smallest among us—Adara. When Rek volunteered to take me, however, no one else protested. And I certainly wasn't going to cause trouble.

But now that one of his arms was around me, holding me steady against him, I had to confess—to myself, at least—that it had been more than agreeableness that kept me quiet. I had always admired Rek—he had been the leader of our childhood games after all, and far more reliable than either of the twins. But even then, he had been set apart—the crown prince.

The twins had been more approachable, as well as being the same age as me, so they had been the easy object of my childish affection. Looking back now, I could also see how liking the two of them equally had helped keep the whole situation firmly in the realm of giddy fun. My youthful self had never truly been romantically interested in either of them as an individual—merely in the idea of them and the idea of romance.

Now, as my breath came roughly and my heart beat quickly, I wondered something about those days. Even as children, Adara had always laughed at me for being too practical. Had I been shielding myself even then? Had I attached my romantic dreams to the twins because some subconscious part of me recognized that Rek was far too dangerous a person to fill that role? Dangerous for my heart, that was.

When I believed myself betrayed, I had certainly been quick to focus my anger on Rek. Had that been a defense mechanism as well?

The thoughts scared me, and I wished I could shove them back down to the hidden corner they had sprung from. Because if the old Rek, still teetering on the edge of manhood, had been a danger to me, the grown version currently holding me against his chest was far more so.

He was confident, thoughtful, and devastatingly attractive. Even the reckless streak that lurked beneath his responsibility thrilled me—calling to the same buried seed within me. Compared to Adara and the twins, we had always been the sensible, responsible ones—but we had still been there, racing into mischief beside them.

And worst of all, Rek was far too pleased to resume our old friendship—when he wasn't forgetting about me entirely in pursuit of his mission. It was just the combination to keep my heart confused, hopeful, and in pain.

I could see it now so clearly. Rek and I had always been the most alike. But I was a servant now. Even before, as the daughter of a junior vizier, I had qualified as a childhood playmate and nothing more. Now, we didn't even belong in the same room.

In the one way that really mattered, Rek and I were nothing

alike. Which is why my heart needed to return to its usual speed, and the flush on my cheeks needed to cool in the night wind.

My heart wasn't listening, however, continuing to beat out its hurried rhythm. I tried to force myself to focus on Rek's question instead.

"It is just a theory," I said and felt his nod of agreement against the top of my head.

I drew a deep breath, trying to suppress my reaction to his nearness. Only when I was sure I could speak calmly, did I continue.

"The thieves brought what they'd stolen—or most of it—to the cave. I was assuming they used it as convenient storage, but Esai—their captain—referred to *feeding* the treasure. As if it was a living creature."

Rek made a skeptical noise, and I hurried on.

"Obviously it's not alive. I'm not suggesting that. But an enchantment could animate it in a way. And if the enchantment required that the treasure in the cave be continually 'fed' new treasure, that would explain why the gang robs travelers over and over, only to deposit their stolen goods in a cave. That was the bit that had me most confused."

"But it still doesn't explain their motivation for doing so," Rek said, clearly wanting to follow every twist of my reasoning. "Why not just keep what they steal and ignore the cave entirely? That was the retirement part you talked about."

I nodded. "Esai referred to a large number of old members who had already retired, and it sounded like many of them are family to the current gang members. I think that if you serve for a certain length of time, you get to claim your share of the treasure."

I paused, feeling the need to add a caveat. "This is the bit where it really does become guesswork. What if, in order for the enchantment to be satisfied that the treasure is being fed, they have to put in more than they take out? That would make the whole exercise worse than pointless *unless* the enchantment has faded to the point where it only recognizes the number of items, not their value. So they feed it a continuous supply of gold coins and simple gems, things like that. But they take items of far greater value—items that, once sold, can keep the thief in question in luxury for the rest of his days."

"Most of the chests and bags near the front seemed to hold basic coins and gems, with a few golden objects among them," Rek agreed. "The further in you went, the more elaborate the items became. Some of them were impressive enough works of art that they would bring their owner status and acclaim, if he valued that over their monetary value."

"Exactly! What if the items at the back are the original treasure of the fabled cave? Treasure that's been sitting there, magically preserved, for centuries. And the chests and bags at the front are what this gang has added over the decades."

"Hmmm." Rek considered the point. "And you believe that if there is ever more taken from the cave than has been added, everything that has been removed turns to dust? And you think that happened? Just then?"

"Precisely. That's why we had to hurry out of there. Combined with what the retired thieves had already taken, the six baskets of gold coins taken by Ali must have come perilously close to tipping the total the wrong way. Not knowing about those baskets, the gang thought it was safe for their retiring member to take his share, removing yet more items from the cave."

"That would be the six baskets neither you nor Navid thought to mention earlier," Rek said dryly.

"It wasn't relevant before now," I said airily. "But now it is, so we told you. I shudder to think how many individual coins were in those baskets. He must have been incredibly near the limit of dusting everything. Close enough that those hundred extra items today set the enchantment into motion. I walked into the cave with a coin in my pocket, but unlike the other coins in that cave, this one had been taken from the cave. It had been marked by the enchantment. And once the thieves rode out, it turned to golden dust. Which means so did everything Joseph took as his reward for service to the gang. It's dark, so I don't know how long it will take that thief to realize his tapestry is gone and his saddlebags are full of dust, but when he does..."

"They'll ride straight back to the cave." Rek glanced to his left where Samuel was leading my horse with its burden. "And they'll find Kasim's body gone. They'll know someone else has been in there tonight."

I grimaced. "Yes, that wasn't ideal. But we couldn't just leave him there! Especially since we have to find a way to conceal his identity."

Rek didn't say anything, but I knew he accepted my point because back in the cave he'd agreed to let us take the body home to Nyla.

"So at some point in the last few decades," I finished up, getting the conversation back on track, "a man somehow stumbled on the secret to opening the cave, but also the details of the enchantment. So he'd found riches beyond measure, but he couldn't take any of them. If he did, he would trigger the enchantment and need to keep continually feeding the treasure. But he's not a principled man, so he comes up with the idea of the gang. By keeping the gang going beyond their own retirement, individual members can retire and have the chance to enjoy their wealth. And they don't even have to worry about being discovered with stolen goods—which is the most common way thieves are caught. Because anything they steal is stashed in the cave, while the wealth they're spending is the original treasure of the cave, not anything anyone else ever owned."

"It's actually a fairly ingenious idea," Rek said with begrudging respect. "It must have taken a charismatic leader to turn it into reality, though—and to keep it functioning all this time later."

"I suspect it was Esai's father," I said. "From the way the thieves responded to the suggestion he might show up, they clearly still fear him."

"The worst of it is that we can't make use of the treasure ourselves," Rek said. "If we were free to take it, everyone ever robbed by the gang could be repaid, and many of the kingdom's most urgent needs met as well. But instead it will continue to sit there gathering dust forever."

"Well, not dust," I said, unable to help myself. "I can only assume from its gleaming appearance that the enchantment keeps that away."

Rek let out a reluctant chuckle. "Not literal dust, then. But it might as well be gathering it for all the good it will do anyone."

"Perhaps we can find a way to break the enchantment? It's getting older and older, and they were able to break the one on the cave in Ardasira."

"I don't know that they so much broke it as triggered it and survived the outcome," Rek said. "But if your coin is anything to go by, there'd be no point our trying the same. We'd end up with a great deal of dust and no treasure."

The walls of the city came into view, and disappointment washed over me. I wanted this ride to last forever—and that despite knowing the danger to my heart of indulging this particular foolishness.

"I hope Benjamin's cousin is still at the gate or we're going to get some questions," I said lightly, my eyes straying to my horse.

"He'll be there."

It was almost certainly my imagination, but Rek's arm seemed to tighten slightly, pulling me marginally closer—almost as if he was regretting the end of the ride as well.

I shook off the thought. *Beware, beware,* I shouted at myself in the back of my mind.

Forcing myself to pull away slightly, I sat bolt upright as we approached the gate. Once again, we made it through without questioning, and the streets between the gate and my home flew past. It seemed impossible that I had thought them so long on the reverse journey.

When we stopped in front of the gates, I twisted slightly to look up at Rek's face.

"This is going to be a very painful scene. And Nyla, Kasim's wife, is not someone who can be trusted with the full story of what's going on. Given that, I think it would be simpler if only Navid and I go in. With…with Kasim, of course. We have to assume he told her about the cave when he collected the donkeys, but I think we should just say that we followed him and found him killed by the thieves."

Rek frowned, looking down at me. "I don't like abandoning you like that."

"It really will be easier if you aren't there."

I honestly couldn't imagine what Nyla would make of the situation if two royals were added to the mix, but I had no desire to find out.

"I agree," Navid said from beside us. He swung down and reached up to help me down as well.

For one second, Rek's arm lingered around my waist, as if reluctant to let go. Then I was sliding down the side of the horse into Navid's waiting grasp, and Rek was nodding.

"Very well, if you judge it best. Does that also mean you don't want either of us to visit you here?"

Navid and I exchanged glances.

"I think that would be wisest." He sounded almost as reluctant as I felt.

"Goodbye for now, then." Adara nudged her mount forward. "I'll make sure you're sent invitations to the upcoming ball at the palace. We can meet there, at least."

"To the ball?" Rek frowned. "Is that wise?" He was carefully not looking at me all of a sudden.

"I don't care," Adara said, tired defiance in her voice. She looked across at us. "I'll send them."

We both nodded, although I couldn't fathom the thought of balls and dancing with this violent night still dark around us, and Kasim's wrapped body on the ground at our feet.

In silence, Navid and I watched the other four ride off, leading our two horses with them. Once they were gone, he drew a deep breath and turned toward the gate.

"We should get inside and out of sight as quickly as possible." He raised his hand to the brass knocker on the gate, but I caught his arm.

"Wait. We don't want to rouse everyone inside. Give me a moment."

I dashed around the corner of the wall and down the narrow alley that ran along the side of the house until I reached the small door that led into the stables. At my urgent knock, it swung almost instantly open, Rowan's concerned face peering out. He must have been waiting there for my return.

"We need your help." I beckoned him to follow me, and he came without question.

When he rounded the corner onto the main street, however, he paused. His eye took in first Navid, and then the wrapped body at his feet.

"Who is that?" he asked, as if afraid of the answer.

I glanced up and down the street, but it was deserted and dark except for the moonlight peeping out from behind a cloud.

"It's Kasim," I said, feeling the weight of the night's happenings all over again.

"Kas—" Rowan cut himself off. "No, we need to get inside."

"Yes, but we need your help to carry him," I said.

Rowan nodded his understanding and crouched to gently lift the wrapped figure from beneath his shoulders. Navid and I leaped to assist, and between the three of us, we managed to carry him around the corner, through the stable door, and out into the courtyard again.

At the quiet sounds of our shuffling movement, the kitchen door swung open, spilling warm, yellow light into the courtyard.

"I've been keeping the fire hot for you," Yara's motherly voice called softly. "You'll be wanting your tea before you head for bed."

I wasn't sure if she was talking to Rowan, to me, or to both of us. But a second later she got a look at us and let out a shocked gasp.

"Hold the door," Rowan puffed, and she quickly pulled back, holding the kitchen door wide for us.

Awkwardly we shuffled through and laid Kasim on the long kitchen table in the center of the room.

"It's Kasim," Rowan said shortly to Yara. "That's all I know."

"Kasim!" Yara's cry seemed painfully loud in the stillness of the night, but she had already closed the outside door, and I knew only Yara's own room lay anywhere near the kitchens.

"We need to wake Nyla," I said. "It would be best to send Layla to do that. No one else can know about this. Not yet."

Both of them must have picked up on the fear in my voice because neither uttered a single protest or question.

"I'll go for Layla," Yara said, and Rowan nodded, saying he would lock the outside door and guard the internal one in case anyone else awoke and came investigating.

Navid and I were left standing over the body, and with reluctance, I began to unwrap his head.

"For Nyla?" Navid asked, and I nodded.

"She'll need to see it's him for herself, of course. And his face looks perfectly peaceful."

"It doesn't seem real." Navid looked down at his uncle.

"If only he had stayed at home tonight." I sighed.

The silent minutes ticked on, only to be broken by a piercing scream. I jumped, caught off guard by Nyla's arrival. Thankfully,

Rowan had already whisked the heavy wooden door closed again, so I turned my attention to Nyla.

"Kasim!" she screamed again, and then promptly went into hysterics.

Even Layla, who had trailed her into the kitchen, pulled back at that, exchanging a panicked look with Yara. I stepped forward, however, and took Nyla firmly by the shoulders.

"You must calm down at once," I said loudly, over her shrieks, "or we'll all end up like him."

She stopped immediately, making me wonder how much of the hysterics had been a performance.

Looking around the kitchen, her lip curled. "He didn't even get any of the gold, did he? I should have gone myself."

Hiding my own disgust at her coldness, I looked her directly in the eyes.

"If you had, you'd be the one lying on the table. And now we need to come up with a plan—quickly—or we'll all be buried beside him."

CHAPTER 14

"That's your second death threat," Nyla said. "I've half a mind to call the guards! Why are you here in the middle of the night with my husband's body?"

Navid took a step forward. "My uncle died through his own foolishness and greed, and I suggest you listen to what Zaria has to say. She's only trying to protect you and this whole household."

Nyla's eyes narrowed as she took in his protective posture, but she remained silent, allowing me to resume.

"The gold you wanted Kasim to claim actually belongs to a gang of thieves. They caught him stealing it and stabbed him. It happened so fast there was no time for anyone to help him—even if there had been help nearby, which there wasn't."

Nyla looked sick, as if the situation was finally sinking in.

"Tragic as one death is," Navid said, "we must act to prevent more."

"The gang don't know his identity, but they're determined to discover it," I said. "They're worried he told others in his household the location of their stolen wealth."

Yara gasped, her hand flying to her mouth. "Are you saying we're all in danger?"

I nodded. "I fear so. Which means we need to decide on a story right now. If rumors spread through the city that Kasim died by violence this night, then we might as well tell the gang his identity ourselves."

Nyla stared at me blankly, contributing nothing. Layla stepped forward, however, talking in her abrupt way.

"So we need a different cause of death, and a different day of death. Illness seems the logical choice. Zaria, you're a familiar face at the market, and the stallholders think of you as trustworthy, so you should go. As soon as it's light, visit Samir and ask for medicine for…"

She glanced at Yara who pulled herself together enough to contribute.

"Powder for a fever. No need to get into specifics."

Layla nodded her approval. "We'll carry him up to his room now and bar the rest of the household entry to his bedchamber. Nyla will visit him, of course, but otherwise I will take on the supposed nursing. Yara will bring his meals herself."

"That sounds sensible," Navid said. "Let the rumor spread today that he is ill, and tomorrow you can announce his death. For now, I need to return home and warn my parents. I'll tell them the truth, of course, and they can assist us. If my uncle was really deathly ill, his brother would no doubt visit. Father can come tomorrow afternoon, after the story has had time to spread."

"Yes, your parents!" Nyla straightened. "We must consider them. I will accompany you."

"You?" Navid stared at her. "You want to come with me now? In the middle of the night?"

"Certainly. Didn't I just say so? We must leave immediately."

Navid glanced at me, but I shrugged.

"I'll need to help carry…" Navid glanced at Rowan who came forward to assist.

It took very little time to get Kasim's body into his own bed. We left him there, with Layla sitting vigil by the door. Navid tried to steal an extra word with me, but Nyla pounced on him and ushered him out of the house.

"What's that about?" Yara asked uneasily when it was just Rowan, her, and me in the kitchen.

"No idea," Rowan said gruffly. "But it sounds like we have a rough few days to come, so I'm going to try for some sleep."

He slipped back out to the stables, where he had a small apartment in the loft, but I hesitated, looking inquiringly at Yara. She smiled and shook her head.

"It's about time to be starting on the dough anyway. There's no point in my going back to bed."

"Or me." I sighed. "It'll be time for me to run to the market soon. I would like to get changed, though. And I should wait in my room as if I have been asleep."

Once I was in fresh clothes, I waited for Layla's inevitable knock. When it finally came, I was more than ready for some action.

"The master has taken terribly ill overnight," she told me from the doorway in a piercing voice.

I peeped into the hall and saw two scullery maids and a groom. They had broken off their conversation to stare at Layla.

"The main apothecary won't be open yet," I said, remembering my line. "But Samir always opens his stall early. Shall I run to the market for some medicine?"

She nodded. "He burns with fever—hotter than I've ever felt—so move quickly."

I scooped up my jacket, making a show of hurrying it on and racing down the hall. But all the way to the market, my mind moved almost as quickly as my feet. I couldn't shake my concern about what had sent Nyla racing off into the night to see Ali and Mariam. She wouldn't turn to them for support in her grief.

Given our already precarious situation, the whole thing made me nervous. But as I approached Samir's stall, I pushed the doubts aside and focused on my performance. Panting for breath and with a furrowed brow, I scanned the various bottles, jars, and pouches.

"You're here early, Zaria." Samir hurried forward, his comfortable face falling into sympathetic lines. "Illness in the household?"

"Kasim himself." I let my frown deepen. "Layla says she's never felt a fever so hot, so I'll need your best powder."

"Of course, of course." He selected a smooth leather pouch and checked it was securely fastened. "I would never send anything else for Kasim."

I nodded my thanks and fumbled as I reached for some coins.

"No, no," Samir said hurriedly. "You mustn't worry about such things in the urgency of the moment. I know I need have no concern that my bill will be paid in time."

"Thank you." I gave him a tight smile and fled with my new acquisition.

I had barely made it five steps, however, before I collided headlong with someone.

"Ouch!" My best friend frowned at me, rubbing at the spot where our two heads had collided.

"Where are you running off to at such an early hour?" Kali asked with a pout. "I spotted you and was hurrying over to say hello, but you weren't looking at all."

"Sorry," I said shortly. "I must hurry home." I held up the pouch. "I've just been at Samir's stall getting medicine for Kasim."

"He's sick?" Kali frowned. "I'm sorry." She hesitated and leaned closer. "But I know you too well to think the worry in your eyes is all for him. What's going on?"

I grimaced. She did know me too well. "I can't say. Sorry, Kali. Not this time."

She rocked back in surprise, and I expected her to press me, but her eyes dropped to the pouch. She placed a warm hand on my wrist.

"You have to hurry. But I hope you know I'm always ready to help you—no matter what trouble you've gotten yourself into. That's what friends are for."

Moisture pricked at my eyes, her kind words balm after the stresses of the night. I wouldn't put Kali at risk by dragging her into my mess, but her willingness meant a great deal.

"Thank you, Kali." I tried to put my feelings into my tone since I couldn't stay to talk.

"Yes, yes, I know, I'm the bestest of friends." She smiled and waved for me to hurry on.

I obeyed, brushing past an elegant middle-aged woman in an elaborately embroidered ankle-length robe. Several servants followed behind her, looking annoyed at the early morning excursion.

"You always get the best prices if there isn't a crowd," I heard her say to one of them and shook my head.

Yasmine, the widow of one of the city's richest merchants, didn't need to worry about bargaining for the cheapest possible price. Such miserly behavior fit all the stories of her, though. Perhaps she had one of her famous parties coming up and hoped to negotiate a better bulk price in person.

I shook off thought of parties, remembering I was supposed to be hurrying back to a sick man. Forcing my exhausted legs into a run, I dashed the rest of the way home.

The kitchen was as full as usual, but an unnatural quiet lay over it. Every conversation was being conducted in a whisper, and no one laughed.

"I sent up my best broth," Yara told me, "but he barely touched it." She looked strained and anxious, but no one would find it odd in the circumstances.

I gave her hand a squeeze before announcing I would look in on Layla when I delivered the medicine and see if she needed any help.

At the door of Kasim's bedchamber, which Layla only opened a crack, I was told in a loud voice that he was worsening, and I should fetch Ali.

I lowered my voice to a quiet whisper before replying. "Nyla came back, I assume? She's not still with Ali and Mariam?"

"She's in here with me," Layla whispered back, her grimace making it clear she wasn't appreciating the company.

I grimaced in sympathy and announced I would run for Ali.

My running pace lagged on the way to his house, more of a jog than a sprint. But it was a longer distance, and I wasn't used to so much dashing around. At least my curiosity helped to drive me forward. With Nyla gone, I could safely ask Navid what she had wanted.

As I ran, I also thought of Rek and Adara. Had they woken up as usual in the palace and easily gone about their days? Or were they struggling to pretend that it had been a normal night spent in their beds?

At Ali's house, I saw the red ribbon had been removed from their front gate. Frowning, I unlatched it and slipped inside without knocking. At the door of the house, I knocked, however, and Agnes answered. One look at her face told me she knew something, at least, although I didn't dare comment without knowing how much.

Navid appeared behind her, clearly relieved to see me.

"I hoped you'd come today." He gestured me into their small visiting room.

I stopped on the threshold, surprised to find both Ali and Mariam inside, wrapped up in what looked like a serious conversation. But at sight of me, both gave a smile of welcome.

"Come in, Zaria," Ali called, his smile quickly falling away again. "It seems impossible to believe that things have turned so quickly from good to bad. I begged my brother not to go to the cave in the middle of the night, but..." He shook his head.

"At least you had the good sense not to go with him," I said. "Or you'd be dead too."

"Dead." He shook his head. "We never had the closeness one would wish to see between brothers, but he helped Navid most estimably. It seems strange to think he's really gone."

"Stranger still to think of living in his house," Mariam said, although she looked more excited than displeased.

"Living in his house?" I asked slowly, trying to make sense of the comment.

"My aunt insisted on returning with me last night because she had an...invitation for my parents." Navid met my gaze, his eyes full of the emotion he was carefully keeping out of his voice.

"An invitation?" My uneasiness grew.

"An arrangement of mutual benefit to all," Mariam said. "Naturally she does not wish to be alone at such a time."

I raised an eyebrow but said nothing. Nyla was hardly alone in her house, even without Kasim. But apparently the servants didn't count.

"Precisely," Ali said. "What could be more natural in the circumstances? We will combine households and be there to comfort our sister in her time of grief and to take the burden of business management from her shoulders. Navid is excellently placed to take on the mantle of his uncle's business, given his training and Kasim's lack of an heir."

"Wait," I said, still struggling to understand, purely because it seemed so unbelievable. "Nyla came here in the middle of the night to ask you to move in with her? To combine households permanently?" I looked at Mariam. "She's willing to share her position as mistress of the house with you?"

"My aunt," said Navid, letting his emotions loose, "claims that it was Kasim who was against offering us a place beneath their roof as family. But she claims that he always intended to make me his heir in the end. She says now that he is gone and she's all alone, she doesn't want to wait but wishes us to share in everything—as true family should. Naturally, she didn't mention anything as crass as the gold my father retrieved from the cave."

I stared at him, struggling to find my voice. "Kasim was dead by mere hours, and she was already here maligning his name? Does the woman have no shame?"

Navid gave me a look. "What do you think? Her greed was always greater than her love for my uncle."

"But..." I looked across at Mariam and Ali. "Surely the gold from the cave must have turned to—"

"Yes," Mariam said quickly, before I could finish my sentence. "But my sister-in-law did not ask about it, and naturally we did not bring up such a topic while discussing the tragic death of Ali's brother."

She met my eyes, and I read the rest of her thinking in her face. Nyla was finally offering to do what Kasim should have done from the moment his fortunes changed. If Nyla was doing it under a false understanding, it wasn't Mariam or Ali's fault, and once she realized the truth, it would be too late for her to kick them out again. Kasim and Nyla had always hovered on the edge of public censure over their treatment of Kasim's brother—it was why they did as much as they did to help him. Casting her husband's family and heir from her household would not be accepted.

"There's no reason Nyla should ever know," Ali said comfortably. "She needs someone to manage the business, and Navid will do an exemplary job, I have no doubt. My brother was rich enough for us all, and our combined household will remain rich enough to cover any desire of my sister-in-law. Whatever her initial motivations, I am sure she will come to find the company and assistance welcome."

"But you…But she…" I tried to imagine Nyla maintaining the façade that she wasn't interested in the gold and failed. I didn't even want to imagine her reaction when she discovered it was gone.

"It was the middle of the night." Navid met my gaze steadily. "And my uncle was lying on the kitchen table. But her first thought—her first action—was to rush here under false pretenses, all to ensure she received a share of the gold. She's been rich since before I was born, but apparently she couldn't bear the thought of my parents becoming wealthy as well—not unless she could share in it."

I understood what he wasn't putting into words. After Nyla's behavior, he wasn't going to intervene to correct her unspoken assumption.

"I know I said I would bring you to work for us, Zaria." Mariam sounded concerned. "I still mean to honor that as best I can. I told Nyla I wanted you for my personal servant, like she has Layla, and she agreed. You'll still be living in the same household as her, but maybe that's a good thing. You'll be able to stay with your friends this way."

I blinked, staring at her. With everything else going on, I hadn't even thought about my own situation. It was kind of her to think of me, but I dreaded being anywhere near Nyla when this drama played out to its inevitable conclusion. But neither could I abandon Navid, or my friends—not when I was one of only two people in the new combined household that knew the full extent of the situation.

I met Mariam's anxious look and made myself smile. Her look of relief stripped away my remaining illusions, however. It hadn't been kindness that had motivated Mariam to include me in the negotiations with Nyla. Mariam was afraid I would tell Nyla about the destruction of the gold and destroy the whole scheme before the announcement of Kasim's death and their move. The possibility of maintaining my current position while working for her instead of Nyla was essentially a bribe.

I sighed and pushed my hair out of my face. I desperately needed a long, hot soak in a bath and uninterrupted time to think. I couldn't put off answering her, though.

I glanced across at Navid who gave me a pleading look. This was his chance at a better life, and I couldn't abandon him. It would be a relief to have him on hand, if nothing else. He shared the burden of knowing the full story, and I relished not carrying it all myself.

"Thank you," I said to Mariam. "I would love to work for you."

It was true, too. Despite her motivations now, there was no question Mariam would be a far more pleasant mistress than Nyla had ever been. And while Nyla would still be part of the household, I didn't doubt Mariam would do her best to shield me from her.

I also didn't doubt Mariam and Ali would have told Nyla the truth if she'd just asked them. If Nyla had negotiated openly, offering them a place in her household in exchange for the gold, they would have confessed. They were honest enough, I could trust in Mariam's offer to me. She wouldn't go back on her word once the danger to them was past.

Nyla had created her own situation, and she would have to live with it as best she could. I had more important things to worry about.

Life was changing so rapidly, it was becoming hard to follow. But in the middle of the whirlwind of change, I couldn't lose sight of the most important point—we were all in danger, and I had to do my part to keep us safe.

CHAPTER 15

My fear kept my acting sharp throughout the following days. I didn't hear a single whispered question or doubt from anyone. Everyone in both the household and the city appeared to believe the situation was unfolding exactly as we portrayed.

The day after my visit to the market, Nyla tearfully announced Kasim's death to the assembled servants. The next day, he was buried. Nyla and Layla had dressed him in ornate clothing to hide his wounds. He really did look as if he could have died of some unknown fever, and for a disorienting moment, even I believed our story.

But the day after the burial, Nyla went into the traditional mourning isolation, and Ali and Mariam moved in. With their constant presence, it was impossible to forget the reality of the situation, even for a moment.

I already had much to be grateful to Mariam for, however. Without children, or any surviving family of her own, Nyla was left to isolate alone, instead of surrounded by family as she should have been. Given she was expected to keep to her suite of rooms for two full weeks, custom dictated she could choose someone to stand in as family and isolate with her. But Nyla had no true friends—certainly no one she wished to be cloistered with for any length of time.

I fully believed her spite was great enough that she would have selected me, just to give her someone to torment. But as Mariam's new personal servant, I was no longer an option, and poor Layla bid us all a gloomy farewell for two weeks.

"I wouldn't mind the task if she were actually grieving," she told Yara and me. "But that woman only truly cares for herself. She's already irritated at being expected to complete the mourning period, and she's only going to get worse as the days drag on."

Yara promised to send all of Nyla's favorite dishes, as well as Layla's, and to include as many treats as she could when the meals were left at their door.

"I don't know how she endures it," Yara confided in me when Layla was gone. "I couldn't work so closely with that woman."

Her words took me by surprise. None of Nyla's servants were fond of her, but I had never heard the head cook speak with such open disrespect. I soon discovered the reason for her new sense of freedom, however.

Nyla's haste in seeking to claim the gold had caused her to make a significant strategic error. Had she realized her mistake now that she had all those long hours to think? Or was she in for a shock when she emerged from her seclusion?

If Nyla had introduced Mariam and Ali to her household at any other time, I could only imagine the battles that would have resulted. But she had gone to them immediately, and they had taken her invitation at its most literal—moving in as soon as she disappeared into her mourning seclusion.

And it was clear from the moment of her arrival that Mariam intended to make full use of the opportunity inadvertently presented by Nyla. While Nyla was absent, Mariam was busily taking the reins of the household and making a great many changes according to her taste.

Given the general dislike of Nyla, the servants were all enthusiastically aiding Mariam. I strongly suspected Nyla would emerge to discover Mariam had taken her place as the true mistress of the household.

I had no doubt she would take the change extremely badly, but she had handed over the reins of the business and household finances to Navid, so she would find it very difficult to reverse matters.

I thought of Rek and Adara every day, but since we'd been the ones to ask them to keep their distance, I couldn't be irritated with them for staying away. My heart leaped, however, when I saw invitations with the royal mark arrive. Adara hadn't forgotten her promise.

The invitation was for four named guests: Nyla, Ali, Mariam, and Navid. But given he was unmarried, Navid was permitted to bring another guest with him, and neither Ali nor Mariam questioned his assertion that he would take me. Both of them knew of Rek's visit to their house, so they likely suspected I was behind the invitation in the first place.

As Kasim's brother, Ali wasn't expected to cloister himself for two weeks, but he and Mariam couldn't attend an event like a ball. Nyla was prohibited from going as well, of course, given she was confined to her own suite. As far as I was aware, she didn't even know about the invitation, and by the time she heard of it, she would have plenty of other options for things to be enraged by.

I received a number of laughing comments and sly looks from the other servants when it became known Navid had invited me to the ball. But they all seemed convinced they knew the reasoning behind it, saving me the need to come up with an explanation.

"You've been friends for a long time," Yara told me, with a

twinkle in her eye. "I'm glad to see you're making the most of the situation. Maybe we'll eventually have a mistress here we can truly love."

I protested, of course, but everyone seemed to expect that, and I didn't protest too hard. They would discover there was nothing of that sort between me and Navid eventually, and in the meantime, it provided us with a reasonable excuse for our odd behavior.

Kali, however, pounced on me the next time I made it to her father's mill. I had managed to tag along with the kitchen hand collecting the household's weekly flour, but Kali immediately dragged me away from the business being conducted.

"Zaria!" Her eyes were wide and her cheeks flushed. "You're going to a ball at the palace!"

I grinned. "Do people really not have anything better to gossip about?"

"Don't dodge the question! You said you were considering emerging from your dark hole and celebrating the next festivity with the rest of us, but this is a different level. Actually going to the palace!" She lowered her voice. "Does that mean you've made up with your *old friends*?" She put heavy emphasis on the last two words as if it was a great secret and someone might be listening in.

"Actually, yes," I said, hating the flush I could feel creeping up my cheeks.

She squealed loudly, jumping into the air before wrapping me in a hug. When she pulled back, she adopted an exaggerated expression of sadness, however.

"Once you're best friends with a princess again, you won't forget your other best friend, will you?" She gave me the most pathetic face imaginable, and I laughed.

"As if I could! I'm only going to this ball as Navid's guest, but if I ever get an invitation of my own, I'll be sure to take you along."

Her eyes gleamed, and she sighed with delight. "Me, at a royal ball! Can you imagine?"

"Easily," I assured her. "You would take the court by storm."

That made her laugh, the dreamy look disappearing. "Now that is hardly likely. I don't think I'm the sort to appeal to all those stuffy, important people."

I laughed again. "Maybe not. But the younger ones would like you. I promise."

She grinned. "That's enough for me. Just promise you won't let all the sadness of the last week stop you from seizing every bit of enjoyment you possibly can."

I solemnly swore I would do my best, and her words came back to me as I prepared for the ball. It wasn't Kasim's death that made it hard to see the event as entertainment, though. Navid and I had been invited there for something closer to a secret war meeting than dancing. And it was hard to forget it with the constant threat hanging over us from the gang of thieves.

Our charade appeared to have been successful, so there was no obvious way they could trace Kasim's identity. But there were too many unknowns. Who had seen Kasim leaving the city in the middle of the night with ten donkeys in tow? Even if it was just the gate guards, it must have been someone. Would the thieves have a way to interrogate them? It seemed impossible, but that assurance didn't stop me jumping at shadows constantly.

Of course I had nothing in my wardrobe that would do for a royal ball, and I caught myself thinking wistfully of the stunningly beautiful ballgown I had briefly owned. It wasn't a memory from my childhood at the palace—I had left there before I turned sixteen, so I hadn't been old enough then for either balls or ballgowns. Rather it was the gift from the girl who was now Princess Cassandra of Ardasira that filled my thoughts, foolish as it was to waste time thinking of such an ephemeral garment. But it had been the most exquisite gown I had seen before or since.

I considered using some of the coins I had received in

replacement of the dress to purchase myself a new gown. While few people knew about my possession of the coins, the local dressmakers would likely assume I had been given the money by Mariam or Navid.

But before I could act on my thoughts, Mariam approached me. She claimed that as a representative of the household, I was obligated to accept her gift of a gown. And then she produced an outfit that took my breath away.

It was as golden as the treasure of the cave and seemed to contain actual gold thread. The two pieces included a long, full skirt and a fitted bodice with elegant, puffed sleeves that pulled together at the wrists with yet more golden threads.

For a moment I imagined arriving at the palace in it, and then good sense reasserted itself.

"I can't accept this," I said, trying to hand it back to her.

She refused to take it, however.

"Yes, you can. And you must. For my sake. I can't go, and so you must represent us all. Besides, I spent hours combing the city's dressmakers to find it for you."

I hesitated, but I couldn't fight both her protestations and my own desires. I would wear the dress.

And when I did, I wouldn't worry about whether her explanations were the truth or not. Whether she still felt the need to keep me on side with subtle bribes, or whether she meant it as a gesture of support for Navid's apparent interest in me, it didn't matter. The result was the same. I no longer had to worry about what I would wear to the ball.

On the journey to the palace at Navid's side, I felt only gratitude to Mariam. I was about to enter a building that had once been my home—a building I hadn't entered for a long time. It helped to have the confidence provided by such an outfit.

"Are you all right?" Navid asked softly as we joined the long procession making its way through the palace gates.

I drew a deep breath and considered his question. Was I all right?

Memories of my father flew at me from every direction, and I kept thinking of the first time I had entered here—an overawed child, clutching her father's arm. On that occasion, he had been there to support and protect me, but I was on my own now.

No. I sternly took myself to task. That wasn't right, and this was no time to give in to maudlin self-indulgence. Then I'd had my father. Now I had not only Navid beside me but Rek and Adara waiting for me. I wasn't alone at all.

Leaving had been painful, and my father's death even more so, but I had already spent years weighed down with the anchor of my past. I couldn't afford to live that way anymore.

I straightened.

"I'm more than all right," I told Navid. "I'm delighted to be back where I spent so many happy years." If I said it enough, perhaps it would become the whole truth.

He gave me an approving nod and a pat on the arm which made me want to laugh. He treated me so much like an older brother that it was hard to believe the entire household thought he was falling for me.

Inside the gates, the first thing to hit me was the scent of perfume in the air. I almost lost my step, swept up into a powerful wave of memory as I remembered countless hours spent in the fragrant garden with its enormous bright flowers and plants in every shade of green.

But I caught myself and looked across the large courtyard to the sprawling palace building with its cream stone and gilt windows. Only after a long look at the building itself, did I turn for a glimpse of the garden which bordered the courtyard on both sides. The angle allowed only a hint of the vast expanse of garden within the palace walls, but nostalgia made me look anyway.

I could see little in the darkness, however, since the moon was the thinnest of slivers and the blaze of lanterns was clustered in the courtyard. I turned away with a sigh, but my sadness passed with the next breath as we crossed the smooth stone of the courtyard to approach the double doors of the building.

Ascending the shallow steps into the palace, time seemed to roll back once more. But then the gleaming flash of my gown caught my eye, and reality rushed back in. I had watched guests arrive for many balls, giggling from above as Adara and I peered over the balustrade of the staircase that led to the royal apartments, but I had never made this trek myself.

Navid handed over our invitation, and we were ushered inside the long ballroom. The carved screens on the row of tall windows were thrown wide to let in the cool night air, and small palm trees in pots had been brought inside, blurring the distinction between garden and room. Servants wended their way through the guests to offer trays of refreshments.

It had been a long time since I spied on a ball from the shadows, and the number of people took me by surprise. I should have expected it, of course, but I had been so focused on seeing Adara—and Rek—again, that I had imagined only a shadowy handful of other people.

In reality, the press of people meant I could see no sign of the prince or princess, and it occurred to me that royal duties might keep them busy for most of the event.

"Do you see them?" Navid asked, revealing his thoughts closely mirrored my own.

"You're the one who can see over heads. I can't see a thing."

He looked down at me with a grin. "It must be hard to be so short."

I turned my nose up at him, spinning away with a satisfying flick of my skirts. The sight of my back only made him chuckle, but my new angle gave me view of a server, and I hurried over to accept a familiar delicacy from his tray.

I bit into the savory ball with a sigh. They had been my favorite as a child, and I hadn't had one in far too long.

"That looks good," Navid said, making me jump.

I pointed in the direction of the disappearing server. "He went that way."

Navid started after him with single-minded focus, leaving me standing alone. My foot started to tap, and I watched those on the dance floor with hidden longing. I hadn't come here for the purpose of dancing, but it was impossible not to be swept up by the music. I missed the hours Adara and I had spent with the dancing master and the feeling of freedom as I flew through the steps, my body responding without needing my mind to direct it, the movements effortless and exhilarating. It had been too long since I'd danced, and I missed it.

I was still distracted by the dance when a woman at least two decades older than me approached. Her extravagant gown was hung with thin disks of gold that jingled as she walked, reminding me of a dancer.

Distracted by the setting and her dress, I didn't recognize her until she was standing in front of me. I had last seen her at the market, on the morning after Kasim's death.

"Zaria, I believe, is it not?" she asked with a smile.

I nodded, wary.

"You'll know me, of course." Her smile grew.

"Of course," I agreed, adopting the respectful tone she clearly desired. "Everyone in the city knows Yasmine, head of Karema's greatest merchant empire."

Her expression took on a self-satisfied air. "Very true. And you'll have heard of my parties as well, I'm sure. You must come to my next one. I'll send you an invitation."

"How kind." I inclined my head respectfully.

Inside, I was feeling more intrigued than flattered, however. It was true Yasmine's parties were famous, but they had a questionable reputation, and I had never desired to attend one. I did, however, wonder about her sudden interest in me.

Something over my shoulder caught her attention, and she floated away, clearly considering a farewell beneath her. I watched her go, my thoughts busy.

"What did she want?" Navid appeared at my side again, his face alight with curiosity and food gripped in both hands.

"To invite me to her next party, if you can believe it."

He laughed. "Of course I can."

"Really?" I frowned at him. "I'm just a servant, remember?"

He raised an eyebrow as he scanned my dress. I flushed and waved a dismissive hand.

"This is just one night."

"Perhaps." He paused and when I said nothing, laughed again. "You really can't see it?"

I shook my head.

"You're always so astute, Zaria—except when it comes to yourself. I suppose it's a charming quality, really."

I rolled my eyes. "Get to the point."

"It's precisely because you're—officially—a servant that Yasmine is so interested in you. I know my aunt spews a lot of poison, but she's right about Yasmine. She did start out as a dancer from a poor family. But she was highly skilled—especially at the more difficult knife dances, from what I've heard—and she attracted the attention of an older merchant. When she first married, it was an enormous step up for her, but she still wasn't rich like she is now. It was her cunning and skill that built their merchant empire, and it's only expanded since she was widowed and is now unencumbered by a husband."

I wrinkled my nose. "That's an awful way to talk about losing your husband."

"I've been to one of her parties, and I can guarantee that's the way she thinks of it. She started with nothing, but now she's rich, influential—a sultana, in a way, of her own social set. But it took her decades to achieve that. And here you are, barely eighteen, and overnight you've gone from being an ordinary servant to this." He waved at my outfit and then at the room in general. "She's vastly intrigued, and she wants to know if you're going to be an ally or a competitor."

"A competitor?" Now I was the one laughing. "I have no desire to compete with Yasmine." I caught a final glimpse of her before she was swallowed by the crowd. "If she was once a dancer, it makes that dress even more audacious. It's certainly eye-catching."

"She likes to remind everyone of her origins," he said. "She wants them to remember it was her skills and acumen that got her this far. And she certainly likes to be the center of attention." He looked at my dress again and chuckled. "Which is another reason she's interested in you. She didn't expect to find anyone here tonight more eye-catching than her. Imagine if she knew you could rival her on the dance floor as well?"

I groaned. "Don't exaggerate. I was never a professional dancer. And unlike Yasmine, I'm not interested in catching eyes."

"Except for one pair, perhaps?" He cocked an eyebrow and gave me a knowing look.

"I don't know what you're talking about," I said in my most dignified tone.

"Then I suppose you won't be interested that a certain someone is just over there?" He gestured behind me and to one side, and I whirled.

"Where?"

He laughed, and for a moment, I thought he had merely been teasing me. But then my eyes caught on a tall, familiar figure, and I forgot about Navid entirely.

Rek.

CHAPTER 16

Seeing him out in the city and on horseback, I had thought this new Rek seemed more grown up. But here, in his home environment—the environment I had known him in for so many years—the change was even more obvious. The boy I had once known was entirely gone, replaced with a confident crown prince who couldn't have been more at ease. One who made my heart beat faster every time I saw him.

He looked up, and our eyes met across the room. My heart stopped beating entirely. For a foolish moment, I thought I read stunned admiration despite the distance. But he didn't even nod acknowledgment. Instead his face darkened, and he turned back to the older man in front of him as if I were a stranger who had dared to catch the prince's gaze.

Vaguely the thought crossed my mind that his companion looked familiar, but it was hard to focus on anything but Rek's unexpected rejection.

"That's Jerome, one of the guard captains," Navid said, kindly trying to cover the awkward moment.

His words jolted my memory. He was the one who had led the guards the day I first saw Rek again. I had only had a glimpse of him then, but I never forgot a face. The captain was dressed as a guest, not a guard, but there was no mistaking his posture. He stood straight, his feet planted firmly, his alert stance giving the appearance he was ready for action at any moment. Whatever they were discussing seemed serious, both of them intent on their words.

Seeing the captain again, I could understand why Rek hadn't included him in the secret of the cave. He had needed not only men who were loyal to the kingdom, but ones whose loyalty to him personally came above everything else.

One look at Captain Jerome, and I could easily imagine how he would have responded to Rek's risky plan—a conversation with the sultan and physical restraint if necessary. Had Rek told him the truth now, or was he still trying to outmaneuver his father?

I took a glass blindly from a passing tray, reminding myself that Rek had important duties here. It was natural he would be distracted. And he hadn't wanted us here anyway.

I needed to keep reminding myself that his arms around me in the darkness, as we rode back to the city, hadn't been an embrace but a practical necessity. He had clearly shown he was glad to regain contact with an old friend, but from the beginning his manner had lacked the open enthusiasm of Adara's. She had been ready to cast Azzam out for his wrongs toward me, while Rek had been measured and practical. I would be a fool to transpose Adara's emotions onto Rek.

"Do you want to join the dancing?" Navid asked. "I know you've missed it."

I hesitated, tempted despite everything. "Actually, I don't feel in the mood for dancing. If you don't mind."

"Oh." He sounded genuinely disappointed, so I tore my attention away from Rek, who I had been watching from the corner of my eye, and looked at Navid properly.

He wasn't looking at me at all. Instead his eyes were on the dance, and after a moment I saw why. Adara was in the middle of it, skipping lightly from partner to partner, as the dance required.

I opened my mouth to utter words of caution, only to be seized by a moment of rebelliousness.

"You can join without me," I said. "I don't mind being left."

"Really?" He looked at me swiftly, his brow creased, and his eyes flicking to Rek. "I don't—"

"Zaria!" Adara's shriek was mostly obscured by the music, so only those closest to us turned to look. She ignored them, breaking free of the dance and hurrying toward us.

"But you're gorgeous!" she cried, indicating for me to spin, which I dutifully did.

"Don't sound so surprised," I said on a laugh.

"I'm not! Of course not!" She gave me a sparkling look. "You know I'm not." She threaded her arm through mine. "Do you remember how many times we dreamed of attending one of these together? I hated turning sixteen so much before you, and you not being able to come." Her words flowed on without pause. "But have you seen the twins yet? I told them you were coming, and they didn't believe me. They've been saying all along you must have been killed by bandits on the road south." Her voice turned disapproving. "I'm sure I never did anything to deserve *two* such brothers. Oh!" She spun us left, waving at someone I couldn't see. "There they are!"

"I'd almost forgotten how exhausting it is just to listen to you," I said with a laugh.

She threw me a smile. "Yes, I missed you, too."

I laughed again. I had almost forgotten that as well: how much I laughed when I was with Adara.

"Xavier, Xander," she said triumphantly, "here she is! Now you can take back everything you said on the topic."

Two young men, dressed identically, turned toward us. My stomach clenched, remembering the foolish, youthful dreams I had woven around them in those final years before I left the palace. They were grown now, too, and everyone said they were distractingly handsome...

Everyone was right. They were. Yet my heart beat on at its usual pace, the only emotions rushing through me the pleasure of being reunited with old friends and the happy warmth of remembered childhood misdeeds.

"Xavier!" I held out a hand to the one on the right and he promptly raised it to his mouth and kissed it.

"Even more ravishingly beautiful than I remember. That dress!"

Still I was unaffected, merely laughing at his usual excessive manner.

"Xander." I turned and offered my hand to the second young man.

"It really must be you," Xavier's marginally more considered twin said with a look of surprise. "You can still tell us apart."

"Of course. You're both taller, but you haven't changed that much."

Adara sighed happily. "Just like old times." She turned abruptly and gave a dazzling smile to Navid, who had been trailing behind us. "But with new friends, of course."

Both twins raised their eyebrows in perfect unison.

"This must be Navid, I presume," Xavier said, in far too smooth a voice.

"Quick, Adara," I said. "Take Navid dancing before the twins can get their claws into him."

"Excellent advice." She dropped my arm and grabbed his, pulling him into the dance without waiting for his response.

Xavier sighed heavily. "The Zaria I remember used to be fun."

"No, no," his twin said. "You're misremembering. Zaria was always allied with Rek *spoiling* our fun."

"Rescuing you from your 'fun', I think you mean," I said dryly, and they both laughed. "So have you both been enjoying being eighteen? All that freedom you always longed for!"

"Actually." Xavier frowned. "It's all turned out to be a big scam. We've been meaning to talk to someone about it, but no one seems willing to take responsibility."

"A scam?" I looked between them. "Don't tell me the sultan is still keeping you chained to the palace? I can't say I'd blame him, but..."

"Personally, I blame Rek," Xander said gloomily. "He was always so eager to take on all those tiresome responsibilities, so it gave a false impression."

"Well, maybe not *always*." Xavier gave me a significant look I couldn't read before nudging Xander, who laughed.

"Yes, maybe not always. But for enough of the time. You should have seen him after you left, Zaria." He shook his head sadly.

"I have no idea what either of you are talking about."

"No one does understand us." Xavier gave a sigh of long suffering.

I gave him an exasperated look. "I'm not some city maiden ready to fall for your act of supposed suffering. I'm still waiting to hear about this apparent scam."

"All those years," Xander began.

"All our long, weary youth," Xavier continued.

"We believed in the mirage of freedom once we turned eighteen. But it turns out that now we're of age, there are all these *responsibilities* and *expectations*. It's not free, at all!"

I laughed. "Only the two of you would be surprised by that."

"But we're the third and fourth children," Xavier told me earnestly. "We're so low down the list we hardly count as royal. Rek and Adara are supposed to take care of all that."

"Well, mostly Rek," Xander said. "Adara can't be counted on for much."

"Excuse me!" I cried, offended on my friend's behalf.

"From the adults' perspective, I meant," Xander explained

earnestly, as if his words would remove any offense. "Naturally she's the best of good companions in mischief."

I wanted to protest again, but I was on shakier ground, so I held silent.

"Did you see that Yasmine's here?" Xavier asked his brother, his attention wandering to something on the other side of the room.

"Yasmine?" I looked between them in surprise. "Isn't she several decades too old for you?"

Both of them laughed.

"Don't worry, Zaria. We aren't about to fall prey to the legendary older woman," Xander said.

"We've just heard she throws the most fabulous parties." Xavier briefly looked away from whatever—or whoever—held his interest to throw me a wink. "There might be a little bit of freedom we can take advantage of."

"Excuse us, old friend," Xander said, giving his brother a shove in the direction of his gaze. "But we must continue circulating."

Both of them hurried away, moving through the crowd with purpose. I was left standing alone, shaking my head and fighting a laugh.

"Could anything be more typical of the twins?" I asked the empty air.

"And what do you know of Their Royal Highnesses?" asked a female voice from behind me.

I turned slowly, wishing I'd kept my thoughts inside my head. I didn't recognize the voice, but as soon as I saw the girl's face, I remembered her. Iola was the daughter of a senior vizier so should have been a preferable playmate for the royal children than me. But she was also two years younger than the twins and me, and more than three years younger than Adara, so we'd only spent time with her at larger gatherings of the palace children.

She must have turned sixteen only recently, so this would be her first ball, or close to it. But she carried herself with the confidence of someone far more experienced. She obviously didn't have my gift with faces, though, because her expression made it clear she didn't remember me.

"Hello, Iola." I gave her a friendly smile, and her look of confusion deepened.

I was about to remind her of my identity when I felt someone approaching from behind me. Iola's posture changed, her eyes brightening as she watched the newcomer.

"Your Highness," she said with a welcoming smile.

A shiver up the back of my neck told me which of the royals it was even before he spoke.

"Rek is fine." Despite the friendly words, he sounded distracted.

"Thank you." She flashed her eyes to me, as if to make sure I'd caught the interchange. She was betraying her inexperience after all, if she thought it important to impress a total unknown like me.

I turned slowly, trying to tame my raging emotions. By the time I'd made it all the way around, I'd settled on a light, friendly smile.

"Good evening." I kept my words as neutral as possible.

"Is it?" He still sounded distracted. Glancing around at the crowd, which was growing more and more tight, he frowned. "We should go into the gardens."

"Rek?" I took an involuntary step forward. "Is something wrong? What's happened?"

He blinked, as if surprised by my words, and I saw the merest flick of his eyes toward Iola.

"No—at least nothing more than yesterday." He gave a laugh which sounded forced to my ear but seemed to satisfy our audience since Iola's concerned look dissipated, and she went back to looking at me with some mixture of jealousy and shocked disapproval.

Rek held out his arm, and when I hesitated gave me a stern look. "Zaria."

I meekly placed my hand on his offered arm as Iola gasped.

"Zaria? I thought you moved to Ardasira!"

I shrugged, but Rek spoke before I could, his voice hard.

"An incorrect rumor as it turned out. She never left Karema."

"But…" Iola's forehead furrowed, and I could almost see the thoughts running through her mind. If I'd been in the capital all this time, where had I been? No one had encountered me at any of the palace's social events in over three years.

Not wanting to get into that particular explanation, I squeezed Rek's arm slightly, and he moved toward the closest window.

"It was nice to see you again," I called over my shoulder to a stunned Iola.

"I think we might have scandalized her." I struggled to keep my voice light and even as we stepped out beneath the scanty moonlight. "Are we supposed to be out here?"

Rek pulled his arm away and gave a shaky laugh as he looked at me in my golden gown. "Supposed to be? That probably depends who you ask."

I frowned, thrown off by his cryptic answer. But looking around, I noticed several other people spread throughout the closer parts of the garden. They stood talking in small clumps or walked down the carefully manicured paths. Lanterns had been interspersed at regular intervals along the sections of walking track that gave easy view of the ballroom.

I relaxed. Clearly the gardens were an acceptable extension of the ballroom still—as they used to be in the days when Adara and I would sneak out to peek in the windows at the dancers. The need to dodge guests seeking fresh air had always made the adventure more thrilling.

I waited for him to speak again, but he didn't. He didn't look at me at all, instead gazing into the darkness of the deeper gardens with the same shaken expression.

"Has something happened?" I asked in a quiet voice. "Your conversation with your captain seemed intense."

"Jerome?" He turned to me with a frown. "Not at all. He just dislikes being forced to attend such events. He's more at home on horseback than in a ballroom."

I bit the inside of my cheek. I almost wanted there to be some fresh disaster to explain Rek's strange behavior.

"Does he know about…" I asked, not finishing the sentence. I didn't want to mention the cave even in a whisper.

"No," Rek said quickly. "If it was possible to empty it, I would have informed my father, of course. But as it stands, it is of most relevance to our investigation, and Father put me in charge of pursuing the gang."

"Of course." My doubt tainted the words, but he didn't seem to notice.

I didn't think the sultan would see it the way Rek did. But I wasn't going to argue in favor of reporting it since that would almost certainly end up involving me.

Instead I copied Rek, gazing out across the garden. A memory vision danced through my mind—two girls creeping around the nearest bush.

"So many memories here," I said softly, mostly to myself.

Rek turned to me, his brows drawn. "You seem to have taken up residence inside my mind."

Confused by his intensity, I barely managed a smile. "Given our shared history, it's no surprise we'd be thinking the same thing."

He opened his mouth as if to speak, only to shake his head and grab my upper arm instead. I looked from his hand to his face, trying to read the confusing emotion in his eyes.

Once again, he remained silent while I waited. When the silence grew too charged, he burst into motion, tugging me down the closest path and behind a stand of trees. Soft lantern light still filtered through, but we were mostly out of sight of the ballroom.

"Rek," I said uneasily, remembering his earlier words. If anyone saw us back here, they might get the wrong idea. "What's going on with you? Are you sure there hasn't been any sign of the thieves?"

"The thieves?" He frowned at me. "I'd forgotten all about them."

"Rek!" Now I was sure something was wrong. "We were just talking about them a minute ago."

"Were we?" He groaned, dropping my arm and taking a step back before abruptly stepping forward again. "I can't remember the last time I was so distracted at a royal function."

"That's understandable." I tried to put my own confusion aside to be supportive. "It's not every day you find a lost treasure cave full of wonders beyond counting that also happens to be overrun with deadly thieves."

"The cave?" He laughed, the sound half pained, half amused. "My distraction began before I knew anything about the cave." He took my arm again, reaching for the other one as well and looking down into my confused face. "As you said, there are so many memories."

"Rek, what is going on?" I gave the words a sharp edge, out of patience with his strange pronouncements and abstraction. "When I saw you in the ballroom, you reacted more coldly than if I were a stranger. And now you've dragged me out here."

"I'm sorry." His voice was soft. "You're right, I'm behaving erratically. And I'm not used to behaving erratically. It's... confusing."

My laugh was shaky. "Yes, it certainly is."

Part of me wanted to pull away and march straight back into the ballroom, leaving him to work out whatever perturbation he seemed to be under alone. But I made no attempt to leave.

Even with his cold behavior, I couldn't help the way everything in me leaned toward Rek. Far too much of me was reveling in being out here with him, practically alone beneath the moonlight. I didn't want him to let go, I wanted him to put his arms all the way around me and pull me close.

I took a slow breath, trying to get myself under control, but the ball and the dress and the look on Iola's face had combined to bring out my inner rebellious streak. I'd stopped listening to my sensible self.

I stayed in place.

Rek shook his head, a sharp movement. "I'm sorry," he repeated. "You don't deserve any of this. But that's the problem. I spent three years thinking you did."

"That's not your fault," I said, trying to follow the thread of his thinking. "You were lied to."

He let go of me again and took several strides away down the path that led into the dark garden. I watched him go in bewilderment, but he abruptly swung back around and strode back.

"I know that now. And I know you were lied to as well. It's not your fault either." His intense, turbulent gaze locked on mine. "Even before I learned the truth, I thought I'd overcome my anger. I thought I'd left it all in the past. But seeing you again in the forest—it all came rushing back as if you only left yesterday. It turned out I hadn't defeated my feelings at all." He cut off abruptly, his gaze dropping from mine.

"That's understandable," I whispered, trying to catch my breath now he was no longer piercing me with his eyes.

"Perhaps." His gaze jumped back to me, a wry smile I didn't understand spreading over his face. "Yes, it's very understandable. But I spent so long feeding that anger. And now that you're back—" He sighed. "For you, all your memories of this place are from *before*. I have those memories, too, but I also have years of memories from after. Years when I told myself I hated you."

He shook his head. "Sometimes when I see you, those are the emotions that come flooding back, and other times—" He broke off awkwardly before finishing. "Most of the time, I remember the truth, and all of that is washed away. But it's hard to turn off such intense feelings."

My brow creased. "I think I understand."

His warm smile enfolded me. "Of course you do. That's one of the things I always liked best about you. I never had to endlessly explain things to you. But this…" His mouth quirked sideways. "I'm not sure even you understand…"

His words trailed away, and the space between us shrank. Where had all the air gone? Every nerve in my body seemed heightened, the warmth of his breath brushing across my cheek making my own catch.

"So many confused emotions." His words were almost inaudible, more felt on my skin than heard with my ears. "But when it comes to you, Zaria, all of them so intense."

Despite myself, despite the sensible part of my brain screaming at me to pull back, my eyes drifted shut. Was it only the false magic of moonlight that made me feel the upcoming brush of his lips against mine?

"Your Highness!" The low call made him jerk away, cold night air rushing in to extinguish the heat in my cheeks.

My eyes flew open, but I couldn't see anyone near our stolen hideaway. Rek leaned to the side, peering toward the ballroom.

"Jerome." He sounded disgruntled. "Did Father send him to search for me?"

I gasped softly, remembering his earlier words. Had someone reported to the sultan that his oldest son had disappeared into the gardens with me? Rek had warned me the moment we stepped outside, but I hadn't been listening. Angrily I stuffed the rebellious part of me back down where it belonged.

But Rek gave me an apologetic smile, not seeming to share my concern. "Father probably wants me to meet some dull dignitary. He'll have to let me free at some point. I assume you still love dancing as much as you always did?"

His eyes invited me to laugh with him, diving into the happier memories. Whatever confusion he'd been feeling earlier, he seemed firmly in control now, remembering me as a friend of his youth. Had I dreamed anything else?

I gave a non-committal answer as he pulled me back onto the main path and into the disapproving gaze of Captain Jerome. I didn't meet his eyes, and his focus quickly shifted to Rek. He spoke rapidly, giving a string of names I didn't recognize, and within moments he had swept Rek away. The prince had time for only a single look over his shoulder in my direction, his eyes sending another apology.

I stayed in place, not moving back toward the ballroom myself. In there I would see Rek again and maybe Iola. Adara and Navid might come looking for me, expecting me to be ready to laugh and dance and joke. Perhaps the twins might come back, ready for further reminiscences.

I couldn't face any of it. For me the night was over.

A server walked the path nearest the windows, a tray of drinks in hand, and I hurried over to her. It only took a moment to leave a message for Navid, asking the servant to inform him I was leaving early. As soon as I had her agreement, I headed for the side of the palace and the front courtyard, fleeing into the night.

CHAPTER 17

The guards at the gate were reluctant to allow a young ball guest out onto the streets alone. But after some persuasion, I managed to escape with just the addition of a small lantern. As I hurried through the streets toward home, I was glad for its light.

The limited moonlight was almost entirely obscured by clouds, making the streets seem dark and menacing. I tried to shake off the feeling, reminding myself the city was my home, and I was more than familiar with this section of it. Still, I moved more cautiously than usual, jumping at any sound.

When I turned onto my street, relief swept through me, the strange dread draining away. The gates ahead of me stood for more than immediate safety. They represented my familiar, stable life, far removed from the palace and the dangerous emotions that swirled around me whenever I was in Rek's presence.

I had to put the lantern down to unlatch the heavy gate, my fingers fumbling in their haste. When I reached down to scoop it back up, however, my eyes caught on something.

My emotions told me to ignore it and hurry inside to the

haven of my bed, but my mind wouldn't let me. Already my thoughts were whirring, my eye catching on the details.

Someone had drawn a mark just to the side of the gate in chalk. It was a strange mark—almost like a roughly etched seal or signature. I wanted to dismiss it as the work of local children, but my sense of dread was back in full force. I didn't understand what the mark meant, but in my years here, there had never been any chalk on our gate before.

Now wasn't the time to ignore oddities or strange coincidences.

Determination filled me, driving out both the primordial dread of the night and the confusing emotions left from my encounter with Rek. My mind—usually so sharp and clear—was restored to me, and I no longer felt the least longing for bed.

I didn't immediately move, however, my eyes locked on the chalk mark as I tried to work out its origin and purpose. If I rejected the possibility of childish mischief, the most logical remaining explanation was that someone wished to distinguish our house from all others.

That idea was highly concerning, of course. I could think of one group who had a keen interest in identifying our household, but how would they have known which house to mark? And why mark it at all? If they'd found us, why not act immediately?

I stood back, holding up my lantern and peering down the street. Its light didn't stretch far, but I could call up the whole street from memory easily enough. Our house itself was distinctive, easy to remember when once you'd seen it, but from the outside, the external wall of the property looked almost identical to all the others on the street. Even the gate was made from the same wood as the next four or five, only the fine details of the latch distinguishing it. Perhaps it would be confusing to someone who didn't know the area well?

The answer came immediately on the back of that thought. Someone wanted to mark our house out from the surrounding properties because they all looked too similar. I could wash away the chalk, and even probably succeed in making sure the wall didn't look too clean afterward. But that would do nothing to tell me who had left the mark. I needed the person who had marked us to find this street, but not our house. That meant I needed to make sure the houses were similar in all respects.

Pulling open the gate, I slipped inside, not bothering to latch it behind me. I would only be gone for a moment. My feet flew across the courtyard, my mind moving even faster, the tang of potential danger mixing with the joy of finding a distraction.

Thankfully I knew where to find chalk since I had seen it recently in the cabinet housing the silverware. Everyone swore it was the best way to keep rust away, and I had noticed the packet of it when I returned the polished items after my unnecessary labor.

Inside the house, I moved more slowly, not wanting to wake anyone. It took me only moments to reach the right cabinet, pulling open both doors and dropping to my knees to find the wrapped package in the bottom.

Unwinding the cheesecloth that kept the chalk from marking the silver, I selected one of the sticks. Within seconds, the rest of the package was rewrapped and put back in its place.

Back out in the street, I eased the gate closed again and stood back examining the mark. For my plan to work, I had to be able to reproduce it exactly. A search along the street produced a slim stick that I used to trace the shape of the mark in the dust. It took me at least twenty tries, but I kept at it until I was sure it looked as close as possible to the original.

Smearing the dust with my foot, I gripped the chalk hard as I walked down to the next closest gate. But the more I thought about keeping my hand still, the more it shook. I closed my eyes and took a deep breath, letting my tension drain out. This wasn't a time for nerves.

Calmed, I used the chalk just like I had the stick, reproducing the mark with strong swirls and confident lines in the wood beside this gate. When I reached the next one, I was ready. By the end of the street, however, my hand had started to ache from clutching the chalk so hard, and the stick was almost too short to be of use.

Retracing my steps, I considered the next part of my plan. There was no point in reproducing the mark if I didn't have a way to watch for who came looking for it. This might be my only opportunity to discover their identity, and I couldn't squander it.

The most obvious course of action was to hide somewhere nearby. But a hiding place was less obvious. The smooth walls of the houses on our street gave little opportunity for concealment.

I turned onto the small alley that ran between our house and the next. Its purpose was to allow direct side access to the stables of both properties, but over the years it had been used as a dumping ground for various items. The issue was an ongoing source of contention between Nyla and our neighbor, and they had recently ramped up the offensive by leaving an entire broken wagon, half blocking the alley.

I experimented with positioning myself behind it. Despite my fear that it was too far back in the alley to be of use, I was eventually able to place myself so that I had a partial view of the street. The dark cloak over my gold dress helped conceal me, but a flash of the material from beneath made me wonder if I should go inside again to change.

But that would take time, and I had no way of knowing when the creator of the mark might appear. If I left my post now, I might miss them. I twisted the material in my fingers. How much had it cost? Would it be easily damaged?

With a shake of my head, I smoothed it out. Protecting our household from the thieves was more important than a gown, regardless of its worth.

Settling in to wait, I wished finding a place had proved harder, after all. How many hours was I going to be stuck here?

Slowly, the sharpness of the moment faded, and my eyes started to droop. Each time they did, I reminded myself about the burly thief and the careless way he had ended Kasim's life. Just picturing his face was enough to jolt me awake each time.

The hour had already been late, so it wasn't surprising when the sky began to lighten, moving slowly toward dawn. Slowly and carefully, I stretched out each of my limbs, not wanting to end up so stiff I couldn't move when the time came.

If daylight arrived fully without any sign of someone looking for the mark, what would I do? What if they weren't coming for days? But rain would wash away chalk, so surely they had expected to be back soon?

The first stirrings of the horses in their stalls reached my ears just as I heard hurried footsteps. I tensed, but it was just the local baker's assistant, running past. If it was already getting light, he must be late. Bakers started early.

I resettled, but almost immediately I heard a larger group approaching. They stopped in front of the neighbor's gate, just out of my sight, and I strained to hear their words.

"Look, this one has the mark as well." The speaker sounded angry.

Every muscle jumped to alert, my body tensed for movement. I didn't recognize the voice, but the cadence sounded familiar. If I could only see them, I was sure I would see a subset of the thieves.

They couldn't have all come. Even if they all entered the city by coming in ones and twos, carefully spreading out their arrival over the course of a day, they would need to keep to small groups in public. Forty men couldn't walk the streets together without drawing far too much attention.

From the sound of the footsteps, I guessed there were some-where between five and ten in this group.

As difficult as it was, I held myself still. I couldn't afford to creep out of my hiding place for a peek when I didn't know their next movements. A moment later, my patience was rewarded.

One of the men strode impatiently past the mouth of the alley, stopping in front of our gate. With an exclamation of disgust, he turned and hurried back, calling softly as he got near the rest of the group.

"That one too. Does every house on the street have a mark?"

"It would appear so," said a voice I did recognize. Esai, the gang's shrewd captain.

"Do we pick one at random?" the first speaker asked, sounding uncertain.

I held my breath, wishing they'd had this conversation in front of some other house. What terrible luck it would be if—after all my efforts—they picked the right house, purely by chance.

"Of course not," Esai's voice dripped contempt. "Davis will be back in the city today. We make no plan of action without consulting him."

Davis. That name was familiar. Davis was the thief who had been sent as a decoy the time Captain Jerome and Rek nearly caught them in the forest. And in the cave, he had seemed the most focused. He must be their master strategist.

I breathed a sigh of relief. We had time, then.

I had been carefully not thinking of Rek all night, but the thought of him leaped to the front of my mind now. He would launch into action the second he heard the gang was inside the city itself. He—I frowned. Rek could hardly knock on every door in the city. By the time he managed to track them down, it might be far too late.

We needed to know their base of operations within the city walls. And the only possible way we were going to find that out was if I followed them now.

Their footsteps were already growing fainter, so I came out from behind the decrepit wagon and tiptoed to the main street.

Forcing myself to move slowly, I eased just my head out far enough to see down the road.

The men were returning the way they had come, never having passed in front of our house, and I didn't need to worry about being seen. Most of them had already rounded the corner. An instant later, and I would have missed seeing which way they turned.

Leaving my lantern behind at the wagon, I shot off after them, relying on the faint glimmer of dawn to light my way.

At the corner, caution returned, and I slowed. Once again, I eased my head around the corner, peeping in time to see them turning yet another corner.

I expected them to head for the back streets of the city—the parts furthest from the palace and the central guard barracks, where the more disreputable citizens chose to live. But instead they moved toward the river—a solidly respectable neighborhood housing mostly tradesmen and skilled workers.

Was someone in Karema hiding them? Someone connected to the traitor, perhaps? We neared the river that ran through the city center, passing close to the secondary small mill used by Kali's father. The sight of it made me feel like the traitor. Many of the people who lived in this part of town frequented the same market I did. Did I really think any of them were traitors?

Reaching the next corner, I stuck my head around once again. A dirty, unkempt face loomed large, almost close enough to collide with mine. Someone was coming in the other direction.

I pulled back sharply, but not before I smelled the drink lingering on his breath. A straggler, returning from a night's revelry.

My abrupt backward movement made my cloak and skirt swish out, around the corner. The man's eyes, which had looked dazed and confused, sharpened as he caught sight of the gold fabric.

"That's a mighty fine dress for these parts." His cackle matched the unpleasant gleam in his eye. "Gold as the sun!"

Fear shot through me. Not because of the man himself—he looked like he was barely staying upright, and I was confident I could easily fend him off and escape if he attempted to rob me. My fear came from the volume of his voice. Anyone within two blocks must have heard him.

I tried to retreat, but he lunged around the corner, grabbing my arm and pulling me around after him. I wrenched myself free, and the sudden motion upset his balance. He fell backward, landing on his rear and staring up at me in bewilderment.

I ignored him, staring down the street instead. The last of the thieves had paused, looking back at us. The corner they were rounding was close this time, and he wasn't far away—easily close enough for me to see his eyes slowly narrow as he stared at me. For a moment, we all remained frozen, then the thief called something to the others, turning back to move toward me.

I fled.

A shout behind me accompanied running footsteps, hurrying in pursuit. The drunk was calling something—either protest or encouragement, I couldn't tell—but he was drowned out by the sound of the thieves.

Wishing I'd taken the time to swap my dancing slippers for sturdier footwear, I retraced my steps, instinctively fleeing for home. But a glance over my shoulder made me rethink my plan.

There were eight of the thieves, and at least two of them were tall, their long legs eating up the distance between us. Even if I could stay ahead of them long enough to make it home, I couldn't risk leading them there. As soon as they realized it was one of the houses with a mark, they would guess the truth.

The rush of the river water reached my ears, giving me another idea. Swerving, I dived down a side street, popping out in front of the water. I fled up the length of the riverbank, dodging crates and early risers. Several yelled after me, but I ignored them.

The miller shouldn't be at work yet, so the mill would be deserted. If I could just get into it before the thieves drew close enough to see where I'd gone...

I ran dangerously near the edge of the river—thankful this stretch was paved. The mill loomed in front of me, the enormous wheel jutting out into the water of the river. It was cradled between the straight wall of the building which lay flush with the river and a small half wall of stone which extended out from the building and then ran down the other side of the wheel.

Without pausing to judge the distance of the leap, I launched off the riverbank and jumped for the half wall. I landed squarely, swaying slightly before I caught my balance. Thank goodness I had spent so many of my rest days here. Kali and I had made the leap many times, sent by the miller to remove some piece of debris jamming the wheel.

I scurried along the thin top of the wall, reaching the end of it and making the right angle turn toward the building. A single large step brought me to the wall itself, and I braced myself against it, trying to catch my breath even as I kept moving.

Crouching, I looked for the hole, well above the level of the river. The miller had been talking about patching it for years, but he never seemed to find the time. Kali said it was because he thought the crown should fix it—given they owned all the city mills and only rented them out to the local millers.

Whatever the reason, I had never been so glad to see a damaged wall. The gap was slim, too small for any but the most petite adult. I couldn't hear footsteps over the sound of the river, but a quick glance back up the shore showed movement coming in my direction.

I pulled my cloak around me, hoping they were too far to have seen where I went. Diving for the hole, I committed myself to the maneuver—the only way to successfully make it as Kali had shown me. My top half disappeared in, my middle catching on the rough stone. I lay there—half in, half out—for a moment before I managed to wiggle the rest of the way through.

I collapsed on the floor, panting. Kali and I hadn't entertained ourselves with the daring jump for at least a year, and it was starting to get tight. I wouldn't fit through much longer. But I had made it this time, and that was what mattered.

Scraping myself up off the floor, I made my way around the heavy machinery to peer through the small, dirty window beside the locked front door. The thieves had stopped not far away. I had hoped they would continue chasing after me in the direction they thought I'd gone, but they'd clearly stopped after losing sight of me, too clever to fall for such a simple trick.

The captain was several strides away, conversing with a local man, and I desperately tried to remember if he'd been there when I ran past myself. Had he seen me?

The captain finished his conversation and rejoined his men. "That fisherman said he saw a girl going into the mill."

I spun away from the window, standing with my back to the wall, my breath coming fast.

"The mill?" The speaker sounded confused, and from the sound of his voice, he'd turned to face the building.

They'd found me, after all. They must suspect I'd been following them—that I had some connection to the house and family they were searching for—but would they go as far as breaking into the mill?

CHAPTER 18

creaking sound on the far side of the building made me start. It was followed by the sound of a door closing. Flinging myself across the mill floor, I sprinted for the small back door that opened into a side room.

The heavy footsteps of a tall man had already exited the room by the time I arrived, but one person still stood there, hanging two outer jackets on hooks by the door.

I leaped forward and clapped my hand across Kali's mouth, stifling the inevitable squeal.

"Zaria!" she shrieked into my hand. "What are you doing here?"

"I'm being chased," I said in a soft, panting voice. "By some very dangerous men. They can't find me, Kali! You need to hide me!"

She pulled herself free, her eyes wide and voice lowered to match mine. "Hide you? Will they look for you in here?"

"They're on the other side of the building. I came in through our hole, and I thought I'd made it in unseen, but a fisherman told them he saw a girl come in here."

"A girl?" A gleam I didn't like entered Kali's eye. "That's easy, then."

She ran lightly around the machinery, making for the main door while I trailed behind.

"Kali! Kali, what are you doing?" I hissed, but I didn't dare raise my voice as we got closer to the main door.

When I spotted someone pressed against the window from the outside, trying to look through the thick layer of dirt, I whisked myself behind a piece of machinery. Peering around the edge, I made one last attempt to call to my friend as she reached the main door.

"Kali! Don't!"

But she was already opening it.

I could perfectly picture her look of surprise and disdain as she gazed at the mass of men on the other side of the door.

"Excuse me?" One eyebrow would be arching, giving her words added hauteur. "Do you need assistance? My father and I have only just arrived and won't be open to customers for an hour yet." The way she said *customers* made it clear she didn't think them likely to fit into that illustrious category.

One of the thieves muttered something I couldn't hear, although Kali's reply reached me clearly.

"Certainly there is a girl here in the mill. As you can see with your own eyes. I'm here many days with my father, but perhaps you would like me to call him so you can confirm I'm not some trespasser?"

I pressed a hand to my mouth, unsure if the laugh bubbling up was one of amusement or horror. Kali sounded so much like Adara on her dignity. She had always been an excellent actress, able to mimic the mannerisms of every class in the city.

This time it was Esai who replied, his words measured and loud enough for me to hear.

"Of course we do not wish to disturb the worthy miller. It is our mistake. Good morning to you."

Kali didn't move for several seconds, presumably watching them leave before I heard the sound of the heavy door closing. I waited several seconds more before emerging.

"Kali! I told you they were dangerous men! You're outrageous!"

She laughed. "I think you meant to say brilliant. They're gone, aren't they? My father and I are both too well known in this area for them to make trouble."

I shook my head although I couldn't deny the truth of her words. Even more than she knew, this group of men didn't want to draw undue attention to themselves—especially from the guards.

"Thank you," I said instead.

"You're welcome." She grinned at me. "My only price is hearing the whole story. How exactly did you come to be pursued through the city by cutthroat villains?"

I walked slowly toward her, buying myself time to think. But in the process, my cloak swished open, revealing the golden material beneath.

Kali was instantly diverted, gasping loudly. Springing forward, she pulled my cloak completely open, gasping again.

"Zaria! It's gorgeous! Where did you get that gown?" She looked up. "Wait! Did you wear that to the ball at the palace? Were you there all night? Surely those men didn't chase you all the way from the palace?"

Her eyes grew brighter and brighter. "And what about the prince? Did you dance with Prince Tarek? Or the twins?" Her eyes grew even wider. "Or all three?"

"Kali." I groaned. "Only you could find me a fugitive in my own city and be distracted by dancing."

"Did you hear me say *three princes*, Zaria?" She shook her head sadly. "Priorities, my girl. You have never looked so fabulous, and such a moment cannot go unremarked. Obviously I also want to hear about the being chased part." She sighed. "Why can't I be the one to have adventures and meet princes? You don't even appreciate it!"

"I humbly apologize for not being sufficiently excited about being threatened with a violent death."

"Ooh, a violent death? Was it as exciting as that?"

I gave a reluctant laugh. "You really are hopeless, Kali!"

"Not hopeless, hopeful," she corrected me. "One day I'll get the chance to travel and have adventures like my mother." Her voice turned wistful at the mention of her beloved mother who had passed away two years previously.

"Of course you will." I squeezed her hand. "Hopefully nicer adventures than my current one."

I bit my lip as the enormity of my so-called adventure hit me again.

"Actually, Kali," I said, "I don't think I can take the time to tell you about it now. I promise I will, but not now. It's imperative that I get back to the palace."

Her face, which had fallen at my initial words, brightened again. "The palace! I understand, of course." She squeezed my arm. "But you will tell me eventually? You promise?"

"Of course." I frowned down at myself. "I don't suppose you have anything you can loan me to wear? Those men didn't get a good look at my face, so if I can get into a less distinctive outfit, I should be safe on the streets."

"Come this way." She tugged me back into the side room. "I've kept a change of clothes here ever since I got covered in flour that time. Do you remember? I dropped in to give Father a message on our way to the market. And flour does not brush off!" She made a despairing face before opening a small cupboard and bringing out a wrinkled chemise and outer robe.

"Thank you, thank you," I cried, changing my outfit as quickly as I could. "Can I leave this here?" I held out the gold gown. "I'll come back for it when I get the chance."

She laughed. "I'll hold it hostage against that promised explanation."

I rolled my eyes before grinning and thanking her a final time.

Although my mind told me I was safe in my new outfit, my eyes and ears were still on high alert as I took the fastest route to the palace. I could feel the fatigue pressing in behind the alertness, but it wasn't yet strong enough to override the fear.

I arrived to find the last of the ball guests long gone, and even the lanterns that had decorated the front courtyard of the palace packed away. It was as if the night before had never happened.

Worst of all, the main gates were closed and barred. They weren't solid, like the walls and gates of most of the houses in the city, but formed of metal strands that twisted together to create beautiful patterns. So I could see through the gates to the palace beyond, but I couldn't reach it. When the gates were closed, the only access was through a solid wooden door on one side of the gate that was flanked by a pair of guards.

It was open when I arrived, the guards talking to a man pulling a handcart piled with crates. I lined up behind him, my heart sinking. My instincts had said to run to Rek, and I hadn't taken the time to think it through properly.

When the cart finally rolled into the palace grounds, I approached the guards. They eyed me up and down in perfect synchronization.

"I need to speak to Princess Adara," I said, deciding at the last minute that I would be more likely to get access to the princess than the crown prince.

"Do you now?" The speaker looked across at the other guard, their expressions making their opinion clear. "And would you have an appointment?"

"I'm an old friend," I babbled. "I was here last night for the ball. Something's happened, and it's very urgent that I—"

"The ball?" He was openly incredulous now, once again looking at my gown—the crumpled dress of a miller's daughter.

"Or Prince Tarek," I said, the exhaustion pressing in on me and making me desperate. "It's a matter of life and death and the good of the kingdom. I must speak to the prince or princess!"

The silent guard cleared his throat. "In that case, you'll need an appointment. You may write to the junior vizier in charge of schedules and request..." He continued on, but I'd stopped listening.

I could ask for Captain Jerome. That might get their attention. But while I'd seen him talking with Rek at the ball, he hadn't seen me, other than one brief shadowy glimpse in the gardens. And he hadn't looked approving on that occasion. If I asked to see him, he might dismiss my whole story as an attempt to get close to the prince. Or he might suspect me of being in league with the thieves and send me straight to an interrogation like I'd feared from the beginning.

Remembering his serious face, I shivered and rejected the idea. Perhaps I should ask for Samuel or Benjamin instead? Instantly I realized that I should have asked for them from the beginning. If I hadn't been so tired, I would have.

But the two guards were looking more and more suspicious. If I didn't get myself out of there soon, they were going to arrest me regardless and let the captain sort it out.

"Can you at least pass on a message to Samuel or Benjamin for me?"

The names of their fellow guards made the ones in front of me pause, looking at one another again.

"Please just tell them that Zaria needs to talk to the prince—or to one of them, at least—immediately. They'll know who I am."

"Will they now?" The first guard asked slowly.

"Yes," I said hurriedly. "Thank you."

Before either could say anything more—or attempt to grab me—I turned and fled from the palace for the second time in less than twelve hours.

All the way home, I kicked myself for handling the situation so badly. In the aftermath of the ball, I had forgotten my new self. I was no longer the daughter of a vizier, who could approach the prince at will.

Walking through the gate of my own home, I dully noted the chalk mark was still there. I had confirmed it came from the thieves—and that they were close to discovering Kasim's identity —but I'd failed at finding anything more useful. There must be things I should be doing now, but I couldn't think of any. The lack of sleep was catching up with me, and I desperately needed a few hours in my bed.

With Nyla in isolation in her suite, no one was watching for me from the front windows. I managed to slip inside, avoiding even the kitchens since Yara would be almost as eager to hear about the ball as Kali.

I heaped silent praises on her head when I arrived at my room to find a plate of date bread and fruit. After inhaling it, I fell into my bed and was asleep within seconds.

I awoke with a start, disoriented, my heart racing. It took me several seconds to work out where I was, what I was wearing, and what had happened. I scrambled up as soon as I did, noting it was late afternoon.

Exchanging Kali's clothes for my own, I ventured to the kitchen, eager for news. Yara was too busy preparing the evening meal to give me a full inquisition, but it was clear from the general mood of the room that none of the servants were aware of any reason to be afraid. Did that mean my stratagem with the chalk continued to be successful?

When I asked if I'd had any visitors or messages from the palace, Yara paused her work to look at me with an astonished expression.

"From the palace? No indeed! And you can be sure I'd remember such a thing."

I thanked her and escaped before she could question me further. Rowan also knew nothing of any message, although his surprised look was more subtle, shot from under bushy brows and unaccompanied by questions or exclamations.

I tried to remember how long the guard shifts at the palace gates lasted. But my world had been inside the palace walls, and I'd never known much about the operation of the guards.

Once the guards had changed, I could try a second, more discreet approach, but I didn't dare go back while the same men might still be there.

Belatedly it occurred to me to ask for Navid. As the heir of a rich merchant, he might be able to gain access to the palace when I could not.

"Navid?" Rowan's mild look of bemusement deepened. "He left first thing this morning. Rode out and told me not to expect him back before nightfall."

"Rode out?" I frowned. It was only a short walk to Kasim's main place of business.

"Didn't say where he was going, but he had an air about him," Rowan volunteered.

"An air?" I stared at him. "What sort of air?"

"Well, now." He chewed on his lip. "Excited, I would say, if I had to give it a name."

"Navid rode out early this morning, excited, and planning to be gone for the whole day."

My mind was blank, my supposed cleverness failing me. He could have no reason to go back to the cave, and I couldn't think of anywhere else that would require a horse. Clearly I would have to wait for his return.

Mariam had kindly granted me the day off to recover after the expected late night of the ball, so I had no responsibilities or remonstrances waiting for me. But it soon became clear I wasn't going to be able to sit still and wait for hours. I needed to be moving.

I didn't have to think long about a destination. If anyone in the city had noticed a group of strangers, acting questionably, word of it would be found in the market. Everything that happened in the city was eventually discussed there.

When I reached it, I scanned the crowd, feeling guiltily grateful when I didn't see any sign of Kali or the miller's wagon. I still needed to work out what I could safely say to her about the situation. The cowardly part of me preferred to avoid her until the whole matter was resolved—one way or the other—and I could tell her the full truth. Assuming I was still alive at that point, of course…

I wandered up and down, looking at the stalls but not approaching any of them. Snatches of conversation drifted in and out of my earshot as the crowd discussed rumors of the ball the night before, Yasmine's upcoming party, and who had secured the supply deals for each of them. Others discussed the incoming cold weather, the state of the roads, or the newly discovered lands across the desert and Ardasira's success at allying with them—all the normal topics of conversation that could be heard on any given day in the market.

I waved a greeting to many of the stallholders, some of whom called back to me, but when I passed Samir's stall, he hurried toward me, his face grave. I moved closer, instantly alert.

"Zaria! Such sad tidings! The most tragic. I was deeply grieved to hear my powder was not enough to save the worthy and estimable Kasim."

I relaxed. I'd forgotten this was my first time seeing Samir since my purchase of the fever powder. Heaving a sorrowful sigh, I tried to look as grieved as I could manage with such distracted thoughts.

"It is sad, indeed, but I'm afraid the fever was too fierce for even the strongest of powders. You, of all people, know that some illnesses rage too hot for any medicine."

"You speak the truth!" he cried, visibly relieved. He must have been afraid of a leading merchant family holding a grudge against him and spreading stories about the inefficacy of his wares.

He continued on for a few minutes, and I nodded in all the right places. Nyla usually purchased her medicines from the more established apothecary who had a full shop on the edge of the market. But it had been early morning when I came, before the shop was open, and Samir must have been hopeful his powder would prove a success and he might gain our business in the future. He certainly worked hard—the first in the market most mornings and the last to leave.

"Samir," I said when he paused, thinking of the long hours he worked. "Have you heard anything about any strangers nosing around asking questions? Rough men, who don't look like they belong to the city?"

Someone had marked our house in the evening, between our leaving for the ball and my return. If they'd been wandering the streets at that hour, perhaps they'd passed through the market.

"Hmm…" His brow furrowed in thought. "I don't know about any rough men. You wouldn't want to be mixing with such people, Zaria. But strangers now, that's another matter."

His face brightened, as if pleased to find a way to be of service to Kasim's household.

"There was a very nicely spoken stranger here just last night. From down south he was and newly arrived in the capital. Said he'd heard about a recent merchant death in the city and was afraid it might be one of his associates. When I gave him Kasim's name, he was most grieved to realize he was indeed one of his merchant contacts. Showed just the sort of interest and respect for his passing as anyone might wish. Of course he wanted to pay his respects, and since this was his first visit to Karema, I was most honored to point out your house for myself—seeing as I was just packing up and heading home anyway. It was hardly out of my way at all."

He paused for breath and fixed me with an inquiring look. "Of course he could not go straight in, it already being night, but I assume you've seen him this morning?"

I cleared my throat, trying not to show horror on my face. "What did he look like?"

"Oh, yes." He chuckled. "Foolish me. I'm sure you've had many visitors since the tragic event, and I was thoughtless enough not to discover the stranger's name. He had a distinctive look, however, so I'm sure you would recognize him. His eyebrows arched, like this." He drew the shape on his own face, looking at me hopefully.

"Yes," I managed, recognizing the thief called Davis in his description and feeling sick. "I believe he has been past the house."

Samir looked pleased and said something else which I didn't catch. I was too busy remembering the conversation I had heard from behind the broken wagon. I had misunderstood their words. I had assumed they were waiting on Davis's input to formulate a strategy, but in fact, they were waiting for the one who left the mark to return and point out the correct house.

He was clearly the most trusted of Esai's men and had been assigned the job of nosing around in an attempt to find Kasim. How happy he must have been to stumble on the stall holder with the most intimate knowledge of Kasim's apparent illness and passing—and one overeager to do some service to the family.

And then Davis had left the city—or separated from the rest of the gang, at least. What could have taken him away? It must have been another task Esai trusted only to him.

"Samir," I gasped, as the full memory of their words hit me. "I'm sorry, but I have to go." I didn't wait to see his reaction, dashing out of the market square in a blind panic.

Esai had said Davis would be back by now. I had assumed that his return meant they would begin formulating a new plan. But Esai had meant Davis would show them the right house when he returned.

The shadows were already lengthening, the day drawing toward its close. While I was wandering the markets, the thieves might have already attacked!

CHAPTER 19

I ran through the streets, furious at my missteps of the morning. If only I had approached the palace more wisely, I might have managed to speak to Rek or Adara.

But I wasn't the only one to blame. If only Navid hadn't left for the day, he might have corrected the issue. Why would he go off like that? Hadn't he wanted to talk to me after my unexpectedly early departure from the ball?

I knew I was being unfair to him, but fear consumed me, sparking an unreasoning fury. As I ran, I pictured Yara and Rowan and Layla lying as Kasim had done, slain by the thieves.

But as the streets flew past, my panic subsided somewhat. Forty men were enough to make a frontal assault on the property, overwhelming the few ceremonial guards employed by Nyla and whatever defense the other servants might attempt.

But it would be a noisy business, sure to attract attention. By the time they were finished, someone outside would have sent for the guards. Sultan Khalil didn't tolerate violent disturbances in his city.

They couldn't just charge in and murder everyone. They would need a more subtle approach. They might even be measured enough to want to seek information first—to find out who in the household were most likely to know about the cave.

By the time I reached the familiar street of home, I was moving at a fast walk. My initial view of the gate provided further reassurance. It looked as it always did, with no visible sign of disturbance.

I wrestled with the latch, pulling it wide and peering inside. For a terrifying moment, I registered a mass of people and objects filling the courtyard. The unusual sight sent fear rushing back through my body like a physical force.

But a second look brought clarity. It wasn't an invading army in the courtyard but an enormous wagon surrounded by moving people. I slipped inside, closing the gate behind me, and looked for a friendly face in the crowd. I found Rowan.

He was standing at the head of a huge workhorse, scratching behind its ear while he whispered to it. A second horse stood harnessed beside it, occasionally blowing a breathy sigh. I smiled, relief making me giddy. Rowan believed it was best to get to know a new horse before attempting to unharness it, so the sight was a familiar and reassuring one.

I hurried over to him. "What's going on?" I watched two servants struggling to carry an obviously heavy trunk between them.

Various bags, crates, and trunks had been placed in piles around the courtyard, and servants were in the process of moving them inside. When I looked more closely, I realized every servant had a familiar face. This was definitely the chaos of an unexpected arrival, not an attack.

Rowan spoke in a softer voice than normal, obviously thinking of the horses. "Ali met an old friend and invited him to stay. Or it might be a new friend. I didn't entirely catch that part."

I hid a grin. Nothing distracted Rowan like the arrival of an unknown animal. No doubt by tomorrow morning, he'd have these two mammoth horses eating out of his hands just like every other creature on the property.

"Is he another merchant, by any chance?" I asked. "Selling oil, perhaps?" I eyed the rows of large leather jars in the back of the wagon.

"Something like that," Rowan said, clearly not really listening.

I turned to watch the other servants, but no one seemed in need of assistance. The feeling of fear from earlier had abated, but it hadn't entirely disappeared. In the current environment, anything unknown seemed suspect.

Idly, while I debated the matter in my mind, wondering what action I should take, I counted the jars.

Thirty-eight.

My stomach clenched, and I counted again. Definitely thirty-eight. It was an oddly specific number—not round, like I would have expected, and it left the rows in the back of the wagon uneven.

"A new friend, did you say?" I asked Rowan in a tight voice, remembering the story Davis had fed Samir. "But also an old one. Perhaps he's one of Kasim's associates, but new to Ali."

Rowan looked up, briefly distracted from the horse. "Yes, now that you say it, that sounds right."

I nodded, feigning a calm I didn't feel. "Where is our visitor now?"

"Eating with Ali and Mariam, I believe." He gave a last pat to the horse by our side and walked around to its pair.

I abandoned Rowan, hurrying toward the house. A small part of me hoped the merchant would be a stranger, and the number of jars a coincidence, but after my run in with the thieves at dawn, I didn't dare trust such a thought.

Some of the other servants gave me odd looks, but I ignored them, making straight for the smaller dining room where Nyla and Kasim entertained when they had only one or two guests.

When I reached it, I found one of the serving girls about to enter with a platter from the kitchen.

Whisking it from her hands without giving her a chance to protest, I walked into the room in her place. The server in front of me stood just behind each guest, offering the platter from their right side without intruding on the table conversation.

I did the same, keeping my head tilted down and looking at the guest out of the corner of my eye. Navid had apparently still not returned, so there were only three around the table.

Ali, Mariam—and Esai, just as I had feared. I moved around the rest of the table with paranoid care, not wanting to put a foot wrong and call attention to myself. Esai never looked my way, however, his focus on charming his hosts. Hearing him laughing and complimenting Ali made my stomach churn, but the thought of all those jars inside the walls kept me from blurting out his real identity. Esai wasn't the biggest threat—his men were.

It was hard to stay silent when I heard Ali refer to him as Esai, however. What effrontery to not even bother with a false name.

As soon as I was safely back out of the room, I dumped the empty platter in the corridor and hurried back to the courtyard. I slowed my steps as I reached it, however. All the bags and crates had now been carried inside, and only Rowan remained with the horses. If those jars had ears, as I suspected, I didn't want them hearing anything that sounded amiss.

I arrived just as Rowan finished getting to know the second horse and finally reached for the halter straps.

"Hold on," I called, making my voice as cheerful as I could manage.

He paused, looking toward me in surprise.

"You need to move the wagon before you unhitch them. They want it around the back after all."

He opened his mouth—presumably to point out that there wasn't room for a wagon that large anywhere but the front courtyard—but I gave him my most deadly glare, drawing my finger across my neck menacingly for emphasis.

My efforts only appeared to confuse him, but at least he closed his mouth again, eventually saying a plain, "Ah."

Miming for him to stay silent and to move away from the horses, I tiptoed close and put my mouth against his ear.

"No time to explain," I whispered at the lowest possible volume. "But we're all in terrible danger. I need you to open the gate without saying a word."

I wanted them to think it was Rowan at the reins—a much less suspicious option than a young girl suddenly commandeering the wagon. Rowan regarded me with concern, and I gave him a pleading look. When he finally gave a small, silent nod, I leaned in to give one further warning.

"Watch out for the guest. He might try to run. Get our guards to stop him, if he does!"

Rowan's eyes widened, his look of concern deepening, but he stepped toward the gates, and I sent him a grateful smile.

Scrambling onto the bench at the front of the wagon, I took up the reins. This was the part that made me most nervous, but they settled into my hands with reassuring familiarity.

I had never driven a wagon in my life, but when Rek turned sixteen, his parents had given him a racing carriage. Naturally, Adara, the twins, and I had all demanded that he teach us to drive it. But he had declared I was the only one sensible enough to be trusted with his horses.

I hadn't actually enjoyed the first lesson because poor Rek was so worried about his new horses that he remained stern and tense the whole time. But Adara insisted I stick with the lessons, purely because of how much it enraged the twins.

As I flicked the reins to get the horses moving, I couldn't have been more grateful to her.

Lurching into movement was a much less smooth process than with the light racing carriage, but the two workhorses stepped forward obediently, and the wagon creaked into motion behind them. Rowan had pulled the well-oiled gates wide while I was accustoming myself to the reins, and I managed to squeeze the wagon through without scraping the sides.

The turn into the street was tight, but I hoped the men inside the jars would think they were turning around the side of the house. I wanted to be well on my way and moving quickly before they realized there was something wrong. I was trusting in a combination of confusion, uncertainty, and speed to keep them all in place.

As soon as the wagon had swung onto the road, I signaled to the horses to increase the pace. Thankfully the early evening was a quiet time on the streets with the main business of the day concluded and most people inside eating. Within minutes, I had the wagon traveling at a dangerously high speed, barely slowing for the corners. Without the weight of all the jars, plus the heavy wood of the wagon itself, we would have tipped on some of the turns.

We passed an occasional other vehicle, but they all took one look at our enormous bulk thundering down the street and hurried to one side or the other to make room for us.

Every creak and slosh from the wagon behind me made the back of my neck prickle, the skin itching. At every sound, no matter how small, I expected a thief to burst from one of the closest jars, knife in hand. If one did, I had no defense.

But we got further and further from the house, and still none of them moved. Esai must have instructed them to emerge at his signal and, lacking that signal, they weren't confident enough to make a move. I had seen his tight rule over the gang. None of them would want to be responsible for ruining his plan, not when they weren't sure what was actually going on. It was a desperate gamble, but I hadn't been stabbed in the back yet.

I made another turn, too fast this time, even for the heavy

wagon. I felt it shuddering under me, the outside wheels leaving the ground as we teetered on the edge of disaster.

I held on to the reins, throwing my body weight toward the far side, for what little good that could do. The horses strained forward, the wheels turned, and we straightened, all four wheels making contact with the paving beneath us again. I took a shaky breath and urged the horses even faster. We had a straight shot to the distant palace now.

As we approached the gates, I finally had to pull back on the reins, easing the horses slower and slower so we could come to a stop in front of them. A wagon this size wouldn't fit through the small wooden door, so I had another gamble before me. This time I would play my hand better.

"Evening!" I called loudly to the guards, relieved to see their faces were unfamiliar. "I have Esai's gift to His Highness, as instructed."

I thought I'd heard a low rumble from the jars behind me, but my loud mention of Esai's name brought silence. My ploy was enough to make them second-guess themselves again.

One of the guards approached closer. "What instructions?"

"Open this gate, or I'll ram it open myself!" I said insolently.

The guard stiffened, sending a signal to the one who remained at the gate which made him disappear through the door. I smiled to myself.

"Climb down immediately," the guard said, directing the sharp end of his ceremonial spear toward me. It might be part of his dress uniform, but it had a deadly blade.

I immediately dropped the superior posture, adopting a serious expression and holding his gaze.

"These jars are a gift for Prince Tarek, and it's urgent that he receives them immediately. Send for Captain Jerome if you don't believe me."

I kept myself still and my attention on the guard, although I was fairly sure several of the nearer jars had rocked at my mention of Rek's name. I held my breath, but none of them broke open. So far everything was going significantly better than my worst fears.

The guard facing me didn't have time to reply before a long line of guards came running through the wooden door, streaming out to surround me and the cart. In a side corner of my mind, I counted them as they came, only stopping when I reached fifty. It seemed an excessive reaction to the apparent threat I presented, but for once I was delighted with the sultan's caution.

"Dismount," the original guard said, sounding more confident now. "And you can speak to Captain Jerome yourself."

"With pleasure," I said promptly and far more loudly than was necessary. "Now that there are so many guards here, I'm handing over the wagon with relief. Although a hundred does seem an excessive number."

The guard gaped at me, probably convinced by that point that I was suffering some sort of delusion. While there might have been more than fifty guards, there were far fewer than a hundred.

I jumped down so quickly I nearly lost control and landed on my rear. I managed to keep my feet, however. The closest guards all swung their weapons toward me, but I frantically gestured toward the jars.

"In there," I said at a more normal volume. Some of the thieves might hear me, but it was too late for it to matter. And if they believed my last assertion, they would know there was no point coming out fighting. "The threat is in there."

PART III
THE TRAITOR AND THE TREASURE

CHAPTER 20

"Stand aside!" A commanding voice made the guards nearest the door part, allowing an older man to stride through. Obviously someone had run for Captain Jerome.

"Captain! I'm glad you're here." I turned to him, but several guards instantly leaped in front of me, blocking my passage to their captain.

"He said *stand aside*," a younger voice said from behind the captain.

The authoritative tones made the guards jump to obey, melting out of my way as quickly as they'd appeared. It took everything in me not to run to Rek and throw myself into his arms.

I settled for a swift walk.

"Thank goodness." I hoped no one could see my legs shaking as the tension of the last hour began to dissipate. "I asked for you, but I wasn't sure anyone would actually deliver the message."

"They probably wouldn't," he acknowledged. "But I happened to be with the captain when they sent for him."

"I instructed His Highness to stay safely behind," Jerome said, "but since you seem to know him, I'm sure you know he's not one to listen to my instructions."

I managed a shaky chuckle, and he gave me an assessing look.

"Now that I'm here," he added, "I can't say I'm too concerned about his presence. For once, my guards seem to have overreacted to the situation."

"I was behaving strangely," I said in an apologetic voice. "And I'm glad they brought so many because there are thirty-eight violent criminals hiding in those oil jars."

"What?" Jerome's voice rang out like a whip lash, his head spinning to stare at the jars.

Rek's eyes grew wide. "The gang?" he asked in a strangled voice. "In those jars? How is that possible?"

"It's a long story." Exhaustion was hitting on the heels of the shaking. "I tried to get a message to you first thing this morning, but the guards on the gate wouldn't let me through. I asked them to pass a message via Samuel or Benjamin, but I'm assuming they didn't."

"Samuel and Benjamin?" Jerome broke his hard stare at the jars to send me a rapid glance. "It sounds like something has been going on here that I should have been informed of." He gave Rek a single loaded look before turning to bark a stream of orders at his men.

I grimaced apologetically at Rek. "Sorry. I think I just got you into trouble."

He laughed, still looking incredulous. "I'm the crown prince, remember? The captain can't yell at me like I'm one of his men." He slipped an arm around my back. "But I'm worried about you. You look like you're about to fall over."

I had been feeling that way, but the sensation of his arm around me sent energy surging back through my limbs.

"I'll be all right," I said, but he was already drawing me away, pulling me back toward the door.

I tried to protest but caught a signal from Jerome. He was

clearly instructing Rek to get me back behind the gate, so I gave up trying to hold my ground. Besides, the captain was likely relieved that I was distracting Rek and keeping him from diving into the thick of any fighting that might be about to occur.

As soon as we were safely inside the palace grounds, peering out through the whorls and twists of the gate, Jerome barked a loud order. The guards took a synchronized step toward the wagon, but several of the jars ripped open before they could get any further, the thieves inside leaping out. Some of them had weighed their options and decided to make a stand.

A shout went up from the guards, and they rushed forward in a more ragged line to meet their foe. The commotion brought the rest of the thieves bursting out as well. Some launched themselves at the closest guards, while others tried to make a run for it, aiming for weaker points of the circle.

None made it out, however. The thieves were at too much of a disadvantage, disoriented from the jars, blinking in the light of the sunset and the blazing palace lanterns, and surrounded by prepared guards. The ring of spears kept them from making much use of their knives, and soon they had all been disarmed and arrested.

Only two guards had been hurt, both by thrown knives, and no one had been killed. I closed my eyes and blew out a long breath. It was the best possible outcome.

"Is that the entire gang?" Rek asked, clearly torn between wanting to go out to join his captain and not wanting to leave me.

I straightened, horrified with myself. "No! It's not! I should have said something immediately. Their captain—Esai—posed as a merchant and used the jars to sneak them past our gates. I knew I had to get them away as fast as possible, so I had to leave him there. Last I saw, he was eating with Ali and Mariam, but anything could have happened by now! We have to get back there."

"You stole his gang from under his nose?" Rek sounded awed.

"I just climbed onto the wagon and drove away," I said. "It wasn't much."

"Just climbed on and drove away—with thirty-eight thieves in jars." Rek shook his head, a laugh in his voice. But when he turned to shout an order, his face was serious.

Half the palace must have been alerted to the commotion at the gates by now, so plenty of grooms were on hand to respond to his command. Within minutes, four saddled horses were pawing at the ground at our sides, two of them already carrying Samuel and Benjamin.

Rek threw me up onto the shorter of the two available mounts, himself springing into the saddle of his white stallion. As we walked our horses out the smaller door, Rek swerved toward the captain.

Jerome looked up, a frown descending over his face.

"Where are you going, Your Highness?"

"To catch their captain—if I can. There's no time to waste. You'll have to oversee the questioning of these prisoners yourself. With any luck, you'll have the name of the traitor by the time I get back, and we'll have eliminated the threat and the gang in one day."

Jerome looked less convinced about the inevitability of a positive outcome, but he was obviously able to read the steely determination on Rek's face, so he didn't protest.

Rek pointed his mount down the street and let him have his head, the rest of us following in single file. Just like with the wagon, the light traffic on the streets scattered before our hasty progress. While the trip to the palace had seemed to stretch on impossibly long, the return journey passed in the blink of an eye.

As we turned down my street, I dared to let myself hope for the best again. If they were all still seated at the meal, Esai might not even realize his men were gone yet. Rek, Samuel, Benjamin, and our household guards could easily arrest one man, no matter how skilled a fighter.

But as soon as I saw the gate swinging loose, I knew it wasn't going to be so simple.

Someone inside must have heard our hoofbeats because a maid appeared, peering out with a terrified look, as if fearing some fresh attack. When she recognized me, she held the gate wide, however, and we rode straight through into a milling crowd of agitated people.

From my vantage point on horseback, I could see into the center of the mass of people. They were gathered around a person lying on the ground.

"Rowan!" I slid off the mare's back, pushing my way through the crowd.

They gave way before me which only increased my fear of what I would find. When I burst through the inner ring, I found Yara sitting on the stones of the courtyard, Rowan's head resting gently in her lap. His eyes were closed, and his face looked strained, but I could hear his rasping breaths.

I dropped to my knees beside him, noting the bandage around his side that was already stained red with leaking blood.

Mariam appeared, Ali trailing behind her, his face full of shock and bewilderment.

"I've reported what's happened through the door to Nyla, so her hysterics aren't our problem any longer, we must focus on—"

She broke off as she saw first me and then Rek pushing his way through the crowd to join me.

"Why…Your Highness!" They both bowed low.

"What has happened here?" Rek asked, not bothering with formalities.

"I'm not entirely sure, Your Highness," Ali said. "It was all very strange."

"It was one of our late brother's business associates," Mariam explained. "He wished to check on his wares during the meal, but instead he appears to have attacked our head groom and run off."

Rowan's eyes fluttered open at her words, and his gaze latched on to me.

"Sorry, Zaria. I tried to stop him, like you said. But my body isn't as spry as it used to be."

Tears sprang to my eyes. "You were supposed to get the guards to do that! Not throw yourself in front of him."

"No time," he answered. "He came out too soon after you left."

I seized his hand and squeezed it, the tears spilling over. His injuries were my fault.

"Tried to stop him leaving?" Mariam stared at Rowan. "Whatever for?"

"Because he's loyal and trustworthy," I said fiercely. "And because I told him to. That man wasn't Kasim's business associate —he was the captain of the gang of thieves who've been harassing the roads of this kingdom for decades."

Mariam gave a small scream, her eyes flying from me to Ali and back again. I had worded the revelation carefully, considering our audience, but she and Ali knew why the gang were interested in our household in particular.

"Every one of those jars had a thief inside," Rek added. "If it wasn't for Zaria's quick thinking in delivering them to the palace, who knows how many of you might have been killed?"

The effect of this news on the surrounding crowd of servants was deafening. Several screamed, and all of them began talking to each other in panicked tones.

"So his wares were stolen!" Ali said, as if that had been the most confusing part of the matter.

I was too busy looking at Rowan's leaking wound to answer. "What's been done for him?" I asked Yara. "How bad is it?"

"One of my girls has run for the apothecary," Yara said. "But his shop may already be shut."

"He needs the palace doctor," Rek said. "And quickly. He was injured in service to the kingdom, and I shall ensure he receives proper care."

"Th...Thank you, Your Highness," Yara stammered, for once overawed into near silence.

"How do we get him there?" I asked, relieved at Rek's words.

"Samuel, Benjamin." Rek signaled the two guards. "I'll mount first, and the two of you can hoist him up to me. I can keep him upright as far as the palace."

As they both pushed forward to join us, Rek looked down at Rowan. "Did you see where he went? Did anyone?"

Rowan grimaced. "I'm afraid not, Your Highness. I went down hard, and he was out the gate quick as anything."

Rek's mouth tightened for a moment, but he didn't ask further questions. The crowd had drawn back, giving us room, so he was able to remount without trouble, holding himself ready to receive Rowan.

The groom didn't complain during the process of lifting him, but from the tightening of his mouth I could tell he was in pain. I turned to Yara.

"Don't worry. I'll take good care of him."

She nodded, hand over her mouth and eyes wet.

I turned to Mariam and Ali next. "Keep that gate locked and the guards on alert." I lowered my voice. "And guard your tongues."

Neither of them protested at one of their servants giving them orders, so I started toward my own mount, only to stop and turn back.

"I assume Navid isn't here because he still hasn't returned from his day's outing? Do either of you know where he is?"

Both of them shook their heads, and for the first time it occurred to me to feel fear for my absent friend. What had happened to him?

But I couldn't stop to worry about that now. Rowan needed our urgent care, and I couldn't keep him waiting.

We rode back with no prisoner, just a gravely injured friend, and I couldn't have felt more opposite to my previous hopeful attitude. Once again, the streets stretched before us, seeming to lengthen as we traveled.

Rek had to ride carefully to keep Rowan steady and to not unsettle his horse who was high tempered and unused to carrying two. But I noticed Rowan's lips moving, despite his closed eyes, and guessed he was murmuring to the stallion.

His efforts must have worked because the horse gave him a smooth ride, following in the wake of Samuel who had shot ahead at a near gallop, riding far faster than was ideal in city streets.

But thanks to his faster pace, by the time we reached the palace, they were expecting us. Two doctors waited in the court-yard, accompanied by several servants bearing a stretcher. They carried Rowan away while I was still dismounting, but I would have caught up to them if Rek hadn't grabbed my arm.

"You stay with your friend," he said. "I know that's what you want. But I have to check in with Jerome and find out what's happening with the prisoners. I'll come and find you afterward."

I nodded and rushed off, having to run to keep the stretcher in sight. But after I'd successfully followed them through the palace, the doctor barred me at his door.

"You'll need to wait out here." He pointed at a bench on the opposite wall. "After I've treated him, I'll give you an update on his condition."

Reluctantly I nodded and took the indicated seat. I was soon on my feet again, though, pacing the corridor. I strained my mind, trying to think what I could have done differently to protect Rowan but also capture Esai. I came up with nothing.

"Zaria?" Adara's voice made me stop. She ran down the hallway and threw her arms around me. "Rek just told me…I can't believe it…You really weren't hurt?"

"Not me, but my friend." I pointed at the closed door. "Your doctor is treating him now. I don't know if he'll…"

"Oh no!" Adara's ready sympathy made her eyes well up, although she didn't know Rowan. "Father's doctors are the best in the kingdom. If anyone can help, it's them."

I smiled my thanks, grateful she hadn't given false reassurances that everything would be all right.

"Who is it?" an equally familiar voice asked, sounding strained. "Who's injured?"

I looked up, startled. I had been so pleased to see Adara, I hadn't even noticed she had a companion.

Navid hung several steps back, looking both uncomfortable and concerned. I gazed back and forth between him and Adara, my mouth dropping slightly open.

"This is where you've been all day?" I asked him, my voice growing heated as my outrage built. "Didn't you even want to check in with me before leaving again? What if something had happened to me on my way home from the ball?"

"Did something happen to you?" Navid asked, the concern on his face deepening. "I assumed you were in bed sleeping, and I was hardly going to barge in on you there."

"A great many things happened," I snapped. "And you can be grateful I did leave the ball early because one of the thieves had found our house and marked it. I had to mark all the surrounding houses to throw them off."

"That was clever." Adara sounded admiring. "I'm sure I wouldn't have thought of that."

"I hid and watched for them," I said, in no mood to acknowledge the compliment. "And I tried to follow them back to wherever they're staying in the city."

"On your own?" Navid sounded horrified.

"Of course on my own!" I put my hands on my hips. "You weren't with me, were you?" I paused before adding, "They ended up seeing me and chasing me through the city." The sourness of my tone was partly directed at him, but partly at my own failure. "I only escaped because I hid in the mill with Kali. So I came straight here to tell Rek, but they wouldn't let me through the gate or even pass on a message."

"Oh no!" Adara looked stricken. "We should have thought of that and instructed that you be given entry."

Her obvious contrition deflated my unreasonable anger, and I continued in a calmer voice.

"I went home after that, of course. I thought you might be able to get through the gates, Navid—or at least help me work out what to do—but you were gone, and no one knew where you were. Although that mystery is now solved." The sour note crept back in as my words concluded.

"I didn't—" Navid hesitated, glancing guiltily at Adara.

"It's my fault," she said hurriedly. "We got talking at the ball, and we're both convinced Azzam is behind everything. But Rek is obsessed with following the gang, so I thought…"

"She asked me to help," Navid said hurriedly. "Obviously I couldn't tell anyone back home, but you're right that I should have thought to leave you a note and a way to contact me. I didn't even think…I'm sorry."

I remembered my own befuddlement of the night before, and the last of my irritation dissipated. I highly doubted Navid's visit to the palace had been motivated by a passionate belief in Azzam's guilt, but I could hardly blame him when I had been as giddy myself with a different royal.

"You had no way of knowing what was going to happen," I said. "It's really myself I'm angry at. I just wish I'd handled the whole thing better."

"If the little bit Rek told us is true, you single-handedly captured the whole gang," Adara said. "Gift-wrapped them and delivered them to the guards! Would it have been possible to do it any better?"

"Their captain escaped," I said. "He was eating with your

parents, Navid, and he realized what had happened—or some version of it—and ran. Rowan was injured in the process. Injured because I told him to keep Esai from leaving."

"Rowan?" Navid looked toward the door, deep lines in his brow. "And my parents?"

"Everyone else is fine," I said wearily. "And they're all on alert now, of course."

I glanced up and down the corridor to check we were alone before continuing. With the gang mostly captured, much of the truth would come out, but I wasn't sure which parts still needed to be kept secret.

"I know you couldn't hear the whole conversation in the cave, but you'll remember what we talked about afterward. We're expecting the retired members of the gang to be congregating here now that their treasure will have dissolved. So even though we caught all the thieves but one, that one will likely have reinforcements soon."

Adara grimaced. "I'd forgotten about that. But even if Esai is still out there, at least the captured thieves might reveal the name of the traitor. Then Father can relax, at least. I'm sure Captain Jerome will have had a chance to—"

"They don't know it." Rek appeared from a side corridor, his face and voice weary. "They've all been offered a reprieve from execution in exchange for cooperating with us. Enough of them took the offer, and their stories are the same, so I'm confident it's true. They *have* been working with someone from Karema recently, but only Esai ever spoke to the person, and only Esai knows their name."

"So we have nothing. Rowan is injured, and we have nothing." I sagged back down onto the bench.

"Today was not nothing," Navid said. "Thirty-eight dangerous criminals are off the streets because of your work today. That has to count for something."

"It's disappointing," Rek said. "But it in no way takes away from your achievement."

The door to the doctor's rooms swung open, and I jumped back up. As soon as I saw the smile on his face, I relaxed.

"It's not as bad as I feared," he announced to the corridor at large, seeming uncertain who to address his remarks toward. "I've sewn him up, and as long as he avoids infection, he should make a full recovery."

"Thank you!" I said. "That's wonderful news."

"Yes, thank you, Doctor." Rek gave him a respectful nod which the doctor carefully returned.

"When can we see him?" I asked.

"He's sleeping now," the doctor said, "which is the best thing for him. I think visitors will have to wait for tomorrow."

I nodded, and the doctor disappeared back through the doorway.

"That's a relief, at least." I sat back down, starting to feel like a jack-in-the-box.

"We'd better get home and let them know about Rowan," Navid said. "And don't worry, I won't leave your side this time."

Rek cleared his throat. "Actually, Zaria is staying here tonight."

"I am?" I frowned at him.

"You're clearly exhausted." He looked disapproving. "The last thing you need is to be swamped with questions by a curious crowd who will likely hound you without thought for your fatigue. I'm making sure you get at least one good night's sleep. We have plenty of guest rooms."

"Did you know she spent last night being chased through the streets by those thieves?" Adara asked Rek in indignation. "And she tried to warn us, but they turned her away at the gate!"

Rek's shocked expression grew cold and angry. "They won't do that again." The threat in his voice made me shiver, although I couldn't tell if he was angry with the guards or with himself for not having foreseen the problem.

Adara saw the movement and put a warm arm around me. "Of course you're not going to sleep in a guest room," she declared. "I have a whole suite with plenty of room for you."

"An excellent idea," Rek said promptly. "You should go and organize a second bed for her." He turned to Navid. "And you should be on your way home. I'm sure everyone there is extremely concerned about Rowan's condition."

"Oh yes, of course." Navid hesitated, looking toward Adara, but after a moment he bowed and hurried off.

"You should go quickly, Adara," Rek said in a pointed tone. "Zaria is tired and needs to get to bed sooner rather than later. Make sure you organize some food, too. Who knows when she last ate?"

I wanted to protest that I had eaten, but I couldn't actually remember the last time I'd sat down to a proper meal, so I kept quiet.

"Oh!" Adara looked at her brother, her voice jumping as she added another, "Oh!"

Giving me a final squeeze, she hurried off in a different direction from Navid.

"Shouldn't I be going with her?" I asked, giving in to my more cowardly emotions.

If I could avoid being alone with Rek, I could avoid a resurgence of the complicated emotions of the ball.

"In a moment." Rek sounded implacable, holding me in place with his eyes. "But first, we need to talk."

CHAPTER 21

I gulped, but there was clearly no point arguing.

"Not in a corridor, though." He held out his hand imperiously, and I tentatively put mine into it.

His grip was strong and steady as he gently tugged me down the hall. We made several turns, but I wasn't trying to track our progress, my mind consumed with the events of the past couple hours and the looming conversation.

When he finally opened a door and ushered me inside, I looked around blankly.

"I don't recognize this room."

"That's because my parents only gave it to me as my private receiving room after I came of age." He shut the door behind us. "None of us ever came in here while you lived here."

"How long ago that seems," I said softly.

"Does it?" He strode over to a window, running a hand through his hair and looking out toward the gardens, although it was now getting dark.

"Ever since the ball I've been able to think of nothing but you," he said abruptly, rendering me silent. "And to think you were at the palace gates, trying to reach me and being turned away." He cut himself off and shook his head. "That's not what matters right now. I tried to explain things last night, but then we were interrupted, and—" He turned to face me with a wry look. "I was floundering even before Jerome arrived. I think my explanations at the ball might have made things worse."

I gave him a small smile. "Maybe."

Rek claimed he'd been thinking of me constantly since the ball whereas I had spent that time trying very hard not to think about him. But despite the intense distractions provided by the thieves, I hadn't succeeded nearly as well as I would have liked.

His eyes caught mine. "All that thinking—I've realized that I can't lose you, Zaria. Not again. And that means I need to tell you everything—from the beginning."

"Everything?" I frowned. "About the traitor and the gang? Is there more I don't know?"

"What? No, I don't mean about the thieves. I mean everything about us—about our history from my perspective."

I wanted to protest that we'd already discussed what happened after my father died and agreed it was neither of our faults. But the look of determination on his face held me silent.

"Do you remember when you arrived here?" he asked but didn't wait for me to answer. "You were five, just a few months older than the twins and a year younger than Adara. I was seven then—nearly eight—and I thought myself so grown up." He laughed.

"But even though you were younger," he continued, "I could tell from the beginning that the twins had found the perfect addition to our small group. You were so small—not to mention alone in a strange place, surrounded by new people—but you weren't afraid to dive straight into our madcap adventures. And yet, at the same time, you had enough sense to balance Adara and the twins' more outrageous moments."

"The four of you were like a whirlwind," I murmured. "You swept me up, and my feet didn't touch ground again for ten years. But you were pulling away from the rest of us toward the end."

"You remember that?" He gave a self-deprecating laugh. "Yes, if I thought myself grown up at seven, I thought myself a great deal more so at seventeen. I was close to coming of age—with all the extra freedoms and responsibilities that would bring—and I wanted to make Father proud."

"That's natural," I said, "and reasonable. We couldn't stay children forever, and you were the oldest of us."

"But then the twins turned fifteen," he said. "Do you remember the celebration for their birthdays?"

"Of course." I laughed. "It was a memorable occasion. I was terrified."

He gave me an incredulous look. "If that's true, you hid it well."

I shook my head. "It was never a good idea to let the twins scent fear."

"Still isn't," he muttered, and I laughed again.

The twins' birthday had been significant because Adara had already turned sixteen. Her entire wardrobe had changed, her outfits redone in grown up styles, and she had started being included in balls and royal events—practice for when she came of age and gained her freedom. For two years she would have one foot in the adult world and one in the world of children.

She had been looking forward to it for years, but she constantly bemoaned the age gap between us, impatient for me to turn sixteen as well. She couldn't bring me along to balls, but when the twins threw their extravagant party—one exclusively for the youthful residents of the palace, since they were yet to reach sixteen themselves—she had been struck by a determination to dress me up to match her.

All my protests were swept aside and ignored. Eventually I gave in and let her have her way, arranging my hair and loaning me some of her clothes. She was delighted with the result, and in private I admitted to being pleased with the effect myself. But when we actually arrived at the party, I was petrified.

"However I looked on the outside," I said, "I was trembling with fear inside. I thought your parents would drop in to wish their sons happy birthday, and I had convinced myself they would be shocked to see me pretending to be sixteen. I was so irrationally afraid, I thought they would instantly dismiss my father and turn us both out on the street."

"When in actual fact, Mother would have taken one look at you and known the whole thing was Adara's idea." He gave me a questioning look. "It was, wasn't it?"

I nodded. "Of course it was. It always was."

A look of arrested surprise appeared on Rek's face. "I wonder if she knew," he said softly. "Then and since. I wouldn't put it past her."

"Knew what?" I asked, confused by the turn in the conversation.

"Knew me better than I knew myself. At least back then." He took a step closer to me, his voice dropping. "Knew the effect you would have on me."

I swallowed, saying nothing.

"It was certainly a revelation to me," he said softly. "For years you had been a friend and companion—so much a part of our group that I never questioned your place at our side. But everything changed that night."

"It…it did?" My mouth had gone suddenly dry, our history new and unknown through his eyes.

"I arrived at the celebration annoyed. I didn't want to be at a party for children—convinced, at the grand age of seventeen, that I had more important activities to occupy my time. And then you arrived, looking nothing like a child. Looking…" He swallowed, stepping closer again.

Where had the distance between us gone? I could feel his breaths now and see the storm in his eyes.

"The instant I saw you, I knew," he said. "And everything changed."

"I…" I licked my lips, feeling like the floor was crumbling beneath me, and wanting to reach out and grab Rek for stability. I kept my arms at my sides. "I don't understand."

"You weren't just a childhood friend to be left behind for grown up pursuits," he said. "In that moment, I knew I loved you. I'd always loved you, of course. I'd loved you for years with the fierce loyalty of children. But after I saw you that night, I knew it was a love to last a lifetime. I knew I wanted more from you than friendship."

He gave a low laugh that was almost a groan. "Suddenly my longed-for birthday felt like a burden because it would cut me off from exactly those events and activities I thought I'd outgrown. Suddenly I wanted to be nowhere more than at that party—with you."

I tried to find words, reminding my frantically pounding heart that we were talking of the past. He was saying he had loved me then, not that he loved me now.

"I think I do remember you being around more in the days after the party," I managed. "But then my father died, so it's hard to remember those weeks. When I think back, that party stands out like a beacon—the last of the happy times."

"And the beginning of all my torment," he breathed.

"I never meant—" I started, my voice shaky, but he cut me off.

"It wasn't torment at first. At first I was…I don't know. Elated? But also terrified? Adara was already planning the celebration for your sixteenth birthday—although it was months away—and I thought I would wait until then to speak to you. I thought that would give me time to—" He grimaced. "Back then, I had the impression you favored the twins over me."

"I did," I whispered and paused. But the charged tension binding us together compelled me to keep going. "At least, I told myself I did. Because they were safer."

Something leaped into his eyes, and he took both my elbows, a spark jumping between us at the contact. When I looked up, his face was far too close to mine.

"I was focused, determined," he said, his voice husky. "Making plans. And then your father died. As soon as I heard the news, I searched for you, full of concern. But you'd disappeared. Adara told me you'd gone to family in Ardasira, and that you'd write as soon as you were settled."

His hands tightened. "I thought those first few days waiting to hear from you were agony. But a letter never came. I wasn't even eighteen yet, so running off to Ardasira to find you wasn't an option. In the end, Samuel went on my behalf. He was the one to teach me to fight, and even back then, he was loyal to me. He could find no trace of you, though. I had to accept that I could do nothing but wait."

He leaned closer still, his face only a breath away. "And when I think," he whispered, "that you were here the whole time—only a few streets away."

"I used to hide," I said, my voice shaking. "Every time I knew one of you was going to be in the city. I thought it would be too painful to see you."

He groaned. "Because you thought we'd abandoned you—just like I thought you'd abandoned us. The twins declared you dead —but I refused to consider it. Even in my anger, that was too painful to contemplate. Adara kept trying to come up with explanations and excuses—loyal to the end."

"She's a good friend," I whispered, caught up in his astonishing story.

"She thought me heartless," he said with a rough laugh, "because I said you had left us behind and were obviously never the friend we thought you were."

"It was a reasonable conclusion given what you'd been told—" I started, but he shook his head.

"Despite being the catalyst for my revelation, she didn't

understand the depths of my emotion. I tried to turn my feelings off, to tell myself you were gone from my life for good, and I should move on, but I couldn't remember a time you weren't firmly planted in my heart. In the end, I couldn't cut out the emotions, all I could do was twist them. I told myself you'd betrayed us and that I hated you for it."

He gave a ragged laugh. "I convinced myself the hate and anger hurt less than the love. At least the hate made it easier to tell myself to move on, to forget you. After three years, I even thought I'd succeeded. That was what I was trying to tell you at the ball. One glimpse of your face in that forest—more beautiful than ever—and all the emotions came rushing back. I thought I'd fought them and defeated them, but I'd merely been suppressing them."

"I remember your anger," I said softly. "I noticed it that day, and I couldn't understand it."

"My anger, yes." He laughed again. "That's what I told myself it was, anyway. I told myself it was anger that made me lie in wait for you inside the city gates. And anger that made it hard to sleep when I got back to the palace. I told myself your presence in Karema was just a further betrayal."

He breathed a soft sigh. "But I couldn't stay away. I would have been at Navid's house earlier that morning if it hadn't taken me a few hours to discover the address of Ali the woodcutter."

"You didn't seem angry that time," I said. "You were very reasonable, in fact, considering the misapprehension you started with."

"After a sleepless night, I was determined for answers." He shook his head. "And desperate to see you, even if I didn't want to admit it to myself. When I discovered the truth…"

"But you were so calm and measured," I said, disbelieving. "You stayed focused on the traitors, even when Adara wanted revenge on Azzam."

"As to that matter…" He drew a steadying breath. "I can assure you I felt far from *measured*. But even in the moment I could tell my rage over his treachery was dangerous. I pushed back against Adara because I was afraid of what I would do otherwise. It would have been so easy to use Father's search for the traitor to punish Azzam, but…"

"You did the right thing," I said firmly. "Finding the traitor is far more important than petty revenge. We need to stay focused."

"Yes, we do." He buried his nose in the top of my head and breathed deeply. "And yet, every time I see you, or smell you, or think about you…"

"Rek." I spoke his name in a last, strangled attempt to be sensible before we were both consumed.

"You're incredible, Zaria," he murmured into my hair. "It would have been so easy for you to grow bitter and jaded from your experiences. But you haven't lost any of the qualities I always loved in you. You've only grown more mature—and even more beautiful."

"But your parents," I managed. "Your position."

He pulled back, looking into my eyes, his voice and face fierce. "I lived without you for three long years. I know what that's like, and I don't want to do it again. Adara can have the throne if keeping it means giving up you."

"Rek, no!" I put my hands on his chest, gripping the front of his jacket. "You were born to rule."

He shook his head obstinately. "I refuse to be like my father, so focused on ruling, he has no room in his life for love. I'm done choosing duty, or anger, or hate. I choose love. I choose you, Zaria."

His face dipped, his lips coming to rest a hair's breadth from mine. "But what of you?" he whispered. "What do you choose?"

"You. I choose you." The words were like an exhale, a relieved sigh as I gave up the fight.

It took only the slightest tug on his jacket to bring his lips crushing down onto mine. His arms swept around me, pulling me close, and the years of sadness and grief and betrayal rolled away. He was mine, just like he'd always been mine—even if I hadn't known it.

The sound of the door being thrust abruptly open broke the reverie. I pulled away, reality rushing back in as I stared in horror at Sultana Rabia.

She stared back, her eyes wide and mouth open.

"Zaria?" Her warm voice was just as I remembered it, although it didn't usually sound so astonished. "I'd heard something from Adara about you being back—or never having left? It was a bit confused, but I didn't expect…"

She looked from me to her son, her surprise swept away by brisk action. Shutting the door firmly behind her, she crossed the room to join us.

"When Adara said you were back, I was concerned," she said matter-of-factly. "But I didn't expect matters to move so swiftly. I wasn't even sure you'd seen each other yet. The twins seemed to think you'd been at the ball, but I didn't see you, and I was assured by several people that you weren't one of Rek's dance partners."

"No." I swallowed, not quite able to meet her eyes. "We didn't dance."

She groaned. "You're the one Jerome found him in the garden with? I should have guessed, but I thought—Never mind that. The question is what are we going to do now?"

"You and Father will announce our betrothal, of course." Unlike me, Rek had no issue holding his mother's gaze.

"My dear son." She raised a hand to cup his cheek before dropping it and sighing. "If only it were that simple."

"It is that simple." He sounded implacable.

"I didn't realize you knew—" My words got tangled, and I started again. "I didn't even know myself about…" I gestured between Rek and me. "How did you?"

She laughed. "I'm a mother, Zaria. I see a lot more than my children realize. I can't tell you how it hurt to see my son in so much pain, but I did wonder if it wasn't all for the best. He was doing so much better, and I thought…" She gave me a sad smile. "Not that I blame you, of course, my dear. I always liked you, or I wouldn't have let Adara adopt you as she did. Looking back, I should have seen it coming, of course. But you couldn't have known what bad timing it was for you to reappear."

"You don't know what you're talking about, Mother." Rek hadn't softened at her speech, his voice still stern. "We owe a great deal to Zaria. She's the one who delivered the gang to us—single-handedly, I might add. I don't know anyone else who could have done it."

The sultana raised an eyebrow. "Is that why the palace is in an uproar? I was just coming to ask you about it, Rek."

"Jerome is interrogating them now," he said. "But thieves or not, it doesn't matter to me. Zaria didn't choose to reappear—she never left at all. We were deceived, and I need to talk to Father about it at the first opportunity."

"Yes, your father." She gave us both an apologetic smile. "He is the issue, of course. I would happily see you take my place one day, Zaria, but the sultan has other ideas."

"Of course he does." I tried to keep any hint of tears from my voice. "Rek will be sultan one day."

"There might have been some hope for you if it wasn't for these new kingdoms," she said. "He's determined Rek will make a marriage of alliance with someone from the Four Kingdoms, just like Prince Zain did. He thinks it's the only way to regain the ground we've already lost to Ardasira. The attack on the Lanoverian delegation only made him more determined. I don't see how you're going to sway him."

The sound of the door opening again made all three of us look up guiltily. To my horror, it was Sultan Khalil who stopped in the entranceway.

I bowed deeply as he began talking, not seeming to have noticed me.

"Ah, here you are, my dear. Someone said you'd gone to see Rek, so I came looking for you. Jerome has—"

"Father." Rek cut him off. "It's thanks to Zaria that we arrested those thieves, and I want your approval for our betrothal."

The sultan took a sharp step inside and shut the door behind him.

"Betrothal?" He looked from his son to me, his forehead creasing. "What are you talking about, boy? Who is..." He frowned at me. "Zaria? Wasn't that Zahir's daughter? The girl who ran off?"

"She didn't run off, Father. She was betrayed. But I've found her again, and I intend to marry her."

"Marry her? Nonsense! You'll do no such thing. I have other plans for you."

"Yes," the sultana intervened. "I've just been telling Rek about—"

"He'll do as his father and sultan commands!"

"I will give up the throne before I give up Zaria," Rek said, calm in the face of his father's anger. "I mean it, Father."

"Give up the throne?" The king's whole body seemed to swell with rage. "I won't allow it!"

"How will you stop me? Do you intend to keep me in chains? Zaria and I are both of age, and I will flee across the desert with her, if I have to." His voice softened. "But I would much rather gain your approval, Father—however begrudging. I'm sure that, in time, you'll see how good Zaria is for me."

"You're the crown prince, Tarek." His father glared at him, never looking my way. "You have to think of your kingdom, not just your own wishes."

"I am." Rek didn't back down. "You've heard what they're saying in Ardasira. The Four Kingdoms have been following the ways of the wise women, and that's why they're so prosperous. They rule through love. Zain told me all their princes and princesses are allowed to marry for love—especially the ones who will one day rule."

"Of course I want you to marry for love," his father said gruffly. "And I have no doubt you will. I'm not demanding you marry any one specific person. None of the Four Kingdoms even have any princesses of the right age. You can choose who you like —just choose someone from over the desert. That's all I'm asking. I know you think you're in love now, but you're young. You'll recover and find love again." He still wasn't looking at me.

"This isn't some whim of the moment, Father." Rek glared at him. "I didn't meet Zaria yesterday. I've known her since I was seven years old. I'm not going to change my mind. Sultan Kalmir let Zain marry the girl he loved. You should allow me to do the same."

I expected a vehement denial, but instead a calculating look came into the sultan's eye, and he actually smiled.

"If you want me to use Prince Zain's example as my model, then fine. You may choose your own bride—as long as she comes with a dowry equal to the one provided by Cassandra of Eldon."

"Khalil!" Rabia glared at him. "That dowry didn't come from Eldon, but from a magical treasure cave within Ardasira itself. You cannot possibly expect any bride of Rek's to match it."

"Tarek is the one who claimed he wished for the same freedom as Zain," the sultan said in a calm, satisfied tone. "I am merely acceding to his request. But I am not an unreasonable man. Cassandra brought a second, less formal dowry with her—a connection with the Four Kingdoms that has already led to a lucrative trade treaty for Ardasira. In lieu of a treasure trove, I would accept a trade treaty as dowry with equal willingness."

"Khalil." Rabia's tone of voice suggested she was unimpressed with his explanation.

When the sultan remained silent, she turned to Rek and me with a sigh.

"I think it would be best if we all took some time," she said. "There is no need for rash actions on either side."

"Certainly not, Your Majesty," I said, speaking for the first time since the sultan had entered. "I have no desire to drive a wedge between Rek and any of his family."

The sultan finally looked at me for the first time since his brief initial scrutiny.

"Well said," he announced. "You're a sensible girl, at least, and I'm sure I wish things could be different. But I must think of my kingdom."

Rek was looking at his mother rather than his father when he replied. "I don't intend to run off to the desert tonight, if that's what you're afraid of. There are matters underfoot here that are more important than my personal concerns—for now. But I won't be patient forever, and I won't give up Zaria."

His mother nodded, seeming relieved to have been granted a reprieve at least.

She smiled at me kindly. "Do you need an escort back to your home, Zaria? I understand it to be in the city somewhere? The moon is still slim, and the streets will be dark at this hour."

"She's spending the night with Adara," Rek said in a tone that indicated the matter wasn't open to discussion.

I bowed to the sultana. "Thank you for the offer, Your Majesty."

Rek put a hand on the small of my back, gently propelling me toward the door. I paused to bow again, this time toward the sultan, before letting him push me out of the room.

It was Rek's receiving room, but he shut the door firmly on

his parents, leaving them inside. I winced, glad not to be present to hear the conversation that must be beginning in the room.

Instead I turned toward Adara's room, the layout of the palace coming back to me more easily than I expected. Rek kept pace beside me, silent at first. After a couple of corridors, he finally spoke.

"I meant everything I said. I knew my Father wouldn't approve, and it changes nothing about my feelings."

"Rek, I can't let you give up not only the throne but your family and your home. We can't run away to the Four Kingdoms."

"It might not have to come to that," he said thoughtfully. "We do, after all, know where to find a dowry equal to the one given to Prince Zain."

I stopped and grabbed his arm, lowering my voice. "Rek, that's an impossible dream! Or are you forgetting that we were relying on *your father* to find a way to break the enchantment? He's not going to consider it a dowry from me when I can't take any of it out of the cave."

"So we find a way to break the enchantment ourselves," Rek said stubbornly. "You found the cave, and if you find a way to access the treasure, he can't possibly deny your right to marry me. Mother heard his promise, and she won't let him go back on it."

"Oh, you have some brilliant ideas on breaking the enchantment then, do you?" I rolled my eyes and started down the corridor again. "It's not as if we have a great deal of time, either. Now that your captain is interrogating the thieves, one of them is sure to mention the cave—if not all of them. It isn't our secret anymore."

"No." Rek looked regretful. "I've already sent two full squads to lie in wait near its entrance. If any of the retired thieves do come, that's the most obvious place for them to go. If we're lucky, they might even manage to capture Esai."

I sighed. "At this point that doesn't seem likely. He's managed to evade the most obvious traps so far."

We reached Adara's rooms. I turned at her door and looked up at him, unsure what to say or do after everything that had just passed between us.

He cast a quick glance up and down the corridor, and when he saw we were alone, pulled me into his arms and pressed his lips against mine. Once again the rest of the world melted away, and no problem seemed insurmountable as long as his arms stayed around me.

A muffled shriek broke the moment. We pulled apart to find Adara standing in her doorway looking utterly delighted.

"I knew it!" she cried and pulled me into a hug.

"I'll, uh, leave this to you." Rek made an almost comically fast escape, leaving Adara free to pull me through her enormous sitting room and into her almost as enormous bedchamber.

"I knew it! I knew it!" she said again.

I fought the flush rising up my cheeks. "Rek wondered if you might have. Even back before…"

"Don't tell me he kissed you back then and you never told me!" Her look of horror made me giggle.

"No, of course not! We were practically children back then."

She waved a dismissive hand. "Hardly. I could tell exactly how you felt back then. You giggled more around the twins, but you saved the heartfelt glances for Rek." She assumed a pained look that was presumably supposed to be an imitation of my fifteen-year-old self.

I dropped onto the daybed that someone had set up for me to sleep on and buried my head in one of the soft pillows.

"I didn't even know it myself back then," I said in a muffled voice. "Or if I did, it was only in some very deep, dark corner of my heart."

"You can fool yourself, but you can't fool your best friend," she said with satisfaction. "And Rek was even more obvious. He always favored you."

I sat up. "That's just because he thought I was more sensible than the rest of you."

"Exactly! Rek likes sensible. And, of course, you're gorgeous. So the rest was inevitable." She sighed with happiness. "And now we get to be sisters."

"Not if your father has anything to say about it." I grimaced, filling her in on the scene with her parents.

"Mother, too?" she asked, horrified. "I thought she, at least, would fight for true love."

"I think she wants to, but she knows how much the sultan has his heart set on an alliance with the Four Kingdoms."

She slowly sat down beside me, all her enthusiasm leaching away. "Four kingdoms, and he has four children. Why limit himself to one marriage of alliance? Sultan Kalmir only has the one son, so here's an opportunity for Father to far outstrip him."

She looked devastated, but I was afraid to ask why the thought upset her so much. After finding Navid at the palace, I didn't want to know the answer. If she was already thinking that warmly of him, I didn't know what I could possibly say that would be encouraging. He was unlikely to be any more of a welcome prospect to the sultan than I was.

But despite the sultan's opposition, and the impediments in front of us, that night I dreamed happy dreams of Rek's arms around me and his lips on mine. Whatever happened, I would always have that moment and the knowledge he truly loved me. Every day that I had endured Nyla's blistering tongue—all to keep some tie with my old life—had been worth it. For one night, at least, I wouldn't think of the future, I would just live in the moment.

CHAPTER 23

*A*dara would have kept me at the palace all day, but I knew Rek would be busy with the captured thieves, and I didn't want to risk running into the sultan or sultana again. Besides, after a brief visit with Rowan—who seemed to be doing remarkably well—I was eager to see my friends and reassure them of his progress.

I found the house returned to its usual state of calm, although when I entered the kitchen, Yara seemed even more volatile than usual, bouncing around as she shouted instructions at her various minions. As soon as she saw me, she stopped dead still.

"You've come from the palace?" she asked. "How is he?"

"Looking very well." I gave her a big smile. "And the report from the doctor was equally encouraging. He'll be back here in no time."

"Oh, thank goodness. When Navid said…I wasn't sure if he was just pacifying an old woman."

"You are not an old woman!" I said sternly. "And Navid wouldn't lie to you. The doctor really did seem pleased last night."

Yara sat in silence for a full minute before standing and beaming around the kitchen at large. "We'll make pudding for dessert, I think. Enough for everyone in the household."

A cheer went up from the servants, and I suspected it was as much for the return of Yara's good humor as the promised treat. I was about to pass through the kitchen toward my room when Yara stopped me.

"In all the chaos, I nearly forgot. Something came for you yesterday while you were out. Nothing like one invite to beget another, I suppose." She waggled her eyebrows at me.

"An invite?" I stared at her blankly before realizing the obvious. "From Yasmine?"

"You already knew about it?" Yara sounded disappointed.

"I met her at the ball. She mentioned sending me one, but I wasn't sure if she'd actually remember."

"Navid has the invitation," Yara said. "He got one, too."

"I suppose she couldn't just invite me." I sighed, not at all in the mood for a party. "Thank you for telling me. I'll go find him."

I found him in one of the front sitting rooms, thankfully alone. There was a surprising amount to catch him up on, given the short number of hours we'd been apart.

He didn't seem surprised at the revelation about Rek and me. Apparently I was the only one who hadn't seen it coming—a willful act of self-denial it seemed. He did appear downhearted at the sultan's response, however, and I once again took the cowardly path of not inquiring any closer.

"And now we have these." He pointed at two gilt-edged pieces of card on a nearby table. "I suppose we have to go."

"Do we?" I sighed, but I already knew he was right. "Of course we do. With Esai still on the loose we need information, and it's just the sort of place where information of a shady nature might be found."

"It's not all bad," Navid said with an attempt at a smile. "She does serve excellent food."

"Surprising." I picked up one of the cards and scanned it. "Given she's so cheap to her servants, I wouldn't have expected anything expensive."

"Oh, she doesn't like to waste money on her social inferiors," Navid said, a sneer in his voice. "But she wants her parties to be the talk of the city."

"Well, she's succeeded in that."

"Mother's already given me permission to escort you to the party," Navid said. "She even said she left something in your room for you to wear."

I raised my eyebrows. Allowing us to go to the palace made sense, but this seemed excessive.

"It's tomorrow night, so we should take our last chance to celebrate anyway," Navid said gloomily.

I shot him an inquiring look.

"My delightful aunt gets out of her mourning isolation the day after tomorrow," he reminded me. "And I'm sure you can imagine what a ray of sunshine she'll bring to the house."

"Oh gracious!" I shuddered.

Mariam's generosity made more sense now. She wanted me firmly on their side when Nyla reappeared.

The outfit she had provided was a simpler one than the gown I'd worn to the ball, the chemise and robe more suitable for an informal party. Kali had sent the golden dress back to me, wrapped in plain cotton, but I stashed the package away beneath my bed next to my small pouch of gold. I wasn't ready to relive any part of that night.

On the day of the party, I received a short note from Rek, but, as I had expected, he was being kept busy at the palace with the thirty-eight new prisoners. I suspected his father had something to do with keeping his son so busy, but I wasn't worried. Rek and I had survived three years apart. We could survive a few days.

That didn't stop me from missing him, though, especially when I left for Yasmine's party with Navid at my side. While I liked my friend's company, I couldn't help wishing for a different escort.

Yasmine's large home was only a short distance from ours, so we walked, accompanied by three guards and a servant carrying a large lantern.

"Excessive?" I asked, watching the servant leading the way.

Navid chuckled. "Just a little. My mother doesn't usually have my aunt's desire for grandeur, but Yasmine seems to have an effect on everybody."

As we neared the wall surrounding Yasmine's enormous mansion, we met a trickle of other people heading in the same direction. I only vaguely recognized some of them—faces I'd seen in the market—but most of them seemed to know each other, calling friendly greetings as they converged on the gate.

I kept my face neutral, although inside I was already regretting the necessity of coming. We were going to be out of place in this gathering.

When the gates were swung wide to grant us entry into the courtyard, my initial impression was confirmed. The party was in full swing, the darkness of the night broken by picturesque torches that burned on long poles scattered throughout the grounds. Between the torches, people called to each other in over-loud voices, drink passing freely among them.

Navid grimaced. "I'd forgotten just how…excessive it is."

"That's one word for it," I muttered as I watched a man who was already staggering take another long gulp from the glass in his hand.

"It might be a good idea if we stay close together." Navid eyed the same man before glancing at a man and woman who stood to one side of the courtyard, their foreheads touching and their arms entwined around each other. They appeared to have lost track of their surroundings, murmuring to each other too quietly to be heard.

"Agreed," I said promptly. "And if we're going to stay here, I need to fortify myself with some of that excellent food you promised."

Our guards and lantern bearer left us at the gate, so it was just the two of us winding our way between the clumps of people. A few called cheerful greetings to Navid, but he kept his replies light, refusing to be drawn into conversation.

Just inside the door of the house we were greeted by Yasmine. I blinked at the sight of her, struggling to keep my face impassive. Her dress at the ball had been daring, but this one was suggestive in a whole different way.

"Navid! Zaria! How lovely to see you both."

We exchanged the necessary phrases of greeting and thanks, extracting ourselves as quickly as possible with the excuse of food. She didn't seem to take any offense, her eyes already traveling to the next arrival as she directed us where we might find the refreshments table.

It was set up in a long room that contained several clumps of chairs scattered throughout. Given the serious conversations going on at three of them, the room seemed a quiet haven from the courtyard.

We both loaded up a plate, finding a place on the edge of the room where a small, raised table gave us somewhere to put our burden while we remained standing with the room in view.

I was only halfway through the admittedly excellent food when Navid stiffened.

"Did you see something?" I asked, looking around the room.

He pointed out to the corridor. "Someone I know from my apprentice days. I didn't expect to see him here, but he's just the sort of person we need. He always knows all the city gossip." He hesitated and glanced at me with a creased brow.

"But he's not likely to open up if I'm with you," I supplied since he seemed reluctant to say it. "You should go on your own. I know we said we'd stay together, but this room seems quiet enough. I'll stay right here and finish eating, and you can come back as soon as you've finished talking to your friend."

When Navid still hesitated, I gave him a small push. "Go! Before you lose track of him."

Reluctantly, Navid hurried away, and I selected a small cake from my plate. My most likely woe in his absence was going to be boredom if he took too long.

Moments later I changed my mind. A group of young men, already singing a bawdy song and leaning heavily on each other, came in, searching for further drinks.

One of them looked my way, and I immediately abandoned my plate and remaining food and made a dignified rush for the door. Navid had only been gone moments, so I should be able to catch up to him easily enough. Better to interrupt his conversation than to end up in some sort of drunken confrontation.

Navid had turned left, so I did the same, but I made it all the way to the end of the corridor without seeing any sign of him. I was standing, debating whether to turn left or right or to risk returning to the refreshment room, when I heard the soft murmur of a voice from inside the room nearest me.

The door was ajar, and I breathed a sigh of relief as I realized the answer to the mystery of Navid's speedy disappearance. Perhaps I could slip inside without his friend noticing and avoid disrupting their conversation.

I eased the door open and peered into the room. It was smaller than I was expecting and completely dark except for the meager shaft of moonlight coming through a large window. Two people stood in front of the window, but they were definitely not Navid and his apprentice friend.

The man had his back to me, but the person wrapped in his embrace, her face pressed to his, was clearly a woman.

As I stood immobile, too frozen with shock to make a hasty exit, a cloud moved, increasing the moonlight. Both of their faces were obscured, but the extra light revealed the deep blue color of the woman's gown. Recognizing my hostess's dress, I took two large steps backward and pulled the door to its original, mostly closed, position as soundlessly as possible.

Silence from inside the room suggested I'd succeeded in my escape. Turning back the way I'd come, I fled the entire length of the corridor. Back at the door of the refreshment room, I nearly ran into Navid.

He took one look at my face and frowned.

"Are you all right? Where have you been?"

I gestured into the room where the rowdy group had started annoying a collection of older men engaged in a serious debate around one of the tables.

"I went looking for you."

He winced. "I shouldn't have left. I'd just promised we would stay together, and then the first thing I did was run off alone."

"Did you learn anything interesting, at least?"

"Nothing of relevance." He sounded depressed. "I couldn't distract him from the latest tale among merchant circles, so I escaped the conversation to return to you."

He glanced into the room again, and I could read on his face that he wanted to leave the party as much as I did.

"Zaria!"

I turned, wondering who in this crowd was likely to know me.

"Xavier?" I stared from him to his brother. "Xander! So you did manage to secure an invitation!"

"You know us," Xander said. "Parties call to us."

I gave them both a disapproving look. "Now that I've seen the party for myself, I'm surprised Yasmine risked inviting you."

Xavier winked at me. "Being of age does allow us *some* freedoms."

"Oh, really?" I raised an eyebrow. "And what would your

father say if he knew you were here?" I gave a significant look into the refreshment room.

Both of them peered inside and gave matching laughs.

"Thankfully our father doesn't concern himself with where we are every minute of the day and night," Xavier said.

"One of the many benefits of having a responsible older brother," Xander added.

"And is that older brother as unaware of your movements as your father?" I asked before giving a theatrical start and staring down the hallway behind them. "Because that looks like Rek now, just over—"

"What?" Xavier swung around to stare behind him, his tone alarmed.

"Rek, here?" Xander peered in the same direction, his brow creasing before he slowly turned back to me, his eyes narrowing.

I gave him a beaming smile while Navid snorted a suppressed laugh beside me. "Sorry, I was mistaken. It wasn't him after all."

"You haven't changed a bit." Xavier sounded accusing. "Are you trying to get your revenge by giving us heart attacks?"

I maintained my innocent expression. As children, Adara and I had been involved in a long-standing game between the two of us and the twins, each pair attempting to turn Rek's ire against the others. The four of us had always presented a united front to the adults, but Rek had been different.

"I don't know what you're talking about," I said. "It was a simple mistake. A man walked past who looked very like him."

"What—judgmental, uptight, and boring?" Xavier muttered, and Navid snorted again.

I glared at them both, trying to think of a fitting defense for Rek that wouldn't give my feelings away to the twins. But Xavier's next words reminded me they had always been more perceptive than their careless manner suggested.

"Navid!" Xavier slung an arm around my friend's shoulder, fixing him with a wounded look. "The real question is what *you're* doing here with Zaria! I'm not sure which of my siblings I should be offended on behalf of."

"Xavier!" I cried before frowning. His words had revealed more than his knowledge of an attachment between Rek and me. "Wait, you all know each other?" I looked between the twins and Navid.

"Know each other?" Xander slung an arm over Navid's shoulders from the other side. "Why Navid here is practically a brother! We certainly trip over him every time we turn around."

Both of my eyebrows slowly rose as I remembered how little I'd seen of Navid at home other than our one morning conversation.

"Just how many days have you been at the palace?" I hissed at him.

He glanced from the twins to me, a slightly frantic look in his eyes.

"We've been investigating Azzam, remember?" His expression turned sheepish. "That's actually why I came tonight."

I stared at him. "You came because of Azzam?"

"When Adara heard I'd been invited, she told me I had to come. We saw Azzam and Yasmine talking at the ball. It was a brief exchange, but it gave Adara the idea he might have received an invitation. She thinks it's just the sort of place Azzam would be found, making questionable deals and amassing contacts."

Xander laughed loudly. "That's our dear sister's best effort at investigating? We've already done a tour of the festivities, and I can promise you there's no one here from the palace except us. Although I'm surprised Adara didn't come herself."

I caught the guilty shift in Navid's eyes. "She would have liked to, it's true, but she didn't have an invitation."

Both twins drew back, giving him mock salutes.

"Very nicely played," Xavier said. "I never would have believed someone could prove such a good influence on our beloved sister in such a short time."

"This would most definitely not be her scene." Xander cast an amused glance at someone who appeared to be sleeping off their drunkenness on the stairway.

"You didn't hear about the party from her, did you?" Navid asked, sounding horrified at the idea that he might have been indirectly responsible for the princes' presence.

"No, no, we heard about it from our newest friends." Xavier pointed through the door at two men standing beside the refreshment table and watching the two clashing groups in the room with amusement on their faces.

My hand flashed to Navid's arm, squeezing hard. He looked down into my face and then back at the men, frowning.

A moment later his eyes widened, and he looked back at me. I nodded slowly.

"And how did you meet these new friends, exactly?" Navid asked, his voice sounding strange.

"Careful," Xavier said with a grin. "If you become too much like Rek, we might have to withdraw our blessing on your suit."

"We met them out and about," Xander said vaguely. "They're merchants, and a good laugh, for all they're a bit rough around the edges."

"Xander. Xavier." I looked from one to the other. "Is there any chance I could convince you to just go home?"

"None at all," Xavier said promptly.

I sighed. I had to be careful what I said. If the twins caught any hint of the truth, they would insert themselves into the situation with gusto.

"I don't think those men are safe," I said. "Could you at least keep your distance from them for the rest of the night?"

The two exchanged lightning fast looks before Xavier gave me an elaborate bow.

"For our dearest childhood friend—"

"—and the woman who holds our brother's heart—"

"—we will do our best in all things," Xavier finished.

I sighed. It was the closest to an agreement I was going to get.

Something over my shoulder caught Xander's attention, and the two disappeared as quickly as they'd materialized in the first place.

"We have to warn them that their supposed new friend is Esai!" Navid whispered urgently. "They could be in danger."

CHAPTER 24

"They'll definitely be in danger if we tell them anything of the sort," I said grimly. "They'll insist on trying to arrest him on the spot, and they definitely wouldn't do anything sensible like wait for guards to arrive first. Esai has someone with him, so it would be two against two, and..." I shook my head. "We can't risk it. We'll just have to keep Esai in sight the whole time. Maybe we can finally work out where he's hiding in the city."

"Who is that with him?" Navid asked. "I don't recognize him from the cave, but I didn't get a good look at all the thieves."

"He wasn't there, I'm sure of it." I examined the man as best I could without approaching closer. "He's older than any of the current members of the gang. But his face is extremely familiar. I must have seen him somewhere before, if I could only remember where." I didn't usually have trouble when it came to faces.

After I'd studied him for another moment, Esai turned to say something to his companion, and I realized why the older man looked familiar.

"Actually, I don't think I've ever seen that man before," I said. "That explains why I couldn't place him at first. It's the family resemblance that makes him look so familiar. He must be Esai's father."

"The one even Esai's own men are afraid of?" Navid asked, and I nodded.

He immediately whisked me to the far side of the corridor, placing my back against the wall. Bracing his arm above my head, he loomed over me with an affectionate smile.

I stared up at him in shock, and he chuckled.

"At least try to look like you're enjoying my close proximity," he whispered.

I dutifully pasted a smile on my face, looking up at him before glancing back into the refreshment room.

"I suppose we need some excuse for loitering," I said reluctantly.

He chuckled. "For all your cleverness, I can't see you with a career as an intelligencer ahead of you. You need to embrace the acting a little more wholeheartedly."

I gave him an apologetic smile and added a giggle on the end.

"Better," he said, approvingly, and the giggle turned real.

"They're leaving," I said suddenly, having thrown another glance into the refreshment room.

"Stay calm," he said. "Keep up the act as they come by, and we'll follow them as soon as they're out of sight."

I checked over his shoulder again, but my vision was blocked by a tall figure standing in the center of the corridor and staring at us. My heart seized, and for a second, shock robbed me of breath.

But the hard line of Rek's jaw, and the way the pulse jumped in his neck, sent feeling rushing back through me. I pushed Navid away, sending him staggering as I rushed to Rek's side.

"Rek! What are you doing here? I didn't know you were invited!"

"I wasn't." His eyes didn't leave Navid, who had recovered his balance and turned to stare at us. "But apparently it's a good thing I decided to come anyway."

He took a stride forward, and I jumped after him, grabbing at his arm. For an unthinking moment, I thought he meant to throttle poor Navid, but he was in complete control of himself as he grabbed Navid's arm.

"When Adara confessed she'd sent you here, I thought it worth coming as back up." His voice dipped lower, the words almost a growl. "What I did not expect was to find you'd been foolish enough to bring Zaria with you. My beloved sister left that part out."

Navid gulped, his wince showing he concurred enough with Rek's sentiment to come up short of excuses.

"It wasn't what it looked like," I said hurriedly. "We weren't actually…"

Rek finally let Navid go, his face softening as he turned to me.

"Of course it wasn't what it looked like." He actually sounded amused. "Are you forgetting how well I know you? I shudder to think what mischief you were so busily trying to conceal with that little act."

I gasped, Rek's arrival having completely driven Esai from my mind.

"Esai!" I hissed, leaning around Rek to peer into the refreshment room. "He's here!"

"Esai? At this party?" Rek's body stiffened, his muscles tense and alert as he smoothly turned, careful not to draw attention with sudden movement.

"I don't think he came past us into the corridor," I said, unable to see either man in the room. "They must have gone directly into the gardens through that side door."

Rek took a step in the direction of the room before stopping and looking back with a frown.

"They?"

"He's with an older man," Navid said. "Zaria thinks he's Esai's father."

Rek gave a long, low whistle. "The original gang leader himself. We've heard plenty of rumors but never been able to confirm his identity. This is pretty brazen, though."

"Come on!" I brushed past him. "We've already lost them. We need to hurry."

I peered through the glass door for a moment before concluding our quarry had already moved on and thrusting it open. Rek was only a step behind as I crossed onto the gravel path on the other side.

Navid followed us, and we all faced in different directions, scanning our surroundings for signs of movement or anyone out of place.

But when I glanced back into the refreshment room, two different people caught my eye. With a sigh, I slipped back inside, away from my companions.

"You two really need to get out of here," I said to the twins in a low voice. "If Rek sees you—"

"Ah, don't think we'll fall for that again." Xavier slung his arm around my shoulders with a grin.

"Fall for what exactly?" asked a deadly voice from behind us.

Xander choked on his drink as we all spun around to face Rek.

"Rek!" Xavier's voice was admirably bright despite the sudden tightness of his arm across my shoulders. "Where did you spring from?"

Rek's icy gaze fastened on his brother's arm, and Xavier quickly let it drop, taking a step back and holding both hands in the air.

"No harm meant, best of brothers."

Xander sent him a wounded look before eyeing Rek.

"I'll warrant Yasmine never gave you an invite."

Rek looked him up and down before raising an eyebrow. "Did you think that would stop me? I'm the crown prince, remember?"

"How could we possibly forget?" Xavier muttered.

"I think it's time the two of you went home," Rek said in forbidding tones. "You have no idea what you've interrupted here. We don't have time to deal with you right now."

Xander looked from Rek, who now hovered protectively at my shoulder, to Navid who was standing in the doorway, his attention divided between the tense scene inside and the occasional passing partygoer outside. Both Xander's brows slowly rose.

"I assure you I couldn't possibly imagine. But it looks a great deal more exciting than anything going on at home."

Rek drew a steadying breath before closing the distance between us, his chest colliding with my back. As his arms wound around my waist, he rested his chin on the top of my head.

"I can assure you, you're entirely out of place and unwanted here," he drawled. "Father, on the other hand, might be looking for you even now. Perhaps someone might tell him where you are." The unspoken threat was clear, despite the change in his tone.

I froze, not daring to move as the twins exchanged startled glances, their eyes lingering on the way Rek held me.

After a charged moment, Xander cleared his throat. "Naturally we wouldn't dream of intruding on your evening." He looked at me, a wicked twinkle in his eyes. "Do enjoy yourself, Zaria."

A flush rose up my cheeks, but I still didn't move. Only when the twins had left the room, appearing to move toward the front of the house and the exit beyond, did I relax, slumping slightly.

Rek immediately let me go, stepping back. I slowly spun to find him rubbing the back of his neck with a guilty expression.

"Sorry about that. But we needed them gone, and fast. The

last thing we need is the twins getting involved in whatever's going on here."

"No, of course not." I breathed a sigh of relief when my voice didn't come out as shaky as my insides felt.

"If you two lovebirds are finished," Navid said in an amused tone, "we need to get moving."

Rek was at his side instantly. "You found them?"

Navid nodded. "They went there." He pointed across a shadowy lawn to a mass of dark garden beyond. "I only just caught sight of them as they disappeared."

"Come on, then!" I stepped away from the circle of light that radiated from the house, hurrying across the grass in the direction Navid had indicated.

The two men had seemed confident inside the house, clearly comfortable in their location. And now they were moving through the dark as if familiar with the grounds as well. Was this their first party, or had they been hiding here under our noses the whole time?

I slowed down as I reached the edge of the lawn, moving as quietly as I could as I stepped along the stone path on the other side. Palm trees lined the walkway, their fronds hanging over to create a low arch for us to creep through.

The light was too low to show the riotous colors of the hibiscus, but I could smell the scent of frangipani on the breeze, a heady fragrance for a night of misdoings. What were Esai and his father doing out here?

We reached a corner, and Rek's hand grabbed my arm, pulling me back before I could leave the cover of the row of palms. Tugging me toward their trunks, he drew me close, a hand on each arm. When he leaned down, his lips brushed against my ear, sending a shiver through me.

"I think I hear them." His words were a mere breath, and I struggled to focus on their meaning as my pulse leaped and raced. This wasn't the first time I had stood close to Rek in a garden at night, but this time was different.

When I looked up at him, catching a gleam of moonlight reflected from his eyes, his arms tightened around me, drawing me even closer. His breath hitched, becoming as ragged as mine, both of us frozen, unmoving in the darkness.

Slowly, too slowly, his head bent toward mine. But just as his lips made contact, a quiet scuffing on the ground to one side made him pull back.

With a single shake of his head, as if to clear it, he took a step back. I glanced across at Navid, mortified despite his pointed focus on the darkness beyond the palms. Both hands flew to my cheeks. How could I lose track of our surroundings like that?

"Can you hear anything?" Rek whispered.

Navid hesitated before replying equally quietly. "They're definitely just around the corner, but I can't make out any words."

We all waited, straining in the darkness, but the murmured conversation remained indistinguishable. I bit my lip. I had nearly lost my head and missed our unexpected opportunity, but I wasn't going to let it slip away.

I stepped quietly forward, and Rek caught at my arm. But I shook him off, creeping slowly toward the bend of the path. When I reached the corner, I carefully peeked around, trusting in the darkness to keep me hidden.

The two men came into view, standing beside a small fountain with the outside wall of the property visible just behind them. But a third man had also joined them.

He stood with his back to me, so I couldn't see his face. His stance seemed tense, though, although I couldn't tell if he was nervous or angry.

I examined the nearby foliage. Would it be possible to get closer without being seen? I desperately wanted to hear what they were talking about and get a glimpse of the new arrival's face.

Before I could decide on a path, however, their manner changed. Seeming to conclude their conversation, they all hurried toward the wall.

As I watched, one of them produced a key and opened a door I hadn't even noticed. Ushering the others through, he closed it behind them, leaving us alone in the garden.

I took off running, and Rek was instantly beside me.

"They went through that door," I panted.

As soon as we reached it, Rek attempted to wrench it open, but it had already been locked again from the outside. All I could hear was the faint sound of disappearing footsteps.

Navid joined us, looking disappointed. "We lost them."

A slow smile spread over my face. "But not for long, I'm betting."

Rek regarded me with a raised eyebrow. "You're thinking that if they have a key for this gate, they must be connected to Yasmine more closely than as mere guests at her party?"

"They're definitely connected with her," I said. "I couldn't get a clear look at that third man, but I recognized his clothes. I accidentally stumbled on him earlier in an…err…intimate embrace with Yasmine."

"You what?" he yelped.

I flushed. "Navid and I were briefly separated, and I was looking for him."

Rek turned toward Navid, his jaw clenching, but I grabbed his arm.

"Leave poor Navid alone. It wasn't his fault. I told him to go and follow a possible lead. I was fine. They didn't see me, and I left immediately. The whole thing seemed very secretive, and I think we just found out why."

"Yasmine in league with the gang of thieves." Navid shook his head. "I never would have guessed it."

"Maybe she wasn't so very shrewd with her business dealings, after all." I looked back toward the house. "Maybe her wealth came from somewhere else."

"We need to send for Captain Jerome," Rek said. "I'll have her arrested immediately."

I shook my head urgently. Something was growing in my mind, emerging from my earlier confusion, but it needed a moment to come to full flower. I held my hand up, and he waited in patient silence.

"That is the last thing we should do," I said at last.

Both of them gave me a skeptical look, so I continued.

"Word of Yasmine's arrest would be all over the city by dawn. Esai and his father would disappear, and we'd be right back where we started—constantly looking over our shoulders."

Rek frowned. "My father is involved now. I can't keep the situation from him this time."

"No, of course not. But we don't want to have Yasmine arrested. We now know she's connected to the thieves, but she doesn't have access to palace secrets. Finding Esai here still doesn't tell us the identity of the traitor. It does give us an opportunity, though. All we need is a day."

"You want to trick her into giving us information." Rek's eyes narrowed. "I don't like the idea of you getting involved in this."

"Actually it's not me we need, it's Navid."

"Me?" Navid stared at me. "What can I do?"

"Tomorrow Nyla comes out of her mourning isolation," I said. "We'll tell your parents to hold a dinner in her honor. We'll have them send an invitation to Yasmine."

Navid's brow creased. "You think you can somehow trick Esai's location out of her over dinner?"

A smile spread over my face. "I'm hoping for better than that. After Esai's failed first attempt, our household is on alert, the gate barred and guarded. So we know Esai and his father will be looking for an opportunity to get inside undetected. And as a widow, Yasmine will be entitled to bring a guest with her to the dinner. I'm hoping that will be too appealing an opportunity for Esai to pass up."

"Surely he wouldn't have the effrontery to stroll in as an invited guest after what he did last time!" Navid cried.

"I believe he would. And I hope he will. We'll invite you, too, of course, Rek. And you should bring Captain Jerome, along with Samuel and Benjamin. The three of them, plus our household guards, should be enough to subdue Esai. But first we pretend to be oblivious and get any information out of them we can. After that, we arrest them both."

"My parents might be a little surprised to discover their social standing has gone up enough to host intimate royal dinners," Navid said wryly.

I grinned. "Never mind that. Rek isn't going to turn down the invitation, are you?"

I shot him an impudent grin, and he shook his head, his lips quirking up in a wry smile.

"I can't deny they'll be delighted enough not to cause any problems," Navid said.

"But are you sure Yasmine will come?" Rek asked. "She won't guess something's wrong?"

I shook my head. "You don't know Yasmine. She would never miss an opportunity to gloat over Nyla. She'll come."

I was proved correct when Yasmine's acceptance came the next morning, only an hour after our messenger delivered the invitation.

I wanted to be the one to take Rek's formal invitation to the palace, but I didn't dare show my face there. If the sultan saw me, he might invent some further reason to keep Rek stuck with him, and we couldn't risk anything going wrong for the dinner.

To his credit, Navid tried not to look gleeful at having an

excuse for yet another trip to the palace himself, and I tried my best not to mope around the house while I waited for his return.

Yara had already kicked me out of the kitchen for distracting her workers. We had received word Rowan was well enough to return home the next day, and Yara seemed to be channeling her emotions at that news into panic at the unexpected dinner party.

I spent the day at Mariam's side, expecting her to need support for Nyla's reappearance. To my surprise, the day went much more smoothly than expected. While there were sure to be battles in the future, Nyla didn't even appear to notice most of the changes Mariam had made, or the way the servants already showed a marked preference for her sister-in-law.

The answer for Nyla's unexpected forbearance soon became clear. Yara—not quite as distracted as she appeared—had given a message to Layla when she delivered their breakfast. After eating the meal, Nyla had emerged into the main house in a glow of triumph. Every other consideration had been eclipsed by the news she would be hosting Yasmine at a select dinner party that was to include—as a surprise to her rival—the crown prince himself.

Although it hadn't been my intention, my plan had placed Mariam and Nyla on the same side, the two of them united in their conviction that a great deal of preparation was needed for a royal visitor. I helped too, of course, running errands for Mariam all day.

Navid returned late in the afternoon, having been gone far longer than needed to deliver a message. He greeted his mother and aunt but carefully avoided looking in my direction. I narrowed my eyes at him as he gave the two older women a charming smile.

"I hope my news will be welcome and won't disrupt your plans too greatly," he said.

"What is it?" Nyla asked sharply. "His Highness isn't coming after all?"

"No, no," Navid said reassuringly. "Quite the opposite. Prince Tarek will be here shortly, but he is not to be our only visitor from the palace."

"Navid," I growled under my breath, but he gave no indication of having heard me.

"Her Royal Highness, Princess Adara is also to attend," he said blithely. "As well as one of the royal viziers."

"The princess!" Mariam clasped her hands together, stars in her eyes.

"That will show Yasmine," Nyla cackled. "She's never had a single royal sitting down at her table, and I'm to have two."

"And what is the name of this vizier?" I asked.

Navid finally looked my way, a twinge of guilt on his face. "Azzam."

I groaned. I should have seen it coming. Of course Navid would have gone to see Adara while he was at the palace and, once with her, he would have told her the entire plan. The rest was inevitable.

Adara had been convinced about Azzam's guilt from the start. She probably thought if she could just get him in the same room as Esai, she would be able to trick them into revealing everything.

I pulled Navid aside as the other two made rapid changes to their planned seating arrangement.

"Please at least tell me everything is set with Rek?"

"Of course," Navid said.

I sighed. "I just don't want Adara to get hurt. There might be fighting by the end of the night. I would have thought you'd want to protect her as well."

"Of course I don't want to see her hurt." His voice turned stern. "But I'm not going to try to protect her by keeping secrets from her. Adara is no longer the child you remember. She's been involved with this since the start, and she deserves to be here tonight just as much as the rest of us."

"I—" I stopped, the protest that had leaped to my lips dropping away. "Actually I have no response to that. You're completely right."

"I am?" Navid did an exaggerated double take and looked over both shoulders. "Are you sure you're talking to me?"

"Oi!" I gave him a light shove. "I don't say it that infrequently."

"Actually," he gave me a broad grin, "I think this might be the first time ever."

I laughed, but when I glanced up and saw Mariam watching us, I cut the sound off and assumed a serious posture. I was more concerned with the indulgence in her expression than the possibility of being reprimanded for over-familiarity with her son, but either way, I didn't want Nyla to notice. I wasn't sure which option she would find more disturbing.

I had stopped not a moment too soon because Nyla glanced our way, her disapproving eyes lingering on me.

"We have two members of the royal family about to arrive in our home! There is much to be done. Don't just stand there!"

I nodded meekly and fled the room. It might be for different reasons, but I was no less eager for the night to go to plan than Nyla.

CHAPTER 25

*R*ek and Adara were the first ones to arrive, and it took all my control not to run straight into his arms. It already seemed like too long ago that we'd stood together in Yasmine's garden.

His eyes flashed when he saw me, standing discreetly behind the family who had lined up in the front hall to welcome them. But his life as a prince had given him as much experience at suppressing his emotions as my employment with Nyla had given me. Both of us held our places and assigned roles.

There was no sign of the three guards who should have accompanied him, but I knew they would have gone straight to liaise with the household guards. I had already had a long conversation with our small group of guards, so they had been ready to receive them. Our men didn't have the experience of the royal guard, but after Rowan's injury, they were eager to prove themselves. Naturally I hadn't told them the full truth about the evening, but it had been essential I warn them to be ready to assist Rek's men.

The royals were led into a receiving room where I served them drinks while they waited for the remaining guests to arrive.

Once the meal began, I wouldn't be able to continue serving alone, but Navid had issued instructions that any other servers should move through the room quickly. Only I would remain with the guests at all times.

Three weeks ago, Yara and the others would have found the arrangement odd enough to fuel a great deal of gossip and speculation. But they had all accepted that I no longer had a simple servant role in the household. Any who might have resented my new status under ordinary circumstances seemed willing to accept it in exchange for the advantages that came with a much more amiable mistress.

The next guest to arrive was Yasmine. She swept into the house wearing a heavily embroidered chemise and a stunningly simple full length red robe. But the superior smile on her face faltered when she caught sight of Rek and Adara.

By the time she'd risen from her bow, the smile was back in place, but I could read a more confusing riot of emotions lurking behind it. The opportunity for an intimate meal with two of the royals was enviable by most standards, but one look at Nyla's triumphant face showed the cost of the offered reward.

Yasmine turned to beckon to a figure standing in the doorway, and an older man came forward to offer his bow.

"This is Isav," she said. "He's a collector of antiquities from southern Kuralan and an old friend. He's making a short visit to Karema, and I couldn't let him dedicate his entire trip to business."

She included the whole room in her warm, gracious smile, but I barely noted it. While I was ostensibly keeping my eyes firmly on the opposite wall, my whole attention was on the man I could see out of the corner of my eyes.

Isav. Or Esai's father. The twins had said he and his son were merchants. Yasmine claimed he was a collector of antiquities. Some combination of the two made sense for someone who had once led the gang of thieves. He must have reserved the rarest treasures from the back of the cave for his own retirement, however many years ago that had been. And even when the items removed from the cave turned to dust, he must have had plenty of wealth left from the treasures he had already sold.

Seeing him standing there beside Yasmine proved my suspicion, but the evening was too precarious to waste time congratulating myself. I might have correctly guessed how the situation would play out, but we still hadn't brought it to a successful conclusion.

It made sense Isav had taken the role of Yasmine's guest instead of Esai. While he had shown himself to be a bold man, his presence at the table would have bordered on foolhardy. Most people didn't have my gift with faces, but even Ali might recognize a man he had shared such an eventful meal with.

Esai had to be here somewhere, though. My eyes flicked to the open door and the corridor beyond, but there was no sign of anyone else.

"Excuse me." Isav rose from his bow with a confident smile. "I was just handing my horse over to your excellent stables. You will think me a foolish old man, and likely you're right, but she is more precious to me than any antiquity. I always travel with my own groom, so I mean no disrespect on your fine establishment."

Ali offered him effusive reassurances of his welcome and their lack of offense while I exchanged a meaningful look with Rek. I couldn't say it out loud, but hopefully he guessed at the likely identity of the so-called groom, as well as the identity of the older man in the room with us.

I wanted to run out of the room immediately to warn the guards, but I reminded myself Benjamin and Samuel were with them and had seen Esai for themselves at the cave. They would give any necessary warnings while also keeping the enthusiasm of our guards under control until the right moment. Jerome's presence would also help with that.

Adara sidled over to Navid, who stood just in front of me, while Ali continued to talk with Isav.

"That's not the captain of the thieves, is it?" she whispered, her tone concerned although a polite smile was still fixed on her face.

"It's his father," Navid whispered back. "I'm guessing Esai is the groom."

I relaxed. I hadn't been sure Navid had gotten a good enough look at Isav at the party to recognize him now.

The sound of a new arrival filtered through from the courtyard, and Adara brightened.

"That will be Azzam." She glanced briefly back at me with a conspiratorial look. "I'll watch his face. Zaria, you watch Yasmine's. And Navid, you watch this Isav. With any luck, their shock at being thrown together will be enough to implicate them on the spot, and we can get this whole charade over with."

I sent her a warning look for talking so openly, even in a quiet voice, but thankfully Nyla had swept forward to give the guests a second greeting, her words easily drowning out our quiet conversation. Movement at the door made me straighten and fix my eyes on Yasmine, as instructed.

In her enthusiasm to prove his guilt, I suspected Adara had forgotten a small but important feature of our history with Azzam. The vizier had a reason to react to this room and the people inside it that had nothing to do with thieves or treason. From her greeting, three years had been enough for Nyla to forget both his face and his name. But even from the corner of my eye, I could see he had not forgotten his connection with this household.

Although I kept my line of sight focused on Yasmine, as instructed, I still caught Azzam's shock. Whatever he'd been expecting, it hadn't been to see me immediately upon his arrival, standing close to both a son of the house and the princess.

His eyes skipped from us to Rek before he recovered himself

and greeted his hosts. Any dismay at Yasmine's presence was secondary to his discomfort at seeing the people he had lied to in contact once more.

By contrast, Yasmine held herself in check much more effectively. As he was announced, she turned slowly, her bland smile of welcome tinged with condescension. But I was sure I didn't imagine the tightening of her smile, or the tiny lines that appeared around her eyes when she heard the identity of the new guest.

The change in expression was gone within moments, but she made no effort to greet Azzam or assert herself in any way, an action more suspicious to me than if she'd greeted him as an old friend.

"Azzam was shocked and possibly scared," Adara hissed in a triumphant whisper as Azzam moved on to greeting Rek on the other side of the room.

Rek responded with perfect civility, but now I knew the truth, I could see the hints of the anger simmering beneath the surface.

"There was something strange in Yasmine's response as well," I admitted, ashamed of how gleeful it made me.

Seeing Azzam again had stirred the deep well of grief inside me, anger quickly springing in its wake. The last time I'd seen him, I'd still been in shock at my father's death, and his face brought back the many horrors of that awful time. I had my own reasons for thinking Azzam was unlikely to be the one in league with the thieves, but if he did turn out to be a traitor, I would get justice enough to satisfy anyone.

"I'm sorry to say it, but Isav had no reaction at all." Navid threw an apologetic look at Adara. "I watched him like a hawk, but he's either an incredible actor and impervious to shock, or he's never seen Azzam in his life."

"Maybe he is an incredible actor," Adara said stubbornly, but I could hear the disappointment in her words.

One of Yara's serving maids appeared in the corridor, sending me a frantic signal. I took a step back from Navid and Adara before clearing my throat and announcing dinner.

Yasmine, who apparently hadn't even noticed me in my servant's outfit, gave me a surprised, assessing look. I ignored her and led the way to the dining room where the first course already waited on the table.

The first clash between Nyla and Mariam arose as both tried to take the place of hostess and usher the guests to their seats. But a deft comment from Isav smoothed over the tension, and everyone was soon eating.

I waited in my place by the door, tense as I tried to watch everyone at once. This was the part of the evening where I had to rely on Rek and Adara's skills. I could do nothing to steer the conversation.

If anyone had the training for it, it was the two of them. But as the courses wore on, my frustration grew. Isav proved as cunning as his son, lightly turning away any attempt at questioning or provoking him.

He also continued to give no indication that Azzam had any special meaning to him. Given my reluctant admiration of his deftness, I might have considered his manner an unreliable indicator, but Azzam was far less capable. And while he was clearly deeply uncomfortable about being at a small dinner party with Yasmine, the royals, and me, he seemed to discount Isav as inconsequential.

Despite my own preferences, the traitor didn't appear to be Azzam. Unfortunately that meant the meal was doing nothing to reveal the truths we needed exposed. The courses would soon end, and we would be forced to call in the guards and see if an imminent arrest made anyone spill any secrets. If the fleeting suspicions that had prompted me to arrange this dinner were correct, then that situation could get very messy.

But I hadn't accounted for the rivalry between Nyla and Yasmine. If Yasmine had brought Isav and Esai here, she must be aware of the dangers inherent in the evening. But apparently that wasn't enough to mitigate her usual attitude.

"It's so nice to indulge in a small dinner," she said in gushing tones. "I'm so used to hosting larger entertainments that I rarely get such a refreshing break. But the whole city seems so enamored of my entertainments, that the numbers always manage to grow. I'm starting to run out of ideas for fresh amusements, although of course I am always partial to the dancers, myself."

She threw an impudent smile around the room, giving everyone a second to remember her own history before she turned an innocent expression on Nyla.

"What entertainment do you have planned for us this evening?"

Nyla and Mariam threw each other identical looks, their expressions frozen but their eyes alive with horror, united for possibly the first time in their lives. Given the speed with which we had arranged the dinner, there hadn't been time to organize any entertainers for the end of the meal.

The two hostesses had likely consoled themselves that it wasn't a grand, formal affair, and they were still in the extended period of mourning. Their guests wouldn't criticize them for failing to provide outside entertainers. But they had forgotten who they were dealing with.

"Yes, of course!" Ali cried benevolently. "The entertainment! No meal would be complete without it. Tell me, my dear, what do you have planned?"

Mariam sent him a furious glare, and his cheerfulness faltered, as he caught up too late with the state of affairs. But a moment later, his eye fell on me, and his grin returned.

"Ah, I remember now," he said. "Since this is, as you say, Yasmine, a small party, we have limited ourselves to entertainment provided by our own skilled household. Zaria is an excellent dancer—trained at the palace, you know—and will no doubt provide a delightful diversion."

Adara and Rek exchanged startled looks while I stared at Ali. But I wasn't cold-hearted enough to repulse his hopeful smile or Mariam's desperate look. Especially not when an equally desperate idea had leaped into my mind. Something was needed to shake up the room, and perhaps this was the perfect opportunity to insert myself into proceedings.

I bowed to the table. "The cakes will be served shortly, and the entertainment with it."

"Excellent! Excellent!" Ali leaned back, his smile regaining its usual good cheer.

Someone must have been listening at the door because I was still standing in the corridor trying to think where I could find a suitable outfit when one of the maids appeared.

"Here!" She thrust it at me breathlessly. "Layla remembered that Kasim used to employ a dancer for this sort of occasion. She didn't last long, of course, but she left some clothes here, and they've been stashed in a back cupboard in case Nyla ever managed to find a new dancer who would put up with her."

I grimaced, thinking of how angry Nyla was going to be with me when this was over. I had purposefully concealed my dancing training from her to avoid being called on to perform at her dinners, and she must be furious that Ali had known when she had not. There was no time to worry about Nyla now, though.

I took the clothes gratefully, racing into the closest empty room to change. When I walked out again, jangling circles of metal chimed as I moved. Their music reminded me of Yasmine's gown at the ball and her old history as a dancer. One at least of my audience was likely to be unimpressed by my performance.

None of the servants were proper musicians, but several played well enough to accompany a dancer. I waited outside the dining room as they tuned their instruments, pulling the door open only when they struck up the beginning of the first song.

My heart beat in my throat, my nerves jangling as much as my skirt as I skipped lightly into the room. It had been far too long since my days of dancing lessons, and my skills were well and truly rusty.

But as the music filled the room, my body took over. My mind might not remember all the moves, but my limbs did, the muscles moving as they had been taught so long ago.

Ali applauded loudly, calling his approval as I spun and clapped, my feet moving in time with my hips and hands. As the room whirled around me, I caught Rek's expression, and warmth flooded me. He appeared to have forgotten all about both Yasmine and Isav, so I could only hope Adara and Navid were less distracted.

As I passed in front of Isav's section of the table, however, disappointment filled me. More than anyone else at the table, we needed him distracted, his alertness dulled.

But if anything, his gaze had sharpened. He smiled in a polite manner as I danced past, turning to Ali at the head of the table.

"Lovely," he said, his tone approving without holding any especial praise. "Your household seems to have a surfeit of lovely women. I saw one just the other day coming out of this house in a most exquisite golden gown. A younger daughter of yours, perhaps?"

I faltered slightly, only just catching the step before I noticeably stumbled. Esai must have told Isav about the girl who had followed him from this house—and charged him with discovering my identity.

Ali, who had never seen me in my ballgown, was cheerfully denying the possession of any daughters, but Mariam was staring in my direction. And she wasn't the only one.

While Mariam might be trusted not to announce that they'd sent a servant to the palace in a beautiful dress, Yasmine had also seen me in my outfit at the ball. And she was now looking most intently at Isav.

Clearly he hadn't thought to ask her if she knew the identity of the girl before tonight, and why would he? There was no connection between Yasmine and me that he knew of. But she must know his wasn't an idle question.

She turned her calculating stare on me just as the song ended. I completed my final flourish, silence falling on the room. Yasmine turned back to Isav, her mouth opening, and I rushed to speak first.

"Yasmine!" My cry effectively cut off any words she was about to utter. "I have long heard that you are the true master of the knife dance, so you will know that a pair of dancers is required for the best of those. Won't you consider joining me for one dance? If we can lure you out of retirement, even for a single dance, it will be talked of in the city for years to come, I have no doubt."

Shock flashed in her eyes, tinged with anger. Yasmine wasn't a woman who liked being surprised. But beneath it I caught the hint of other emotions. I had seen the buried longing in her face as she watched my first dance. She might have truly enjoyed dancing, if she missed it all these years later. And even the great Yasmine wasn't entirely impervious to flattery.

"Yes, indeed, you must humor us!" Rek said into the silence that greeted my words. Ever since Isav's mention of my gold dress, he'd been tense, ready for action. "I never had the pleasure of seeing you in your past career, but I have heard many tales, and I would give much to see the famous Yasmine perform with my own eyes." He turned the full force of his devastating smile on her, and despite the gap in their ages, a flush rose up her cheeks.

"How could I refuse a request from my prince?" she purred, rising to her feet in one graceful movement.

Looking around the table, she gave a musical laugh. "But you mustn't be spreading the story around. I shan't allow myself to be tempted again."

It was clear from her manner that while she might not intend to come out of retirement a second time, she most certainly expected us to do the opposite of her instruction and spread the story far and wide.

I wasn't worried about what came after tonight, though. All that mattered was that I had separated her from Isav before she could reveal my identity, potentially unraveling our entire charade. And now I had the length of the dance to come up with something that would expose the secrets being so carefully guarded around the table.

The fact I was also now able to arm myself was just a secondary bonus.

Rek himself stood and offered me the knife from his belt with extravagant gallantry. I slipped into the role of a dancer, giggling coquettishly and swinging my hips as I approached to accept it.

But for the briefest second, the bare skin of my hand brushed against his as the knife changed hands, and a rush of real emotions nearly caught me off balance. A heady mix of admiration, alarm, and caution shone from his eyes, and I knew it was taking everything he had to keep his distance and allow the charade to play out.

I gave him a reassuring smile, before flicking my eyelashes ostentatiously and brushing unnecessarily close to him on my way around the rest of the table.

Some dancers used false, blunted knives when they performed these routines, but the professionals always used sharp blades. They knew that a hint of danger added to the excitement of the entertainment.

When I took my place beside Yasmine, I saw she had also acquired a very real looking weapon from somewhere. Had she been carrying it on her person?

There was no time for speculation as I found my balance. Given my lack of recent practice, it would take all my ability to complete the dance safely while also paying attention to the movements of the room.

Adara watched with wide eyes, likely remembering the times

we had practiced this traditional two-person dance in her sitting room. I wanted to smile at her, but the music began, and I lunged into the first movement.

Our elegant lines and swishing skirts transformed the lunges and turns of a typical knife training routine into a graceful performance. And as the music built, our synchronized moves changed. Instead of an individual training routine, we now mimicked the movements of a bout, lunging for each other in a choreographed whirl of moving arms and legs.

Yasmine was rusty, too, or I would have been in trouble. Every one of her motions was crisp and smooth, but her speed suffered from her age and lack of practice. It made us better matched. The double knife dance required both dancers not to miss a step, or they ran the risk of dancing into the others' blade.

As the music built, the room fell silent, our watchers captivated by the gleaming dance of the blades as they whisked near our hands and throats, always close but never making contact.

"You really were trained at the palace," Yasmine whispered as the dance brought us within an inch of each other. "What secrets are you hiding, Zaria?"

I whirled away, lunging at her and then ducking down in a flying circle of material.

"What secrets are you hiding, Yasmine?" I breathed back as we danced close again.

Something almost like fear flashed in her eyes. Had she finally realized there was more going on here tonight than she understood?

The music changed again, and we darted around the table, improvising somewhat to adjust to the layout of the room. But a truly enthralling knife dance required proximity with the audience, so they could experience some of the thrill of the blade for themselves. We didn't have an aisle to dance down, but we made our way around separate ends of the table.

Passing one of the doors, I saw we had acquired a larger audience. A crowd of servants had gathered just inside the doorways at both ends of the room, watching the unexpected spectacle with appreciation.

As I turned down the end of the table, passing Ali at the head and reaching the far side, the third, hidden door in the opposite wall moved, its creak lost to the music. This door opened into a small room for the use of guards, complete with concealed spyholes. It allowed guards of both the host and the guests to watch their charges without casting a pall over the tone of the meal.

The room had been unused by the current owners of the house for as long as I'd been here—usually put to use by the maids for extra storage—but I had instructed the household guards to wait there along with the reinforcements from the palace. If there was trouble, they needed to be on hand.

Apparently the flash of blades in the room was enough to prompt further investigation because the guards all appeared, clustered in the doorway with Captain Jerome at the front. His eyes met mine across the room before traveling on to Yasmine, but he didn't move, perhaps unsure if we represented a threat or not.

Responding to a swell of music, my knife swung toward the closest guest, who happened to be Isav. It dipped close enough for the air of its passing to touch him without actually putting him in danger, a move mirrored by Yasmine toward Navid on the other side of the table.

But while her knife held steady, veering neither too close nor too far from his skin, her eyes had latched on to me. I could see her clearly, directly across from me, Captain Jerome and his guards behind her. And as the simple but evocative music filled the room, I caught the tiny tells of emotion that gave me the final confirmation I needed. The time had come to act.

Abandoning the orchestrated moves of the dance, I leaped

closer to Isav's seated back, whipping my arm around him and pressing my sharp blade to his throat.

The music screeched to a halt. Several people shouted, and everyone who was seated leaped to their feet except for Isav, who stayed frozen in place.

"Let me guess," he said lightly, although I could see the strain in the way his hands gripped the arms of his chair. "If I looked in your wardrobe, I would find a dress as gold as the sun."

"Of course." I kept my voice equally light as I replied to him, my words for him but my eyes locked with Yasmine's across the table. "I didn't manage to apprehend your son on that occasion, but I think I'll manage to get you all tonight."

Nothing in Yasmine's stance gave warning of her movement before she suddenly launched into motion, her arm swinging back and sending her blade flying straight for me.

CHAPTER 26

asmine threw knives as well as she danced with them. The tip shot toward me without wavering, and it would have made contact if not for Rek.

He must have sensed something because he was moving before she was, his sword springing from his scabbard and leaping up to shield me.

It intercepted the knife just in time, knocking it off its trajectory. Rek didn't pause, springing onto the table and across it in one leap to face Yasmine. She shrank back before his blade, now weaponless, but she didn't stand alone. Jerome lunged forward, his sword aimed at Rek as he leaped to her defense.

Rek didn't falter at his captain's betrayal. Lightning fast, he brought his sword around to block Jerome's thrust, the two blades clanging together in a loud clash of steel on steel.

Distracted, my knife point had wavered, and Isav seized the opportunity. Driving his elbow back into my gut, he sent me staggering away from his chair.

I gasped, my body panicking as I fought for air, and the knife fell from my grip. Seizing it, Isav spun to face me as I stumbled backward, still doubled over.

His knife stabbed toward me, its tip only just missing the material of my dress. Out of the corner of my eye, I could see Rek still fighting Jerome, with Samuel and Benjamin rushing to his aid.

But somehow he was still keeping an eye on me. With a shouted command, he sent Samuel away from his own fight, the guard running around the table toward Isav.

I dropped to the ground to escape the next strike, hoping either my breath or Samuel arrived in time for Isav's next attack. From my prone position, I caught the swish of skirts as Yasmine rounded the end of the table and raced straight for the closest window. She thrust it open, as if she meant to escape into the night, and I tried to call a warning, but my lungs weren't cooperating.

But Navid had followed close behind her, and he drew his sword, advancing on her menacingly. She fell back from the window, reaching out with her arms placatingly.

His weapon dipped, his eyes jumping over her shoulder to where Adara must be, further back than me. But just at that moment, a figure leaped through the now open window beside them.

The purpose of the open window served, Yasmine's meekness dissolved. She lunged at Navid, despite her lack of a weapon, reaching for him with clawed fingers. Esai, the new arrival, drew a sword of his own, hurrying to join her in the attack.

Adara screamed, and the household guards surged forward, shaken from their shocked immobility. Three of them converged on Navid, one seizing Yasmine from behind while the other two faced Esai.

Only Rek and Benjamin were left to face Jerome, but the captain's blade spun and slashed so fast, the three of them dancing around each other at such speed, that it would have been difficult for anyone else to intervene.

Scuttling backward while I took in the rest of the room, I collided with something solid. I had reached the far wall.

Isav continued to advance, moving more slowly now that he had me cornered. Samuel had never arrived, caught in a press of crying, screaming servants, who were all trying to flee the room at the same time.

But Adara appeared, a short dagger clasped in her hand, her feet in a fighter's stance, and a determined look on her face.

Admiration filled me. She had continued her training in my absence. But Isav was taller and stronger, and his reach was longer than Adara's. She wouldn't be able to protect herself.

"No," I tried to cry, but it came out as a wheeze, my body still recovering from the winding.

The sound was loud enough to attract Navid's attention, though. With the assistance of two more swordsmen, he had already disarmed Esai, and the guards were in the process of binding his hands.

His fight over, Navid had sheathed his sword in order to usher out the servants on his side of the room, as Samuel was doing on the other. But he spun around at my gasping cry.

Taking in the danger, he raced for us by the most direct route —across the table. Scattering dishes, glasses, and food in all directions, he slid across the width of the mahogany wood, catapulting straight into Isav's side.

Navid knocked the older man away from Adara, and the two men went down in a tangle of limbs and flashing knife.

"Navid!" Adara screamed, rushing toward them.

A grunt from the other side of the room sent my attention flying back to Rek, Benjamin, and Jerome. Their blades still flashed in a dizzying bout, the two younger men circling the older, lunging for every opening. Jerome fought with a grim determination, bringing every bit of his experience and skill to bear.

I wanted to run to Rek, but any interruption could prove fatal. Instead, having finally recovered my breathing, I ran to Adara.

She was kicking Isav's back as he tried to untangle himself from Navid and push up off the floor. Navid was also trying to get loose, but blood was seeping from one of his arms at an alarming rate.

Isav's attention suddenly focused on the floor at a point halfway between the fight and me. I followed his gaze and saw my knife lying where it must have landed after being flung from his hand.

He tried to lunge for it, but I was faster. Scooping it from the ground, I gripped the hilt in both hands, and steadied myself on my knees, the blade tip pointed toward him.

His body stilled, but his eyes still flashed, jumping from me to Adara as if searching for an escape. But one of the guards appeared in our line of sight, the longer blade of his sword now steady as it pointed at Isav.

The thief still hesitated for one final moment before letting out his breath and slumping to the floor. I risked looking up in time to see Jerome block Benjamin, only for Rek's blade to slide in and flip Jerome's from his hand.

All the fights were over.

I rocked back on my heels, breathing freely at last as Samuel finally thrust the final servant out of the room and arrived to help the household guard arrest Isav. But a moment later, I jumped to my feet.

"Yasmine!" I cried, looking around. "Where's Yasmine?" Had she slipped away from the guard trying to hold her and made her escape after all during the chaos of the fighting?

"Over here," said a voice of vindictive satisfaction.

I hurried over to peer out the opened window.

Yasmine had made it outside, but someone had followed her. In the light that spilled out from the room through the row of windows, I could see Yasmine lying in the dust of the darkened courtyard, Nyla sitting on her back.

I made a whimpering sound of relieved amusement, but it must have concerned Rek.

He strode to my side and caught me in his arms. "Are you hurt?"

I shook my head and pointed out the window. He followed my gesture, giving a bark of surprised laughter.

"What about you?" I turned in his arms to face him. "Are you hurt?"

"I'm fine." His eyes moved to the other side of the room, briefly meeting Benjamin's before lingering on his prisoner. "I just don't understand. Jerome? Is he the traitor, then?"

"I'm afraid so." Weariness filled me.

"And you knew it?" Rek stared down at me in confused wonder.

"I guessed it," I corrected. "But it was nothing more than a hunch based on his stance. I didn't want to accuse him on a vague suspicion, and the only way to confirm it was for me to see them together."

"Who?" He frowned. "Jerome and Esai?"

"Actually Jerome and Yasmine. And Yasmine and Isav, too."

Rek still looked dazed. "What's Yasmine's connection to either of them?"

"That was also mostly a hunch. We should go to the others so I can tell everyone at once."

Rek nodded agreement, but he kept talking as we moved toward the huddle of people by the far door. "I just can't understand it. Jerome has been loyal to my family for decades—he was only sixteen when he joined the guards as a young recruit and worked his way up. He's had access to sensitive information ever since he became a captain, but there's never been any trouble before now."

"I don't think he turned against your family specifically," I said. "Or the kingdom. I just think there are some loyalties stronger than anything else." I looked up at him. "You should understand that. You told your father so yourself."

"My father?" Rek frowned, looking at the cluster of prisoners being herded into the small guard room.

Jerome was at the rear, holding his back straight and his head high as he walked, despite his bound hands. When Yasmine appeared in the doorway, dragged by Nyla and a groom, he froze, however.

I caught my breath at the look on his face, but Benjamin shoved his shoulder, and Jerome looked down, shuttering his emotions as he disappeared into the room.

"We sent the household messenger to the palace," Benjamin called across when he saw Rek looking. "Reinforcements should be here to transport them soon."

Rek nodded, putting one arm around my waist, as if he didn't want to risk our being separated, and leading me the rest of the way to join the others.

Yasmine had also reached the group and stubbornly stopped, clearly trying to resist being lumped in with the prisoners.

"I've never been treated so terribly in my life," she said in strident tones. "Why am I under arrest, may I ask?"

Rek gave an incredulous laugh. "You tried to kill Zaria when she arrested a thief and a traitor. What did you expect to happen?"

"I don't know what you're talking about," she said. "I didn't attack anyone. My knife simply slipped during the dance."

"You can drop the act. We know about your treachery." Rek was even better than Yasmine at adopting a haughty, commanding manner, and faced with his stern authority, she wilted. Tears appeared in her eyes, tracking down through the dust on her cheeks.

A single, pathetic sob shook her body.

"I've been so lonely since I lost my husband. I never wanted to do anything wrong, but he said he loved me and that we could be together if I just—"

Nyla shook her arm roughly, cutting off her speech. "That will be enough of that. I don't know what's going on here, or who you're claiming to be in love with, but His Highness doesn't want to hear any of your lies."

Yasmine turned on Nyla, fury in her eyes, and I noticed the moisture had completely disappeared.

Nyla just gave her a sly smile. "I may not be as rich as you, but at least I'm not a traitor!"

Ali cleared his throat, reminding me we still had an audience. With the rest of the bystanders gone, only Ali, Mariam, and Azzam huddled in the corner, accompanied by the lone remaining servant. Layla had staunchly held her ground through the fighting and was still positioned defensively in front of Mariam, wielding a solid candlestick from a side table.

The sight of her made me grin. I didn't know how much longer I would stay in this household, but I suspected Layla would soon be taking my position as Mariam's personal servant —a worthy reward after the ordeal of isolation with Nyla.

"Would it be too much to ask what's going on?" Ali asked tentatively. "I can only assure Your Highnesses of my household's complete loyalty to the crown and express my horror at the happenings here." He looked from me to Navid, as if reassuring himself that we seemed to be aligned with the correct side of the battle.

"Of course." Adara swooped in, her manner both regal and reassuring at the same time. "It is we who must apologize for disrupting a most delightful meal. But we knew a loyal citizen such as yourself would be willing for us to use your home to capture a dangerous group of criminals."

"Yes, yes, certainly," Ali said quickly, although he threw an uncertain look at Yasmine, as if he still couldn't quite believe she fit the description.

"Did you actually love Jerome at all?" I asked Yasmine. "Or was he only ever a tool?"

"I don't know what you're talking about," she said, but her act had shattered, and I could see the fear in her eyes.

"I saw you together at your party," I said. "You were, ahem, embracing, so I couldn't see either of your faces, but I recognized your gown."

"So the third man who met with Esai and Isav at the party was Jerome?" Navid asked from his place at Adara's shoulder. "Why didn't you say anything?"

"Because I didn't actually see his face." I sighed. "I recognized his clothes, so I knew the man with Yasmine and the one who met Esai were the same. But I couldn't shake the feeling that something about him was familiar. It was his stance that clued me in—so like the way he'd stood at the ball the night before. But I couldn't be sure. I needed to see him and Yasmine together."

"There's no question you were right," Rek said quietly.

He met my eyes, and I knew he'd just seen the same thing I had on Jerome's face. I had never witnessed such intense longing or such impotent fury. How long had she dangled him on her string? She had clearly been expert at it, to so consume a man like Jerome that he would aid her in her crimes.

"So Jerome knew about the delegation," Adara said. "He provided the information from the palace. That fits. But what's the connection with the gang?"

"There is no connection," Yasmine said. "This is all a fairy story. I—"

"Have been flaunting your history as a dancer in everyone's faces in order to hide the earlier history you didn't want anyone to know," I finished for her. "I thought at first that I must have met Isav before because he looked so familiar. But then I realized it was the family resemblance confusing me."

She flinched at the word family, and I nodded knowingly.

"Initially," I said to Rek, "I thought it was just the resemblance to his son, Esai, that made Isav so familiar. But it later occurred to me that it was more than that. The second resemblance was less immediately apparent, but once I realized there was a connection between them, I could see it. We have two of Isav's children here, not one."

Everyone turned to stare at Yasmine.

"Yasmine is related to the gang?" Navid sounded dazed, struggling to absorb the enormity of it.

"Based on their apparent ages," I said, "I would say she's the older sister." I looked at her. "Did it always enrage you that the gang should have been yours? That if you hadn't been born a woman, you would have been their leader, sharing in the wonders of the cave, instead of being forced to seek a life as a dancer?"

"I'm not saying anything," she muttered, but it sounded petulant, and Rek seemed to take it as confirmation. Her background explained a lot about her endless desire for both money and power, although I couldn't help a twinge of sorrow for her. If only she could have truly left her family and early life behind, choosing to be a different person from the one they had tried to shape her into.

"I suppose you started by inviting Jerome to your parties," I said to her. "You must have realized how helpful he could be in your efforts to quash your business rivals."

She sniffed, lifting her nose up into the air, but I read the truth on her face. Nyla did too.

"Oh ho," she crowed. "So that's why Tristan was barred from operating as a merchant on a fraud claim, despite his continued denials of having done anything of the sort."

I vaguely remembered a scandal with a merchant named Tristan, but it had been more than a year ago.

"I know you had your eye on Kasim," Nyla continued, "but I was watching you closely."

I hadn't realized the extent of Yasmine's criminality, but it made sense.

"For someone who'd been ruthlessly eliminating her rivals for years, it must have been very threatening to hear of new trade treaties being planned with the Four Kingdoms," I said. "There could hardly be a bigger threat to your supremacy. I suppose that's when you decided it was time to rekindle your connection with your family." A horrifying flash of inspiration hit me. "I suppose you were responsible for eliminating your husband, too."

Yasmine remained silent, but she hadn't been able to hide her reaction to my words. Nyla drew back from her, looking shocked.

"Murderer!" She spat at Yasmine's feet, her abrupt action sending a ripple through the people around her.

"Murderer!" The cry went up from voice after voice.

Yasmine's careful control split further, panic hitting her as she looked at the expressions around her and heard their voices proclaim her new title. But when her eyes fell on Azzam, joining the chorus from his place by the nearest wall, she erupted into anger.

"You dare call me Murderer?" she spat out.

He drew back, the fear on his face as great as what I'd just seen on hers. I stiffened, suddenly finding it hard to breathe.

She continued spewing words at him. "Don't think they're taking me off to prison, while you go back to your comfortable life at the palace. When they interrogate me, I'll be telling them all about the money you paid me to procure you liquid nayera. I would never have poisoned my husband if you hadn't shown me how easy it could be."

Azzam looked ill, his eyes flying around the room. But when they latched on to me, his queasy expression grew. The whole room spun around me.

Rek's arm caught and held me, preventing my knees from giving way.

"Zaria?" He leaned over me in concern. "What is it? Are you all right?"

"My father." I struggled to get out the words, my eyes finding Azzam. "It was my father you poisoned, wasn't it? His death was so sudden! I thought you were his friend, but you were always his rival."

"No, no," Azzam protested, but his voice sounded weak and unconvincing.

"Zahir was about to be promoted to senior vizier." Rek sounded horrified. "But after he died, Azzam was moved up instead."

"That's why he moved you out of the palace so quickly!" Adara cried. "And why he lied to us about it. He didn't want you around—or talking to us—when you were the one person most likely to ask questions about your father's death."

"I don't know anything about that," Yasmine said, "but he certainly killed Zahir." She eyed me up and down. "So you're his daughter, then? Back before he cut contact between us, Azzam did like to go on about how the royals only favored Zahir because of your friendship with the princess."

"That's not true." Rek gave Azzam a murderous stare. "Zahir was one of my father's most promising viziers. His advice was always balanced and helpful. His position had nothing to do with Zaria."

"He murdered him," I said faintly. "I can't believe my father was murdered."

Rek's arm cradled me even closer. "I'm so sorry, Zaria."

With difficulty, I pulled myself together, willing strength back into my legs. I would process the news later. For now, nothing had actually changed. My father was dead, as he had been for years, and the truth about his passing didn't bring him back.

And for all my blinding anger toward Azzam, there was a strange comfort in finally understanding the incomprehensible events that had seen me lose not only my father but my home.

At a signal from Rek, Benjamin seized Azzam by the arm and hauled him toward the small room being used as a temporary prison. The vizier tried to protest, but his thin wails left everyone unmoved.

Before Benjamin could return for Yasmine, however, the sound of wagon wheels made us all turn toward the windows. A solid, wooden wagon rolled into the courtyard, disgorging a stream of royal guards.

They marched inside, a flurry of chaotic voices and movement overwhelming the room. But within minutes, peace had returned as Esai, Isav, Jerome, Azzam, and Yasmine were loaded into the wagon and escorted onto the street, the wagon accompanied by a circle of guards on foot.

I stared out the window even after the wagon had disappeared, still seeing Yasmine's straight back and the way she turned her face away from her father and brother. Even now, she wanted to distance herself from them, and yet everything she'd done had been because of them. She'd left them behind physically, but she'd never truly left behind their teaching or their values.

She had been given the chance to move on, but she'd rejected it—just as I had. The thought hit me hard.

Was I really any different from Yasmine? Was my refusal to let go of my father going to send me down a dark path as her own past had done to her?

But as soon as I remembered my father, I realized the nonsense of such thoughts. I had allowed the darkness of his death to poison everything else, until I thought my past was something that needed to be left behind. I hadn't been able to bring myself to do it, and I'd thought that a weakness.

But faced now with what it truly meant to walk a dark path, my error seemed obvious. Yasmine should have rejected her family and her past because they brought death and pain. They had never truly loved her.

I couldn't reject mine because it was the opposite. With my father and my friends, I had known true love. And I had seen what it meant to spend your life in service. To love others more than you loved yourself. Of course I couldn't let that go and walk away.

My loyalty to Karema and the palace that did so much to serve its people wasn't a weakness. It was part of who I was—a part my father had shaped with his own years of service.

I had thought it childish to cling to my past, but my naïveté had been thinking you needed to move on from losing the people you loved and who had loved you. Those people formed you as a person—you didn't grow past them, you built up from the foundations they'd given you.

I didn't need to leave Karema to grow into my full potential. I could do that by honoring my father's legacy and becoming the kind of person he had showed me how to be—the kind of person who gave their life in loving service to others.

My eyes went to Rek, standing in the doorway in conversation with Samuel and Benjamin, who had remained to guard him and Adara. It wasn't only my love of my father that had tied me to Karema. But even if I could never marry Rek, loving him had changed me. I wasn't denying it or hiding it any longer. This was my home, and I would fight for my place in it.

Ali cleared his throat, attracting the attention of all of us who were standing idly in the dining room, unsure what to do next.

"I still don't understand everything," he said. "But it appears you have once again done this family a great service, Zaria. You cannot possibly remain our servant any longer."

"What?" I stared at him, caught off guard.

"What I mean to say is that we must welcome you as a daughter." He beamed at me. "Many happy wishes on your betrothal to Navid."

CHAPTER 27

"*Be...*trothal?" Adara was the first to speak into the ringing silence that followed Ali's announcement. She looked faint, so Layla whisked forward a chair from the table and deposited her into it.

"Father!" Navid looked frantically from his father to me, clearly unsure how best to repudiate his father's words.

"Excuse me?" The cold words came from Rek. I hadn't seen him move from the doorway, but he had somehow appeared at my side, his narrowed eyes passing slowly from Ali to Navid.

"It may be a little irregular," Ali said hurriedly. "But you must admit, she's more than earned it with her services to our family. Even before tonight there was the treasure cave." He froze, his eyes jumping to his wife. In the confusion of the night, he'd clearly lost track of who knew what.

"The treasure cave? Don't tell me that's been found?" Layla sounded as if nothing could surprise her after the happenings of the evening.

"Well..." Ali stuttered. "That is to say..."

"Certainly it has been found." Rek still sounded cold. "But anyone who approaches it will find it is well guarded."

"Indeed, indeed." Ali nodded vigorously, although I suspected Navid hadn't passed on that piece of information. But after Kasim's fate, plus the gold all dissolving into dust, I was fairly certain Ali meant never to set foot in the forest again.

"Well, that's a pity," Layla said, her tone calm and even despite her words. "I wouldn't have wasted my time if I'd known that."

"Wasted your time?" I asked. "What do you mean?"

Focusing on Layla seemed easier than dealing with the mess Ali's betrothal announcement had unleashed.

"I had to do something with all those days I was locked away," she replied, still standing protectively over the shocked Adara. "I took a look at all those musty old books Kasim liked to collect and decided the most useful endeavor would be looking for information about that lost cave. Finding it would have been one way to ensure I never ended up in such a situation again. Of course, if I'd known it wasn't lost, I would have thought of something else to do."

"You spent your two weeks in mourning isolation researching information about the treasure cave?" I asked, fascinated despite myself.

She shrugged. "Like I said, I had to do something."

"I suppose so." My brain didn't seem to be functioning properly. I told myself sternly to pull it together.

"Did you find anything?" Rek asked, his intent gaze switching to her.

She blinked once in surprise, waiting for a moment as if to confirm he was talking to her.

"Nothing that made much sense," she said at last. "Although if the tales are true, the youngest brother who created the caves seems to have been a very paranoid sort. But I suppose if you pile all your treasure in one place, you have to be worried about someone else finding it. He seemed to have a veritable mania about no one carrying the stuff off except him."

"Except him," I said slowly.

"Well, yes, of course he still wanted to access it himself," she said sensibly. "That stands to reason. But all the enchanted objects that were required to set it up! You wouldn't believe! We all know about the nonsense with his ring and lamp, of course—they found those in Ardasira—but there were all sorts of other objects used to create the caves. It would be fascinating if it wasn't all made up, but it probably was. And none of it was very useful."

She shrugged and returned to stand beside Mariam, who was regarding her in astonishment. Hopefully the astonished wonder of someone who'd just discovered a much more useful treasure than gold.

"But the betrothal," Adara said faintly. "I don't quite understand."

"There is no betrothal," I said firmly, finally recovering my wits. "It's very kind of you, Ali, but I'm not interested in marrying Navid."

"Nonsense!" Mariam stepped forward. "The two of you have always been fond of each other."

"We're good friends, but neither of us want to get married." I looked to Navid. "Do we?"

He nodded vigorously. "I would never dispute Zaria's worthiness, but I'm not interested in marrying her."

"I should hope not since she's betrothed to me," Rek said.

"What?" Nyla's shocked exclamation echoed through the room, reminding me she was still present, over by the window where she'd been watching her rival carted off by the guards.

"Rek!" I glared at him before turning to Ali. "It's not official or anything."

"But it will be as soon as I speak to my father." Rek sounded determined.

I eyed him uneasily, but he refused to back down.

"Ali has the right idea," he said. "What you've done for the kingdom is worthy of a great reward. Even Father can't deny it now."

"I think we might find he can," I murmured.

Rek must know his father wouldn't be easily swayed. If he didn't, he wouldn't have been so interested in what Layla had discovered about the cave.

But to my surprise, a grin was growing across Rek's face.

"Actually, he can't," he said. "You heard what he said. For your dowry he requires a treasure cave's worth of valuables—or a trade treaty with the Four Kingdoms. Thanks to you, we've now identified and arrested the traitor and arrested every member of the gang who attacked the delegation. The way is now clear for our treaty. And we wouldn't have succeeded at any of it without you."

Hope blossomed in my chest and spread outward. "Do you really think…It's not what he meant."

"Mother was there," he said with a satisfied smile. "She'll make him stick to his words."

"Let me be the first to congratulate you both," Navid said, sounding more relieved than congratulatory.

I sent him a teasing smile. "Do you have someone else in mind for yourself, Navid?"

But Rek gave me a disapproving look, and I subsided. Navid had helped us, but Rek was right. If the sultan was going to be forced into agreeing to our marriage, he was likely to turn his hopes for a marriage alliance to Adara.

A cloud passed over my happiness. How could I be happy when my friends were denied the same joy?

But Rek's arm slipped around my waist, and I couldn't keep the smile from my face. The day hadn't been without its grief and pain, but that didn't erase the joy that came alongside it.

My father had died serving Kuralan. And now I hoped to serve it as he once had. Back at the palace, with Rek at my side, the part of me my father had nurtured could live once more.

Nothing would bring him back, but his legacy would live on and bless the kingdom and people he loved for years to come—many years, I hoped.

Rek pulled me around to stand against him, encircled in his arms despite our audience.

"You are incredible, Zaria," he murmured. "Thanks to you, our people are safe again."

"Not just me." I looked down, feeling the flush stealing up my cheeks. "I couldn't have done it without you."

"Exactly." The smile in his voice made me look up again, the flush bursting into hot flame at the look in his eyes. "I think we make a good team. Don't you agree?"

I nodded wordlessly, and he pressed his lips gently against mine. Pulling back slightly, he left just enough room between us for him to speak, his lips brushing mine as he did.

"Be warned. I'm just as determined as the youngest brother to keep hold of my treasure. I'm not letting anyone carry you off again."

I smiled, even that small movement turning his words back into a kiss. But this time I was the one to pull back.

He looked down at me quizzically.

"I've just had an idea," I said breathlessly. "I might be wrong, but—" I stopped and looked up at him. "Sorry!"

He laughed. "Never apologize for being you. I love that mind of yours that moves at twice the speed of anyone else's."

"Actually," I lifted my face toward his again, "I think one more kiss should be sufficient."

"Sufficient for what?" he asked on a chuckle, already leaning down toward me.

"To erase everything else from my mind completely."

I pressed my lips to his, and the rest of the world melted away.

EPILOGUE

I peered through the door at the chattering crowd circulating in the ballroom, letting my nerves wash through me and then dissipate. It was hard to believe two months had passed since we dismantled the gang, but at the same time, so much had changed.

Rek had insisted I move into the palace immediately, and they had even given me back my old rooms, the ones I had shared with my father. For the first two weeks, the tears had flowed constantly—but they were healing tears. I could now move around the palace and remember my father and my past years here without the memories being tainted with darkness.

Rek stepped up beside me, his familiar, warm smile bringing light to both my past and my future.

"Are you ready for this?" he asked.

I laughed. "What if I say no?"

He pretended to consider. "It's not too late to run off to the Four Kingdoms."

I fought a smile. "Every person in that room is there to celebrate our betrothal. I think it is too late."

He sighed. "That's a pity."

I wound my arms around him, resting my head against his broad chest for a moment. "Don't pretend you don't love it. You've been preparing yourself to fill this role for years."

"And with you by my side, I have no regrets," he said. "Despite my father's example, I'm convinced it's possible to rule with both love and care for the kingdom."

I looked up into his eyes. "I know it is. In fact, I'm not sure it's really possible to do one without the other."

A fanfare sounded, and I quickly pulled back, returning to my place at his side and frantically patting my hair. He was still laughing at me when the herald announced our names, and we walked into the room.

I saw little of him after that, despite it being our betrothal celebration. As the guests of honor, we were constantly busy meeting dignitaries from near and far.

I took extra time with the ambassador from Arcadia, knowing she was in the final stages of negotiating a treaty with Sultan Khalil. She was the first ambassador from beyond the desert to establish a permanent presence in our court, but we had high hopes she wouldn't be the last.

But the dignitary I was most excited to see came from closer to home.

"Princess Cassandra! I'm so glad you made it. When your delegation didn't arrive until last night, I feared—"

She cut off my words by pulling me into a hug.

"Sorry," she said with a chuckle when we separated. "But after all those letters, I feel like I'm seeing an old friend. I felt it the first time we met, you know—that we could be friends."

"Me too! Only you ended up as a princess, so I assumed it was just wishful thinking on my part."

It had taken courage to send her a letter after my unofficial betrothal to Rek, and only necessity had induced me to do it. But her reply had been more warm than I could have imagined, and our correspondence had become a pleasure.

Cassie laughed again, her eyes finding her husband across the room. Prince Zain was deep in conversation with the ambassador from Arcadia and didn't notice her looking, but she smiled affectionately anyway.

"Sometimes I still can't believe I'm a princess. Then I remember there are fewer crowns and a lot more talking about irrigation than you might think, and it becomes easier to believe." She gave me a confiding look. "He's talking about it right now. I can tell by the spark in his eyes."

I giggled. "But if he really can reclaim the desert, it will all be worth it."

She sighed. "I know. Ignore me. I love it, really." Turning back to me, she brightened.

"I know we didn't get here as early as I hoped, but how did that prince of yours go with—"

"Excellently," Rek said, appearing beside us and handing me a bundle wrapped in plain cloth. "It all went exactly as you said. I will never again doubt the genius of either of you ladies."

"Yes!" Cassie crowed before nudging me toward the other side of the room. "Go on! The sooner you deliver that, the sooner we can all be celebrating together."

I glanced at Rek, and he nodded his agreement, falling into step beside me as we wove through the crowd. It took determination not to get caught in multiple conversations, but we finally reached our target.

"Well?" Navid looked between us anxiously. "Did it—"

"It worked." Rek grinned at him. "And don't worry. We'll be right behind you."

Adara appeared at my side, her fingers digging so sharply into my arm that I winced.

"Sorry," she said without looking my way, her wide eyes focused on the bundle in Navid's arms.

He drew a deep breath and led our small group the short

distance to where the sultan and sultana were in conversation with the Lanoverian ambassador to Ardasira.

As soon as he reached them, he dropped to one knee, bowing his head respectfully. Those closest to us all turned to look, curious, and the sultan broke off mid-sentence to stare at him disapprovingly.

Navid looked up, his gaze steady although he stayed on his knee.

"Your Majesty, I request your blessing on my betrothal to your daughter, Princess Adara."

The sultan's face darkened, his eyes flashing, but his wife put a hand on his arm, her eyes jumping between all of us, a crease in her brow. She knew nothing of our scheme, but she sensed something bigger was going on.

Navid spoke again into the silence.

"I know the price of marrying one of the royal children, and I come prepared to pay it." Unwrapping the bundle, he held out an ordinary looking brass lamp. "I present to you the key to unlocking the treasures of the second cave."

The sultan sucked in a sharp breath, his eyes going to Rek.

"It's true, Father," he said. "It was tested earlier today. In two months, we have found no way around the enchantment, but with the use of this lamp, the entire treasure can be retrieved."

"I have loaned the lamp to Navid," Cassie said, joining us. "Since the idea of using it comes from his inheritance. But when the cave is empty, we would request it be returned to Ardasira. It is no longer able to be used as it once was, but it has historical significance to us."

"I don't understand," the sultan said gruffly, directing his words at his son. "How is this lamp the key, and what does it have to do with him?" He wouldn't even say Navid's name, but after two months, I had started to get to know my future father-in-law, and I could tell he was softening.

"The lamp was one of two personal enchanted objects of the

youngest brother," Rek said. "Some ancient texts belonging to Navid's family showed us that the brother tied the enchantment on the second cave to those objects, to ensure he could retrieve the treasure himself."

"If you accept Navid's gift," Prince Zain said from behind his wife, "then of course you may keep the lamp for as long as you need to empty the cave. I understand it is very full."

Despite his grave tone, I caught the slightest twinkle in his eyes. The sultan regarded him suspiciously for a moment, as if he saw it too, and then he suddenly released his breath.

"How could I turn away a son-in-law who comes bearing such a gift?" He raised his voice. "We celebrate two betrothals today. My son's and also my daughter's to Navid of Karema. And we may also celebrate the turn in our kingdom's fortunes."

"Thank you, Father." Adara ran forward to embrace him, tears in her eyes. "You'll grow to love him, I know you will."

The sultan made a non-committal grunt, but I caught a soft look in his eyes as he watched his daughter return to her new betrothed. Adara was a hard person to resist.

And the expression grew to a bright gleam as he turned back to the Lanoverian ambassador. The ambassador, too, seemed more animated. With the cave unlocked, the treaties would soon be flowing from all sides.

"This really is a day to celebrate," a satisfied voice said from just beyond our circle.

I turned in delight to welcome Yara, Rowan, and Layla.

"Congratulations, my dear," Yara said as she enfolded me in a warm embrace. But after a moment, she pulled back. "Am I allowed to hug you, now that you're a princess?"

I laughed. "Of course you are. You're like a mother to me, Yara, so your hugs will always be welcome. And besides, this is only a betrothal. I'm not a princess yet."

"Congratulations all the same," Rowan said from Yara's side.

"I should be the one congratulating the two of you," I cried, seizing Yara for another hug. "I'm glad you finally decided to bow to the inevitable."

"The cheek!" Yara said, but her grin didn't falter.

She might be older than the usual bride, but she was just as happy as Adara or me. I didn't know whether it had been Yara or Rowan who had first spoken up, but I knew Rowan's accident had been the spark. After his near death, they couldn't go on telling themselves that their comfortable friendship and shared life was enough.

Now they were married and had an apartment in the palace servants' wing, in keeping with their new royal roles in the kitchen and stables.

"Congratulations from me as well," Layla said with a brisk nod. Unlike the other two, she had chosen to stay with Mariam, and I worried she might be lonely without her old friends. But she gave no indication of discomfort whenever she visited. Hopefully she would be happy with her new mistress.

According to Navid, she was indispensable in the house due to her expertise in keeping the peace between Mariam and Nyla, so maybe she liked knowing she was valuable and needed. And her task should be easier now that Navid was betrothed to Adara.

Since the eventful dinner party, Nyla had already half-forgotten her old objections to her husband's relations. Their upcoming marriage alliance with the royal family would ensure the final transformation. I had no doubt Nyla would soon believe she had invited Ali, Mariam, and Navid to join her household out of a true sense of family connection.

"Where's your friend, Kalila?" Adara asked when Yara, Rowan, and Layla moved away. "I was hoping to finally meet her."

My face fell. "She isn't here. I have a letter explaining why not, although half of it didn't make sense. It seems she got swept up into her adventure a little earlier than planned."

"Adventure?" Xavier popped up, his twin not far behind. "I've been thinking of just the same thing myself. And since you've decided to shirk your family responsibility, sister, it seems it falls on us to be the dutiful children and seek marriages of alliance in the Four Kingdoms or even beyond."

"The two of you are thinking about getting married?" I gave them a skeptical look.

Xander returned my gaze, his own full of earnest sincerity. "Naturally we wouldn't risk our kingdom by marrying for any but the truest of loves. So we may be searching for a long time."

"A *very* long time," Xavier added. "So it's a good thing there are so many kingdoms to be explored."

"Visited, brother," Xander said solemnly. "You mean visited." He looked back at the rest of us. "As Xavier said, we are ready to do our duty."

Adara and I burst out laughing at the same time. The twins gave us identical hurt looks and sailed away, muttering about ungrateful relatives.

"Somehow I don't think they're planning to go as part of any official delegation," Rek said wryly when we finally stopped laughing.

I mopped at my eyes. "No, I don't think so."

"We may even have to rescue them at some point," Rek said to me.

I slipped my arms around him and started laughing again. "And perhaps have an adventure or two on the way? You have more of your brothers in you than you like to admit, my love."

He chuckled. "So do you. And that's why I need you by my side." He stole the briefest of kisses. "For the moments of good sense and the moments of adventure."

"And may we have a great many of both," I said with a sigh of perfect satisfaction.

Head back across the desert to Lanover and the desert traders with Kali and the twins in The Rogue Princess: A Retelling of Puss in Boots.

Or if you missed Cassie's discovery of the first treasure cave, read The Desert Princess: A Retelling of Aladdin.

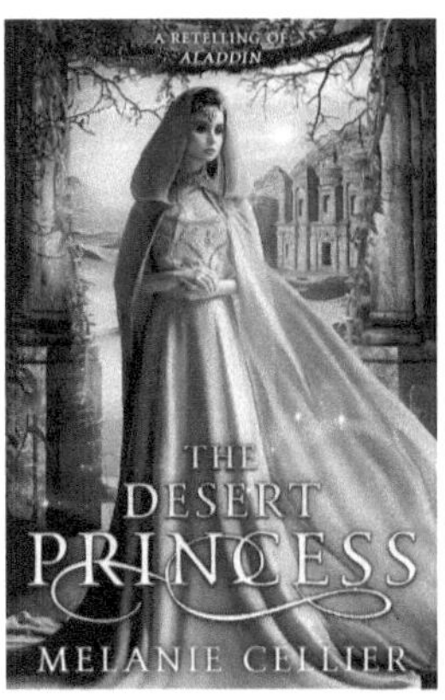

To be informed of my new releases, as well as new bonus shorts, please sign up to my mailing list at www.melaniecelli er.com. At my website, you'll also find an array of free extra content in my Four Kingdoms world.

Thank you for taking the time to read my book. I hope you enjoyed it. If you did, please spread the word! You could start by leaving a review on Amazon or Goodreads or Facebook or any other social media site. Your review would be very much appreciated and would make a big difference!

ACKNOWLEDGMENTS

The original Ali Baba tale is one with a brilliant heroine at its center, and I had a lot of fun bringing her to life in a new way in Zaria. I hope you've enjoyed exploring more of the new lands across the desert, as well as getting an introduction to the hero and heroine of my next fairy tale.

Writing The Golden Princess was particularly rewarding as it helped me discover a new, more enjoyable writing process. (Hint: it involves yummy food and drink, as good plans should.) I'm already looking forward to going forward in my fairy tale world with renewed creativity and focus.

But, of course, I can't move forward without taking a moment to look back and thank my brilliant team. As well as my usual beta and editor superstars—Rachel, Greg, Priya, Katie, Ber, Mary, Deborah, and my dad—I've had the pleasure of working with a new editor on this book. Thank you, Laura, for bringing a fresh perspective and lots of experience to the manuscript.

Thank you also to Karri for another eye-catching cover, and to my author friends for keeping my spirits buoyed, and my sanity mostly intact.

And thank you to my gorgeous, beautiful family—all my writing is for you. And thank you to God who is always gracious far beyond what I deserve.

ABOUT THE AUTHOR

Melanie Cellier grew up on a staple diet of books, books and more books. And although she got older, she never stopped loving children's and young adult novels.

She always wanted to write one herself, but it took three careers and three different continents before she actually managed it.

She now feels incredibly fortunate to spend her time writing from her home in Adelaide, Australia where she keeps an eye out for koalas in her backyard. Her staple diet hasn't changed much, although she's added choc mint Rooibos tea and Chicken Crimpies to the list.

She writes young adult fantasy including books in her *Spoken Mage* world, her *Mage's Influence* world, and her various *Four Kingdoms* and *Kingdoms of Legacy* series that are made up of linked stand-alone stories that retell classic fairy tales.